THE EMIGRANT'S FAREWELL

THE EMIGRANT'S FAREWELL

Liam Browne

BLOOMSBURY

First published in Great Britain in 2006

Copyright © 2006 by Liam Browne

The moral right of the author has been asserted

Bloomsbury Publishing Plc, 36 Soho Square, London W1D 3QY

A CIP catalogue record for this book is available from the British Library

ISBN 0 7475 8022 7
ISBN-13 9780747580225

10 9 8 7 6 5 4 3 2 1

Typeset by Palimpsest Book Production Limited, Polmont, Stirlingshire
Printed in Great Britain by Clays Ltd, St Ives plc

All papers used by Bloomsbury Publishing are natural, recyclable products
made from wood grown in well-managed forests. The manufacturing
processes conform to the environmental regulations of the country of origin

For my mother, Joan Browne,
and in memory of my father, Jimmy Browne

Once or twice as I have gone about the circuit of Ireland I have noted down something like this: 'A setting for a novel.' Youghal was one, Clonmel another, and I would now add Derry . . . What I meant by that, I think, was that something in the atmosphere of these places – indefinable, impalpable – clustered life into articulate and significant relationships. Perhaps it was the atmosphere of history; or that the people have adopted a certain kind of position, almost a pose, appropriate to the dramatic meaning of their own kind of life; and this had gone into the very stones of the town, all its ways and outer signs, as the face and body of a man reveals his inner nature. Why should it not be so? We say of a man that he has a strong personality. Why may we not say it of a town?

Sean O'Faolain, *An Irish Journey*

The poetry of history lies in the quasi-miraculous fact that once, on this earth, on this familiar spot of ground, walked other men and women, as actual as we are today, thinking their own thoughts, swayed by their own passions, but now all are gone, one generation vanishing after another, gone as utterly as we ourselves shall shortly be gone like ghosts at cockcrow.

G. M. Trevelyan

PROLOGUE

The River Shannon, 1821

THE BOAT CAPSIZED as if in slow motion. For a moment the customs men were framed against the heavy sky, each in sharp relief, frozen in exaggerated attitudes of terror like figures on an ancient frieze, and, as the boy watched from shore, the boat toppled from the great wave that briefly held it and tossed them almost casually into the seething waters of the estuary.

The wind blew hard, forcing the boy to take sudden half-steps to stay upright. Occasionally it shrieked, high-pitched and vicious, like a bird of prey fastening upon its quarry. The storm had come up fast, rainclouds racing from off the ocean, throwing shadows over land and sea. The boy stood alone, peering into the blur of waves, praying desperately that he would see the head and shoulders of each man striking out towards him.

But he knew that the majority of those who worked on the river and the estuary could not swim a stroke. He stood there, his pulse outstripping the seconds. If he shouted with all his strength could anyone possibly hear him? If he ran for help, surely the men would perish?

In his mind the boy had yearned for something like this.

He was of an age when adulthood was just beyond his grasp. He walked the banks of the river, talking to anyone who would give him the time of day, captivated by the seafarer's life. He was always available with a helping hand. This was the life he desired. But the men told him by certain gestures – the close eye they kept upon him, the over-genial nature of their regard – that, at fifteen, he was not yet one of them. He therefore invented vivid dramas in which, as others prevaricated, he strode centre stage and through extraordinary physical courage or presence of mind saved the day.

But now that such a drama had presented itself, all he felt was nausea. He looked around again, desperate to find someone to whom he could pass on the responsibility of this moment.

With these thoughts racing through his mind he barely registered that he was undoing his boots, throwing off his coat and moving quickly towards the water. The first wave hit him in a shock of cold and he plunged beneath the next, kicking through the darkness. Surfacing he could see the boat, upside down now, lifting high into the air. Each wave seemed intent on picking him up and throwing him back on shore but he struck out fiercely. This was a river he had never swum in before, a river terrifyingly different from the placid one that he had come to know so well; it was as if he swam now above the void.

A face reared up before him in the water. The mouth opened as if to speak but no words came and it promptly sank from view. The boy dived after it, grabbed at the clothing, and as they surfaced he leaned back and kicked the few yards to where the upturned boat reared above them. As it dropped from the swell he reached out and found a grip with his free hand. Hold tight, he yelled to the man, do you hear me, hold tight.

Through the spray he made out another clinging to the side of the boat, an old man, grey hair plastered to his head, the thin face drawn with fear, the outline of the skull clear to see. I'm no use, I can't swim well enough, he shouted across at the boy. In the name of God do what you can.

Twenty yards from the boat two men were struggling to keep each other afloat in what looked more like a frenzied fight; each in turn would sink and rise, arms flailing, head thrown back. Sucking the air deep into his lungs, the boy struck out towards them. The moment he drew near an arm lunged at him, he felt it slip round his neck and fingers tighten in his hair. Easy now, he shouted, treading water, trying to turn the man nearest him. A wave broke over them and they were briefly submerged. He reached down and grabbed the man's belt, pulling upwards to lever him flatter in the water. He leaned back and kicked out with all his remaining strength, his free arm cleaving the water. The second man was clinging on to his colleague with one hand and paddling frantically with the other. They inched towards the boat. Between waves they gulped for air. A dreadful tiredness threatened to pull the boy below. He could hear the men clinging to the boat shouting encouragement.

Closer they got. Closer. He tried to separate himself from his body; it felt like a cable tensed to the point of snapping. A terrible loneliness filled him and he longed to hear someone say his name with affection.

He kept going.

And then a voice spoke. Good on you, it called out, you made it.

And he realized that it was the voice of the old man and

that he had reached the boat. He opened his eyes and saw close up the face of the man he had just saved, wild-eyed and contorted, like someone in the throes of seizure.

The old man spoke again. You can let go now. And William felt the hand that had clutched on to his hair finally loosen.

His body was shaking uncontrollably. He stared at the grain of the wood on to which he clung, the lines and circles like markings from another world, comforting him, offering him a reassurance that solidity and permanence still existed.

As one, the men and boy rose and fell, clinging desperately. Now and then they glimpsed the shore, saw the trees thrashing in the wind.

They can't have forgotten us, called one.

Is the storm easing, do you think? called another.

As the minutes passed, the cold turned their bodies numb. Each retreated into his own mind. William looked along the line of them and, despite everything, was moved by a strange elation. For the first time he felt accepted as an equal. No word or gesture distinguished him. He was bound to them by their shared fate.

Blessed God, I see a boat, shouted the old man. They all looked in the direction he looked.

I can't see anything, said the man next to the boy.

It's there, I tell you.

They strained to see a true, weighty shape amongst the watery delusions.

You imagined it only, one of them informed the old man.

Trust me, damn you all, the old man cried out. His gaze never left the spot he had fixed on earlier. There, he shouted, there!

Now they all saw it: the man at the prow pointing in their direction, the rowers with their backs turned towards them, the boat clambering over each wave.

For an eternity they waited for it to reach them, beginning to doubt it existed at all.

Finally it drew alongside. Ropes were thrown over, the rowers braced the boat as best they could against the swell, and one by one the men were pulled aboard. The boy tumbled over a hunched figure and collapsed. The rescued lay at the bottom of the boat, flapping occasionally like landed fish. The rowers glanced dispassionately at them as they turned the boat. The boy, beyond caring whether he lived or died, gazed up at their implacable faces and at the great bulk of their upper bodies as they strained through each stroke.

Suddenly the head of one of the customs men popped up before him, just as it had in the water.

What's your name? He asked.

William Coppin, the boy whispered.

William Coppin. The man repeated it, nodding to himself. He grinned down at William. I'm going to remember that name, he said, believe me I am. He said the name again, as if savouring it, as if to ensure that he had it fixed in his mind once and for all.

PART ONE

HE RESTED HIS arms upon the railings, his upper body canted forward, gazing over the expanse of river. The dark waters gave nothing back but he enjoyed their fluidity, time sweeping past him, busy and full of purpose, towards Culmore and the open sea. The Foyle began life as a trickle in the foothills of Tyrone but by the time it passed through Derry, past his leaning figure, it was over a thousand feet wide.

The city rose behind him, height upon height.

Once more, against his will, the river's history possessed him and he visualized the Elizabethan fleet coming upstream four hundred years ago, sixty-seven ships carrying four thousand foot and two hundred horse under the command of Sir Henry Dowcra, intent on establishing a permanent garrison in Derry. Twice they had run aground on the uncharted waters of the Foyle but eventually the final bend was navigated and Culmore sighted. From deep within the undergrowth the natives fired a volley of shots then promptly fell back. They had never seen anything like it; perhaps they sensed that their world was about to be transformed, their days numbered.

He was intimate with the history of his city, its rings of

growth, so that, as the poet's eye sees symbol and metaphor in the everyday, his eye saw distant battles, vanished buildings and old ghosts: the past and present overlapping. And he understood, with unwelcome clarity, that a sense of belonging could, as surely as economics or responsibility, tie you to the one place for life.

A swan emerged into midstream. Four centuries ago this area had teemed with wildlife: barnacle geese, godwits, quails, long-eared bats, plovers and otters had all been common, and the river itself full of salmon. Now there was only the odd swan and a few seabirds fastidious in the mud of low tide.

The far bank had belonged to the O'Cahans, his ancestors, who had fought with a fervour greater than most yet, inexorably, they had been forced to concede until finally even their name was taken from them as O'Cahan was anglicized to O'Kane. The O'Kanes though remained obstinately thick on the ground. He had increased the tribe himself, marrying a Sweeney and then fathering a daughter. His path to marriage followed that of countless others: the first meeting in a pub, a date for further drinks, the cinema, parties, snatched expressions of affection, unease miraculously transmuted into an unnerving intimacy before the inevitable drift into the comfort of familiarity. His courtship dance had suffered from a lack of confidence; no bravura flourishes from him, a display of homely rather than brilliant colours.

The night he first met Eileen he had been out with a group of male friends in the Dungloe Bar. The barman shuttled back and forth as the empty glasses piled up. The others became boisterous, emboldened by drink, and the two women at the next table were lured into conversation;

it was the usual drunken banter, thick with sexual innuendo, the men like children with a new babysitter, seeing how far they could go. His future wife sat through all of this like a woman listening to a Mozart symphony and he'd marvelled at her calm. Her eyes, never downcast, ranging about the bar and her words seemingly unclouded by drink. She was small of figure, dark hair cut short, an impish, fine-boned face that grew more and more attractive each time he glanced in her direction.

After a while she bent towards him. Are you the quiet one, then? she asked, smiling.

To be perfectly honest with you, he replied, I don't exactly shine in a crowd.

She paused. Then why don't you come out with me on your own some night, she offered, and you can just be yourself.

After another pause he managed a sound from the back of his throat that he hoped signified assent.

Always insecure about his own attractiveness, he'd been unaware that such insecurity can be an attraction in itself. He entered every relationship at a gallop, it being the only pace he knew. Declarations of intent issued all too quickly from his lips, he promised the moon and the stars, love wasn't love if you didn't declare it twenty times a day.

In the deep and treacherous waters of romance he was a swimmer who knew only the frenetic activity of the front crawl. But Eileen introduced him to other, gentler rhythms and he took to them with delight, relishing the easy glide of the breaststroke, one muted surge after another, or the stately progression of the backstroke, his arms wheeling in slow motion through the water like a paddle-steamer.

In the early days, though, he'd still to learn and Eileen

was forever cooling his ardour. At the end of an evening when he lunged for her lips she would adroitly turn her head to receive his kiss on the cheek. After two weeks of going out together his declarations of love inevitably started but she paid them no heed, staring him down like you would a growling dog until, contrite, it turns and slinks away. Would you give over, she would add, you hardly know me at all.

And indeed she was right, for every time he thought he had her measure she unbalanced him by smoothing out another fold in her personality. He began to distrust appearances and first impressions. She had an air of disengagement that touched an erogenous zone in his mind for there were times when he flailed beneath a tidal wave of impressions. He studied her with scientific zeal, believing everything indicative, though of what he could not always say. A lovely wee girl, was his father's considered appraisal of her, you've fallen on your feet there. But the chanciness of it all took his breath away; two people leave points a and b independently and meet accidentally at point c, whereupon, if all goes well, they inform each other, in the face of all evidence to the contrary, that this was always meant to be. Chance transmuting into serendipity.

He knew, after only a few meetings, that he wanted to marry Eileen. Knew it with the certainty of an evangelist. And he would have stood on any platform, such was his passion, and declared it to the world. But the world was one thing and Eileen another. Though women were supposed to encourage men to express their innermost feelings, Eileen seemed in no rush to hear his. Don't say something you'll regret later, she warned him. This admonishment continued to pinball around his brain. He was the first to admit that he sometimes got carried away but not all sentiments, he believed, should be given careful consideration – some demanded assertion in the flush of the moment. But he knew that to propose to Eileen, after such a short time together, was just asking for trouble. She would only accuse him of being frivolous.

Over the following months he restrained himself by picturing the withering look any proposal would undoubtedly receive. And then, on a late summer's afternoon, they were sitting on the beach at Portsalon after a swim and as Eileen dried her hair she remarked matter-of-factly from beneath the towel,

Are you ever going to ask me to marry you or will I die in the waiting?

What was that? he said in astonishment, leaning forward, convinced he'd imagined it.

You heard.

Holy God, Eileen, have you any idea how much I've wanted to ask?

Well don't let me stop you.

So there and then he proposed and there and then she accepted and they lay stretched out together on a virtually deserted beach, blue sky all they could see, allowing future scenarios to run unchecked through their minds.

They were married the following winter on what turned out to be the coldest day of the year. Outside the church, the photographer had no difficulty getting everyone to move in close together for the wedding photos; they were captured for posterity huddled together, blue-lipped, their wedding finery almost foolhardy in such weather, all poised to rush indoors the moment they were given the nod.

For their honeymoon they went to Amsterdam for a week. An odd choice for a honeymoon, people said, but on their first date together the city had come up in conversation and when both of them confessed to not having been there it was agreed, half-jokingly, that if things went well between them they would go together one day.

They arrived on a bank holiday Monday and took a tram from Centraal Station to their hotel. A misty morning with barely a soul about, the shops closed, the tram drifting slowly through the deserted streets, he and Eileen feeling as if they'd stepped into someone else's dream. For a week they walked by the edges of the canals, discovering bars and cafés they would return to repeatedly in the course of their wanderings, drinking dark beer or hot chocolate, gazing out at the glass-topped tourist boats plying up and down, the few passengers at this time of year obediently turning their heads to left and right as requested. In the small streets the cyclists whizzed along, often perched on antiquated, high-handlebar bikes, their breath curling behind them like steam from a train. The women, radiating from their high seats an aloof and unapproachable air, flicked a disinterested eye over Joe, then were gone.

On their final day, at Eileen's instigation, they visited Anne Frank's house.

A nice cheerful way to end a honeymoon, Joe remarked, laying down his money.

Did you never read her diary? asked Eileen.

Not that I recall.

It's one of my favourite books. Aren't you even a little bit curious to see the house?

No, he said, not really.

Reluctantly he followed Eileen through the restored warehouse and offices, gazing with little interest at the exhibits in the display cases: identity cards, a typewriter, an example of the yellow star the Jews were forced to wear on their clothing, photographs and certificates. But the moment he stepped behind the moveable bookcase into the secret annex where the Franks and others had been forced to hide, he felt the force of their constrained lives press against him. Black net curtains on the windows muted the light that fell on the bare, ordinary rooms. They walked through the empty spaces that for just over two years had sheltered eight people; the only confirmation of this previous existence that still remained was on the walls: a map of Normandy, on which Otto Frank kept track of the Allied invasion, thin pencil lines that marked the children's growth, the postcards and film-star photographs that decorated Anne's bedroom.

They gazed out at the chestnut tree in the back garden, upon which Anne Frank had also gazed, striving to fathom her life within this house. For two whole years she had never once stepped outdoors; always tiptoeing from room to room, mindful of every creak, fearing that those below might hear. All her girlish energy held within these walls. Her ambition reduced to a pale face at the window.

On their way out Joe bought a copy of the diary in the museum shop. He stepped to the edge of the canal and looked up at the entire house.

You look very stern, said Eileen.

I was just thinking, he replied, and I know this isn't a very original thought, but I was just thinking how lucky we are.

Just over a year later their daughter, Ciara, was born and his luck seemed even greater. As he walked the floor with her at night, a tiny bundle almost weightless against his shoulder, he felt more important than at any time previous in his life. And he felt, in a way he didn't fully understand, answerable to his daughter for the life he intended to live in the years ahead.

Five of those years had since passed and the word 'father', once so strange on his tongue, now had a sweet familiarity.

The Guildhall clock struck the quarter hour and brought him back to the present moment and to the realization that Ciara would shortly be getting out of school for her lunch break. As he moved along the quay the seagulls perched on the railings flexed their wings and shrieked at him and one by one, with the precision of a row of chorus girls, peeled off the line and settled on the water.

Beneath his feet the river flowed, cutting further into the land and in times of extreme rain flooding the cellars of houses and pubs close by. Where he now walked had been, a hundred and fifty odd years ago, the brief flowering of William Coppin's shipyard; from here the *Great Northern* had been launched. The quay, a portal to new worlds and ways of living, had always suggested to Joe a certain otherness, like stepping into a foreign embassy in your home country. As a boy he had found that strangeness intoxicating; he remembered peering down between the gaps in the old planking of the quayside, thrilled by the slap and swirl of riverwater, perched as if over the abyss, increasingly aware that the world was laced with dangers yet still distanced from them by a child's assumption of invulnerability.

But such immunity from fear had long since disappeared and the birth of his own child had if anything propelled him to the opposite extreme. Now he saw danger everywhere, it haunted his steps. He observed natural and man-made catastrophes on the television and was appalled at how easily, and with what indifference, everything you held dear could be plucked from you; husbands and fathers scrabbling amidst the rubble for buried wives and children, or men, forcefully separated from their families by some local warlord, turning to the camera in paroxysms of grief and impotence. And though geography might protect his own wife and child from the likelihood of earthquake or genocide, a terrifying array of dangers still lurked. On the day he and Eileen had carried the newborn Ciara from the hospital entrance to their waiting car, an innocent walk of no more than a hundred yards, it had suddenly dawned upon him that the world he had once known was no more; overnight it had changed into a war zone, a land of tripwires and booby traps in which he must remain ever vigilant.

He turned into William Street and lengthened his stride, not wanting to be late. His eyes fixed on those he passed. Upon faces that told their own kind of truth, the skin stretched taut like a drum on which life beat its own remorseless rhythm. And with the sapping of strength came the lowering of expectation. Life as a slow swan-dive.

And yet they retained an indefatigable humour, he had to give them that. Dark and vexed one minute, inspired and jubilant the next. The jokes were local, often cryptic to the outsider. The town played at being a secret society, enjoying a role that invited its own code of language and gesture.

At the corner of Sackville Street a group of men stood chatting and from their midst a hand reached out to detain him.

What about ye, O'Kane?

He recognized Declan Brady, an old schoolfriend.

How's it going, Declan.

The bulky man in front of him was far removed from the whippet-thin boy he had once known. Only in the face was there still something familiar, a trace of an old shyness.

What are you up to these days, Joe?

Nothing much, Declan. Nothing that I couldn't be doing anywhere else.

Don't talk. Sure that's true for all of us. Grown men wandering the town like teenagers.

The others spoke quietly amongst themselves. One of them said something in a low voice and they all laughed appreciatively, pleased at their collective wit.

I was away you know for the last year, said Declan. Romford in Essex. A wile place, it was. I wouldn't go back to that hole again, not if they paid me in gold bars.

Joe placed a hand on Declan's arm to forestall him and started to move away.

Sorry, Declan, but I'm really late picking the wean up from school. I'll see you about.

He reached the school gates just as the children were beginning to spill out. Some of them were chatting earnestly to each other, oblivious to all else, others struggling into coats, one or two walking reflectively like monks in cloister. He spied her amongst a group of girls and felt the same old kick of surprise and concern, out there fending for herself when she didn't seem able.

Hello, Daddy. She eyed him anxiously.

What's that in your hair?

It's just a bit of paint. It'll wash out so it will.

I should hope so, he said gruffly. Did you have a good morning?

It was all right. What's for lunch?

Fish.

Fish fingers?

No, fish.

Oh. Her mouth twisted downwards, sulky.

Well, if you don't like it complain to your mother. I'm only the cook.

They set off for home, hand in hand, the child swinging along beside her father. A haze of coalsmoke drifted across the low ground of the Bogside. What sun there was shone on a distant hill.

Once inside Joe started lunch whilst Ciara watched television. He dampened a cloth and, standing over her, began to remove the small streak of paint from her hair. Oblivious, her gaze remained trained on the television. He lifted the hair away from the nape of her neck and saw the white, flawless skin beneath. His hands seemed enormous upon her. He touched her tenderly, astonished that she was his.

Sometimes such moments seemed all he possessed as there settled over him the dark thought that his hopes were irreversibly in retreat. Nebulous dreams of elsewhere fretted against all that he knew. The facts of his native town had embedded themselves in his brain like grit in a child's knee after a fall. His father had versed him well, almost too well, for he had ended up knowing his place in more ways than one.

So naturally he had turned his gaze towards opposites, envying the nomadic life, drawn towards all those unfettered by the word 'home'.

He had it seemed, almost without knowing it, stayed too long. Now all he had were Eileen and here, beneath his hands, his daughter.

Patsy O'Kane sat on the back seat of the bus from Dublin, from which vantage he could survey his fellow passengers. His long frame, not meant for the restrictions of public transport, was folded into the seat and his legs, nonchalantly crossed, protruded into the aisle.

Since retirement he could travel the whole of Ireland for next to nothing and Patsy had set his heart on finally seeing something of his own country. Place names that had haunted him for years – Kinsale, Carrickfergus, Lough Corrib, Dingle, Valentia Island, Arklow, the McGillycuddy's Reeks – he now knew with the peculiar intimacy of the stranger.

He would stay in cheap bed-and-breakfasts whose owners eyed with some puzzlement this sprightly man belying his years who was often first down to breakfast and last in at night. Patsy strode belatedly across his native land, the wind whipping at his thinning hair, in his element.

At night, once he'd found the right bar, he would talk without prejudice to whoever caught his eye. In Kinsale an old man recounted the story of the famous battle in the town in 1601 as if he were an eyewitness to the proceedings. He told of the Spanish forces trapped in the town while the English waited on the hills above, of O'Neill marching reluctantly from the north towards a confrontation he'd neither wanted nor relished and then, on Christmas Eve, the battle itself and how in the space of one hour the Irish were routed. The old man described them fleeing into the countryside chased by the English on horseback. One of the most decisive moments in Irish history, he says, shaking his head sadly, and it all over in an hour.

Then for Patsy the walk back through the dark to a strange bed.

Above him, on his travels, paraded the Irish sky in all its variations.

He fell asleep to the boom of the sea, the exclamations of night-birds, or the steady drone of traffic. He woke to gulls squalling, cows desperate to be milked, or drivers in traffic-jams hooting fractiously. Each day away from home he stepped forward into something new or unexpected, life surprising him with its casual abundance.

And all of this augmented by the pleasure of return. As the bus now approached the outskirts of Derry he straightened up in his seat. The road ran parallel to the Foyle and the city was visible only on the far bank, the buildings spread against the hillside. The Prussian helmet of Austin's department store, the two cathedral spires, in the distance the Inishowen hills, near at hand a solitary moorhen dipping. High up, a sprinkling of white denoted the Catholic cemetery; the dead, had they been at all interested, enjoying one of the best views on offer.

Come night, the reflection of lights on the water suggested that a second city lay beneath the waves.

The road followed the river; as travellers must once have done, knowing that eventually they would reach a settlement. Years ago, during his working life, Patsy had stood on the skeletons of growing buildings and wondered why he had been set down on this exact spot on the planet. Or why this planet even? That wonder had never left him and though he had tried to pass it on to Joe, he, with typical guile, had only turned it upside down to remind himself how easily he might have been born elsewhere.

He had never known what to say to Joe; it was as if, instead of encouraging his son through life from the touchline, Patsy found himself outside a locked stadium while the game continued within. From an early age his son kept his own counsel, a self-contained, self-sufficient boy prone to daydreams. Patsy had wanted to knock the dreaming out of him, afraid that otherwise he'd never get on in life. But

Marie wouldn't hear of it. Leave him alone, she'd say, as long as the child's happy. But Patsy could never tell if his son was happy or not, one emotion seemed much like the next.

It probably didn't help that he was an only child – a brother or sister might have forced him to confront the world more, but by the time Joe was born Patsy and Marie had virtually given up all hope of ever having a child, and after Marie had gone through a difficult birth Patsy accepted, with profound gratitude, that his wife was still with him and that he now had a son.

When the bus finally pulled into the station, Patsy stepped down and immediately felt at a loss, reluctant to return to an empty house. He hoisted his small rucksack over a shoulder and wandered towards the river.

The quayside had been transformed in his lifetime. A walkway now stretched alongside the river, following its curves. Families actually chose to stroll there on a Sunday. Their walk took them past the spot where the coalboats had unloaded in a swirl of dust and soot, enveloping the dockers as they'd leisurely watched proceedings. Past where the sheds and the cattle-pens had stood; over ground where rail-lines for the goods trains had once lain.

Patsy followed the walkway, his imagination brimming. Great grain ships arriving from the River Plate, steamships crossing the Irish Sea. The transatlantic liner waiting in the deeper waters of Moville for its human cargo to be ferried out to it. During the war they had stood five abreast: destroyers, corvettes, frigates, minesweepers and submarines.

Across the river from him, as if in remembrance, the chimneys of the banked row of houses smoked in unison.

When war was declared and, after a fashion, his own

town invaded, Patsy was in the process of taking his first faltering steps in the world of romance. Finding a girlfriend had become a Holy Grail but he had not reckoned on competition from the bulk of the Allied Fleet. Like many another local lad he'd suffered accordingly. The sailors brought a touch of the exotic with them, the strange music of their voices drawing the outside world closer with every sentence. Their very presence had put Derry on the map and had granted the town, though it scarcely dared to believe it, the novelty of full employment.

The most intimidating of the new arrivals were the Yanks, stepping down from the cinema screen into his home town, and suddenly the talk was of prairies and rodeos, baseball and soda-fountains. Hick towns in Idaho and Nebraska could, in the hands of the right teller, become Parises of the imagination. The Americans, sure of their place in the world, displayed a certain swagger that the locals sorely lacked.

Yet there were few fights. A truce of sorts reigned in the dancehalls. The music of the big bands soothed belligerent hearts and the local factory girls danced with one and all, revelling in this counterpoise to their working lives.

From memories and stories, smells and sounds long since gone, the pickings of another's brain, Patsy had constructed a town that, for him, contained as much substance as the one he walked through every day. A town though that could never be altered or knocked down but would remain for ever inviolate.

As he aged, and shrank in the world's eyes, life, and his own part in it, seemed more and more extraordinary. Out of nowhere there reared up before him visitings from early years; he stood again in a sweetshop he had entered as a child, around him the shop's dimensions and merchandise perfectly imagined, still able to name the exact order in which the sweets were ranged along the counter; or crouched over marbles with friends in a laneway off Stanley's Walk, noses close to the ground, concentrated, inhaling the damp humus; or walking past the abattoir on the way to school, hearing the panicky shiftings of the poor beasts within while the blood trickled from beneath the gate to circle and pool in the roadway.

It was being given back to him now, memory after memory, beyond all expectation.

Eileen O'Kane earned her living amongst Derry's sick and infirm. The job itself, working as an assistant in a doctors' surgery, pleased her. In a small, undramatic way she felt present at the gates of Life and Death. The dizzying variety of human ailments kept her alert to life's brevity; she watched certain elderly patients, fragile as bone china, take their seats in the waiting room and marvelled at their continuing presence on this earth.

The surgery itself was in the basement of a large nineteenth-century house; patients left street level unobtrusively, with an almost illicit air as if descending into a speakeasy. Inside they sat pressed shoulder to shoulder, flicking through out of date magazines or gazing resolutely ahead, refusing to let anything distract them from their ailments.

Eileen's employers, Doctors Connolly and Hutton, were both in their mid-thirties, forward-looking, assiduous, keen as mustard. The other assistant, Karen, was barely twenty and younger, Eileen felt, than she had ever been. Though only nine years separated them their preoccupations were poles apart; Karen lived for nightclubs, alcohol, fashion and boyfriends, the rigours of motherhood or mortgage-payments meant nothing to her. On weekend nights she met up with her friends, all of them young, confident and dressed to kill, walking down the street with the barely contained energy of racehorses in the parade-ring.

She described to Eileen an array of boyfriends who, despite her age, seemed to come out of a dim and distant past, their names sometimes unremembered, spoken of in the world-weary tones of a veteran socialite.

Against this, Eileen had little comparable to offer. She fished from her brain a few images of Sean, her first boyfriend, and from her bag a photograph of Joe and Ciara taken a couple of years ago at Bundoran; Joe sitting on a rock, Ciara perched on his long legs like a bird on a branch, a white sunhat shadowing her face and her right hand reaching eagerly for the camera.

She told Karen of the nightmare journey down, of Ciara throwing up every half-hour or so until she was lifted out, white as a sheet, on to the main street of Bundoran. And then later, her colour regained, the three of them paddling at the water's edge, dropping a shrieking Ciara into the small waves, and Joe recounting stories of the Mayo woman, Grace O'Malley, who centuries earlier had plundered the Elizabethan ships further down the coast.

In these conversations, held during quiet moments in the surgery, the two women developed an unexpected regard for each other. A regard quickened by mutual envy: Eileen yearning, as she had since puberty, for a vivacity exempli-fied in Karen, and Karen, for all her talk, desiring Eileen's natural candour.

Regard became friendship, symbolized by the shift in their conversations from fact to fantasy, Karen looking forward to what could be and Eileen looking back at what might have been. But though Eileen had regrets, she acknowledged that there was little in life she could or would change. After the heat and confusion of adolescence, awful ineffectual days when nothing had gone right, she now had her place in the world. Even more than marriage, her daughter's birth had been the decisive event. The earth spinning through the blackness of space made sense to her now, her mortal life, the generations to come.

Joe and Ciara leaned against the wall opposite the surgery, waiting for Eileen to finish work.

What kind of pizza are you going to have? he asked

Hawaiian, she said, like always.

D'you think one day you might try something else?

But I like Hawaiian.

Where is that mother of yours? She's late.

Why don't we ever go to McDonald's?

Because McDonald's food isn't very good for you.

But all my friends at school go there. You get toys when you buy a burger.

We want you to grow up to be strong and healthy.

Angeline goes there all the time, and she's never sick.

To Joe's great relief Eileen emerged from the surgery. Sorry I'm late but for some reason the phones are always hopping on a Friday afternoon. She smiled at Ciara. Hello, sweetheart, I hope you're hungry.

Ciara took hold of her mother's hand. Can we go to McDonald's, Mammy?

No, we can't. I don't want you eating their food.

But everyone at school goes there.

Ciara, said Joe, we've already had this conversation.

Not with Mammy we haven't.

Listen, said Eileen, we're not going to McDonald's and that's that. Anyway, I thought you liked pizza.

I do, but I think I might like McDonald's as well.

In the pizzeria, as the waitress stood by to take their order, Ciara made a show of studying the menu, running her eyes up and down the various options, before deciding on a Hawaiian.

Let's have some wine, Joe, said Eileen. I could do with a drink after the week I've had.

As they ate, the restaurant began to fill up and a hen party, all talking at once and wearing angels' wings, burst through the door. Ciara studied them with interest.

Why are they wearing wings? she asked.

One of them is getting married, said Eileen, and they're all celebrating together.

But why are they wearing wings?

Eileen paused for a moment. Joe, why are they wearing wings?

I haven't the faintest idea, he said, but it's not because they're pure and innocent, I can tell you that.

Ciara continued to gaze at him, waiting for an answer. Don't you know? she said.

No, Ciara, I don't. Not everything has a reason.

She received this information with some scepticism. Can I go and ask them?

Over my dead body you will. He looked across at Eileen. How did the pair of us ever rear such a precocious child? You know, when I was her age you wouldn't have heard a peep out of me.

And now look at you, said Eileen dryly. She leaned towards

her daughter. Your Daddy's an oul grump, isn't he? Ciara nodded her agreement. But we still love him, don't we? Ciara nodded once again, smiling at her father.

I'm glad she's curious, Eileen continued, that's how I want her to be.

Joe watched his daughter pick up a slice of pizza and, as its end drooped, adroitly manoeuvre her mouth beneath it. She was changing at such a speed that he could not keep up. Her ability to converse and argue amazed him; that this child, who for so long had offered only rudimentary noises, could now give voice to such vivid thoughts and impressions seemed nothing short of miraculous.

A verse that he used to recite over and over whilst bouncing her on his knee came to mind.

Do you remember this? he said to her. To market, to market to buy a fat pig. Home again, home again, jiggedy-jig.

Ciara looked at him as if he'd taken leave of his senses. No, she said.

I used to say that to you when you were a baby.

I'm five and a half now, she reminded him, as if to imply that no-one could reasonably expect her to remember that far back.

So it seems, he said, though I can scarcely believe it.

By the time they finally left the restaurant the temperature had dropped considerably and they shivered in the sudden cold.

I think I'll light a fire when we get home, said Joe, it's certainly the night for it.

Can I ride home on your shoulders? said Ciara.

Are you not getting a bit old for that?

Please, she pleaded, drawing the word out as far as it would go.

So they set off up the gentle incline of Clarendon Street, Joe walking with the measured tread of a camel crossing the desert and Ciara bobbing happily above. It was a cloudless night, luminous with stars.

Be sure and look in the windows, said Joe, and tell me what you see.

Joe, said Eileen, don't encourage her.

Once indoors, Joe immediately began laying the fire, their first since the previous winter.

I'm running your bath, said Eileen to Ciara, and then it's bed for you, young lady.

Can I help? said Ciara, hunkering down beside her father.

You can be in charge of the sticks. You lay them crosswise, like this.

Her face was a study in concentration as she built a cat's-cradle of sticks across the layer of newspaper.

That's it, he said, now we need a couple of firelighters in there, like so, and last of all you want to get the coal nicely balanced on top of everything.

One by one, he lifted pieces of coal from the bucket, placing them precisely.

A work of art, he said, holding the box as Ciara struck the match. Pleased with themselves, they sat back and watched the fire crackle and flare into life.

Eileen called out from upstairs.

Your bath must be ready, he said. Give me a big kiss before you go.

As he washed his hands at the kitchen sink he could hear Eileen and Ciara involved in an animated discussion immediately above him, with most of Eileen's contribution consisting of the phrase 'no you can't'.

The fire had settled; he watched for a few moments the

coals pulse with heat before picking up the novel he was reading.

When Eileen came back downstairs she stretched out on the sofa where he was sitting and rested her bare feet on his lap. He took a hand away from the book and stroked her feet. A shiver of pleasure went through Eileen. You have your uses, Joe O'Kane, she said, I'll give you that.

The fire made them feel drowsy and languorous, their movements slow as under water.

A faint call reached them.

Oh for goodness' sake, said Eileen, what's the matter now? Do you mind going up to her, Joe?

On the landing he paused to pull the curtains. There was a glimmer of stars and he could make out the tops of the trees rocking in the wind. On the other side of the river a moving pinprick of light continually vanished and re-appeared, a car travelling the main road before turning and dropping down towards the bridge. He pressed his forehead for a moment against the cool glass of the window. A girl's high-pitched squeal of protest reached him from a neighbouring street, followed by drunken laughter. A dog barked. He felt come over him a familiar, sweet melancholy that he loved, felt his bowels loosening slightly, gazing out at the lights of his homeplace.

An impatient Ciara called again.

All right, said Joe, coming into the room, pipe down.

I can't sleep.

Why not?

Just.

He settled himself on the edge of the bed. Your mother will have my life if she thinks I'm sitting with you. She wriggled under the bedclothes in delight and slid further down, her face full of colour from the bath she'd had earlier.

He told her a story his father had told him, of two ships, the *Saldanha* and the *Talbot*, that sailed out of Lough Swilly on a fine day in 1811. Of how three days later they were caught in a terrible storm and blown along the Donegal coast towards Portsalon where the *Saldanha* crashed into the rocks, the ship disintegrated, and the crew were all flung into the sea.

He told her that the stormy sea and the great wind meant the people of Portsalon were unaware of the tragedy happening before them and it was only days later, when parts of the ship were discovered on the beach, that they realized what had happened. Two hundred and seventy-four people drowned. Only one sailor came ashore alive, crazed by shock, senseless for the rest of his days.

Eight months later, he continued, in the garden of a rich man's house in Burt, an employee of the owner saw a bird high up in a tree and, thinking it was a hawk, decided to kill it. He got a gun from the house and shot the bird. But when he approached it he discovered that it wasn't a hawk at all but a beautiful parrot. And around its neck was a gold ring that had written on it, 'Captain Packenham, the *Saldanha*'. A workman came up to the man and told him that he was listening to the bird while working in the next field and all the time it was talking to itself in a strange language.

No-one in the neighbourhood had seen the parrot before. The rich man's house was about twenty miles from the shipwreck so the bird must have flown off the sinking ship in the midst of the storm and, somehow or other, through the cold of the Irish winter, it had managed to stay alive.

Joe pushed the hair out of Ciara's eyes. Isn't that amazing?

She nodded agreement. It's wrong to shoot birds, she declared.

True enough. But some people are very cruel.

She nodded again as if already perfectly aware of this, then, satisfied, puckered her lips for a goodnight kiss.

From bed Joe watched Eileen undress. One by one the clothes were tossed on to the nearest chair. Her bra was discarded. She crimpled the baggy T-shirt like a concertina and allowed it to collapse down her length.

They had only known each other a couple of weeks when she stayed her first night at his flat but he had spent those weeks holding and turning her body in his mind. His fierce desire and his absolute nature convincing him that she was without compare. And desire in turn fuelled by the simplest of her movements: the inclination of her head, or the way, when she spoke, she held her hand palm out in front of her as if the words rested there for his inspection.

She flopped into bed beside him.

When she'd undressed that first night, he had wanted to help but hadn't dared touch her. Finally seeing the longed-for body, the mystery of the veils falling from the dancer. He had reached towards her tentatively as if not fully convinced that she was there. As if she might be only a mirage. But in the morning he woke to find their limbs marvellously entangled and her face inches from his.

He wanted now to remind her of that first night but she was already asleep, her breath hoarsened into faint snores. She lay with her back to him and he fitted himself in against her. Her physical presence was enough; he listened contentedly to the rise and fall of the passing cars and to a chorus of drunks who sang with the bravado of soldiers off to war.

During the first week of their marriage he hadn't slept much and, in morning light, had watched her face. There were dark circles beneath her eyes but the eyes themselves when they opened were animal-bright. With time his mind, hungering for its own religion, turned from a celebration of mystery to a celebration of the familiar.

When he asked Eileen 'Why me?' she just laughed and lovingly listed his failings until he began to wonder if she was joking at all. No praise was tendered without equivocation, as if to guard against complacency.

On Saturday morning, enjoined not to disturb her mother, Ciara sat on the living-room couch with a bowl of cereal balanced on her lap, watching a video of *Snow White*, whilst Joe read the paper. He flicked through the usual embellishments of restaurant reviews, wine columns, how to get the best out of ridiculously large gardens, which lipgloss was right for you, until his eye was caught by a photograph of a middle-aged man standing on rocks by the edge of the sea. His hands were resting on his knees, his body slightly bent, and he was shouting with all his strength at the sea beyond. Joe read the text beneath: the man's father had died when the plane he was travelling in crashed in the Taiwan Strait on its journey from Taipei to Hong Kong, killing all on board, and the son was calling out his father's name to summon his spirit home.

Which religion did the son practise? Buddhism, Taoism? There he stood, a middle-aged man in a baseball cap, engaged in a gesture, a belief system, that dated back thousands of years, his responsibilities to his father in no way ended by the presence of death.

Carefully Joe tore the photograph from the newspaper.

What are you doing? asked Ciara, her attention caught.

Nothing, go on and watch your film like a good girl.

Is it something rude?

Of course it's not. Whatever gave you that idea?

She resumed watching her video but a minute later turned to him again.

Can you whistle, Daddy?

What?

Can you whistle?

Yes, of course I can.

Show me.

He demonstrated with a few notes.

I can't, she said sadly. Kevin Mullan said that girls can't whistle.

And who exactly is Kevin Mullan?

He's in my class.

Well I wouldn't believe everything Kevin Mullan tells you. Of course girls can whistle.

What about Mammy?

Mammy too. In fact – Joe leaned forward confidentially and lowered his voice – I'll let you into a little secret. When we were younger your Mammy used to whistle at me all the time.

Why?

Because she thought I was very handsome. But in those days she was too scared to speak to me. Whenever she comes down you ask about all the times she whistled at Daddy.

I will, she promised.

The doorbell rang. A tall figure shuffled impatiently on the other side of the glass door. It could only be his father.

All right, son? I was just on my way up the town. His father stepped past him into the living room and looked about. Where's Eileen?

She's having a lie-in. D'you want a cup of tea?

I'll only have tea if you're making it, he said to his son's retreating back. I don't want to be any bother.

He turned to Ciara. And how are you getting on at school, blossom?

He ruffled his granddaughter's hair and then lifted her up extravagantly on to his knee.

OK, she said.

In silence they both watched *Snow White* for a few minutes.

When Joe returned, Patsy deposited Ciara back where he'd found her and reached for his mug of tea.

How's it going, son. Any sign of work?

I've a couple of interviews coming up.

That's good to hear. After all there can't be much satisfaction for you in keeping the house tidy and cooking the odd dinner?

Do I look like I need convincing?

Patsy shook his head as if baffled at the direction his son's life had taken. I've never understood why, when you had a good job, you suddenly decided you needed a degree after all.

I've told you enough times why, I was going nowhere in that job.

And since when did any of us in this town ever get to pick and choose our jobs?

Da, it's half past nine on a Saturday morning, would you just give over and drink your tea.

I suppose he passed some remark about you still being unemployed, said Eileen, finishing a late breakfast at the kitchen table.

He means well, Eileen. It's like he says something the once and doesn't realize he's said it a hundred times before.

Funny how you can say whatever you like about your father but the minute I criticize him you leap to his defence. She offered Ciara the last spoonful of egg. Irish men, she informed her, are thick as thieves.

Joe leaned towards Ciara. That, he said, pointing to the eggshell, is what's called an ovum. It's an egg that never fertilized.

For God's sake, Joe, the child's just eaten it!

What harm will telling her do?

You'd put anyone off their food. Eileen dropped her dishes into the sink.

I'm only trying to educate her.

I'm sure there's some things she'd rather not know. She swept the crumbs off the table into her cupped hand. God, but you can be an irritating man at times!

In the afternoon, glad to be out of the house, Eileen took Ciara up the town to buy her a pair of shoes. Wrapped up against the unseasonal cold, they inspected a blanched, distant sky while their breath spumed in the chill air.

Wouldn't the weather founder ye, commented the assistant in the shoe shop as Ciara extended her foot like a timid Cinderella. Mark my words, it'll snow yet.

Shoes bought, they took their time, holding hands, dodging the harried shoppers, reacting like magpies to a glimpse of bright colour. It was as if Ciara intuited her mother's bad mood, her need for affection, and Eileen laughed with love, knowing it was turning into a memorable day after all.

What am I going to do with you, she said, pulling Ciara to her.

They ended up in Fiorentini's, treating themselves to ice cream in defiance of the weather.

As they walked back through town a steady stream of shoppers emerged from the supermarkets pushing trolleys stacked with bags of groceries towards the various taxi stands. No-one lingered, driven home by the cold. Amidst this quickened tempo a young child fell and lay sprawled on the ground before them. His mother, in the vain hope of forestalling tears, picked him up and showed him the palms of his hands.

Look, son, there's not a mark on you!

The light was leaving Derry, hastening across the Atlantic, and in the augmenting darkness the shop windows glowed like shrines. Drunk men tottered from the pubs in search of food, growling to themselves like bears in the forest. The starlings chattered ceaselessly in the bare trees and below them Eileen and Ciara, mother and child, made their way homewards, chatting also, debating what they might buy people for Christmas.

Joe was stretched out on the bed reading when they returned. Ciara hurtled up the stairs and clambered on to him, waving her right foot in his face.

Look what I got, new shoes!

Joe examined them carefully. They're lovely. D'you think they'd do them in my size?

Daddy, they're girls' shoes! She looked at him closely to see if he was serious or not. And we had ice cream in Fiorentini's, she added as an afterthought.

Once she'd jumped off him and gone back downstairs, he became engrossed again in his book, so much so that when minutes later he heard the distant tinkle of breaking glass it didn't properly register with him. But a moment later his name was screamed – Eileen's voice – and as he moved towards the door a cold, primitive fear burst from his heart and flushed through his arteries.

Downstairs he found Eileen cradling Ciara in her arms. A yellow towel was pressed against his child's forehead and neck.

Ring for an ambulance, she's fallen through the glass door. Eileen's voice was low and controlled but he could still detect the terror beneath.

He made the call, blurting out the information so quickly that the operator made him repeat everything. When he returned to the living room the yellow towel had turned almost completely red.

Sweet Jesus, he whispered.

Eileen was talking continuously to Ciara, telling her not to worry, that everything would be all right, Mammy loved her, there was no need to be scared. Ciara's face was a transparent white, as if her bones had risen to the surface, but she lay perfectly still in her mother's lap, moaning occasionally to herself. Her very stillness was terrifying.

He hovered uselessly about them.

Go on out to the door, Joe, and watch for the ambulance. Please!

Outside, incredibly, the street was normal, just the odd figure slipping into the corner shop. Across from the house, beyond the playground, the lights of the town quivered in the freezing air and somewhere out there amongst them an ambulance was speeding towards him. Nearby, the tapering, muted shape of the cathedral pointed towards one kind of salvation but he rejected any thought of prayer; instead he willed the ambulance towards him.

His body was tensed like a wild animal, listening. And then, miraculously, he heard it, the wailing rise and fall, and he shouted back inside 'They're coming' before hurrying out into the road and frantically waving his arms when the ambulance turned into the street. Eileen was at the door immediately, still whispering to Ciara, whose white face, Joe saw as he approached, had settled into a mask.

With professional haste the two ambulance men wheeled a stretcher out of their back door and as they lowered Ciara on to it the towel momentarily came away from her face and Joe glimpsed a long gash on her forehead, like raw meat sliced open, and below, on her throat, a further wound from which the blood bubbled.

You go with her in the ambulance. He managed to catch Eileen's eye. I'll follow in the car.

Come with me, Joe, she pleaded.

I'll be right behind you, love. I promise.

Eileen clambered into the back, the door was slammed, and the ambulance raced away with a long wail. Joe went indoors for the car keys, stepping on the splinters of glass in the hallway and on the blood-flecked carpet. He walked as if wading through water, a ponderous, slow-motion progress that was in vivid contrast to the acrobatic tumblings of his terrified brain.

A few neighbours had gathered at the front door.

Is it Ciara? one of them asked. Aghast, they studied the evidence before them.

I have to get to the hospital, said Joe, suddenly panicking.

Sure one of us will take you.

No, no, I'll drive myself. He held up the car keys as if to convince himself that this was a genuine option.

There's no need to worry about anything here, Joe, we'll mind the house.

In the car he fumbled with the controls while his mind plotted ahead, reminding himself of the quickest route to the hospital. He drove through the Bogside, up the flyover, slowing briefly at the top before dropping down towards the bridge. He crossed on the lower deck but once over his body began to shake violently and he was forced to pull in at the railway station.

Gingerly he walked to the water's edge, trying to regain some physical control, thinking of Eileen having to cope with everything alone, his daughter perhaps at this very moment stretched out whilst doctors gathered around her. He had to get to the hospital. Across the river he could see the spot where he had stood less than a week ago in what seemed now another life entirely.

The night was numbingly cold, the river surging unseen beneath his feet. All certainties had crumbled within him, whatever ambitions he had nurtured now meant nothing at all; fear swept through him like a flash flood that obliterated everything in its path. His past had become sundered from his present. Where was his courage now when he needed it most? – for others as much as for himself.

*

In the waiting area of casualty Eileen sat alone, bent forward as if winded. Joe stood over her and softly spoke her name. She lifted to him a slack, distant face.

I think she's dead, Joe. God forgive me but I think she's dead.

Don't go imagining the worst, love. They'll look after her here.

But she lost so much blood. You didn't see it. It was just pouring out of her.

Tentatively she pulled at her blood-soaked blouse. Look at the state of me.

Joe, close to tears, scanned the waiting room. Would you like a cup of tea or something?

Why didn't you get rid of that glass door like I asked you to? How many times did I say it was dangerous? But oh no, you have to have your own way.

Joe said nothing.

They sat in silence until Eileen whispered, I'm sorry.

Joe took her hand in his. What exactly happened, love?

I don't know myself. I was in the kitchen and she was playing some game in the hall, I could hear her talking to herself. I didn't pay any heed, why would I? When the glass broke I thought at first it was next door up to their usual antics and I kept on doing the dishes. By the time I reached her she'd managed to pick herself up all on her own and she turned to me and her face was just cut open, Joe, you've never seen anything like it. My wee Ciara. And she wasn't even crying or anything, which somehow made it worse, the look on her face was just pure astonishment. I'll never forget that look, Joe, as long as I live I won't.

They held on to each other and waited. They both

shivered with fear, their worst imaginings encroaching again and again.

I'll get us a cup of tea. Joe crossed to the machine, feeling weightless enough to float away. He wondered where Ciara was at this moment, nearby or upstairs perhaps in one of the wards? As he waited for the tea he prayed that someone would bring them news soon. Anything but this waiting, he prayed.

He turned to see a nurse talking to Eileen and immediately hurried over.

The doctor wants to see us, Joe. They followed the nurse towards a door marked 'Private'.

In a small office the doctor was waiting for them.

Mr and Mrs O'Kane. He greeted them almost familiarly, as if they'd met before, gesturing them towards a pair of chairs. I'm Doctor Mulvey.

How is she, Doctor? Eileen reached out a hand as if transfixed by the whiteness of his coat.

Please, Mrs O'Kane, why don't you sit down.

There was a dark square of window behind the doctor and in the silence they could hear something swish and rustle outside, could sense its bulk. The doctor took off his glasses and peered at them.

I haven't been doing this job very long, he said, as if to no-one in particular.

He paused.

I'm afraid I've very bad news. He leaned towards them. Your daughter died a short time ago. The loss of blood, it just put too much strain on her heart. I'm truly sorry.

The chair creaked as he shifted position.

Joe leaned forward. Did you say she's dead, Doctor? Dead?

I'm afraid so.

But she's a young girl. She's full of life.

Her injuries were just too severe, Mr O'Kane. She lost too much blood.

Joe was conscious of trying to think, the effort of it, his brain encased in ice so that the fluids moved sluggishly if at all.

He heard Eileen say, In my heart I knew it all along. She stood up decisively. Can we see her?

Of course you can.

They made their way along a corridor of pure white, past windows that looked out on the darkness of early evening. On through a swing door whereupon Dr Mulvey stopped.

Are you sure you're up to this?

They nodded and he led them into a windowless room filled with artificial light, in one corner of which stood a trolley with a white cloth over it. Dr Mulvey walked over and pulled the cloth down the length of the trolley, then quit the room.

She was still in the clothes she'd worn to town, the new shoes still upon her feet, but there was no doubting their daughter had gone from them. She lay strange and trans-figured upon the trolley. The gashes on her forehead and throat had been sutured and were already paling into the surrounding skin. Her limbs neatly arranged as they had never been in life.

They cradled her in their arms, her body still warm from its final emissions of heat, and her clothes still bearing a fragrant, vernal aroma that had been for five and a half years the smell they'd best associated with love.

To think that she died on her own, said Eileen. I can hardly bear that.

They remained beside her, time passing, the hurt beginning to swell inside them until it seemed there would never again be room for anything else. Eileen began to recite a 'Hail Mary'.

After a time Dr Mulvey returned.

Would you like somewhere to sit for a while?

No, thank you, Doctor, said Joe.

Can we call someone for you?

I don't think there's any need, we'll have to tell them soon enough. Joe looked about him in bewilderment. What happens now? he said. Do we stay here?

You need to make arrangements, Mr O'Kane, for Ciara to be brought home.

You mean we just leave her here in the meantime, said Eileen, on her own?

It'll not be for very long, but I'm afraid everything has to be done through the undertakers.

It doesn't seem right, said Eileen, just leaving her like that.

She pushed the fringe out of Ciara's eyes and they both bent and kissed her forehead before Dr Mulvey covered her again with the cloth.

As they made their way back down the corridor Joe stopped and leaned against the wall.

How are we ever going to manage without her, Eileen?

Passing back through the waiting room they felt completely severed from those who still sat in hope. They stood bereft, awaiting instructions from the doctor, heedless of everything else.

Mrs O'Kane, said Dr Mulvey, could we not get you something else to wear home?

Eileen glanced down at her bloodied top. Sure what does

it matter now? she said, I may as well stay as I am.

Do you want reception to order you a taxi?

I'd far sooner go in our own car. She turned to Joe. Are you up to driving?

We'll manage, Doctor, said Joe.

At the exit Dr Mulvey shook their hands and offered his sympathy once again. The sliding doors opened and they stepped out into a swirl of white.

It's snowing, said Eileen, astonished. The snowflakes fell in small ellipses, out of a dark sky, through the brief illumination of streetlights, to disappear at their feet.

This isn't meant to hurt you, Joe, she continued, but I've never felt so alone in my life.

They stood in the lee of the hospital, loath to leave, all urgency in life dissipated, and watched the snow erase the familiar as if it were an Old Testament affliction upon the face of the land. Finally they slipped an arm around each other, hunched slightly, and started out across the cold, white ground.

The snow fell all night, growing in intensity, and by early morning, as Joe stood at the bedroom window, the familiar world had entirely vanished. The snow removed all thought of distance and perspective; the Guildhall, only a few hundred yards away, was something intuited rather than observed, while both river and far bank had disappeared altogether.

Eileen's grief had finally given way to exhaustion and behind him she lay sprawled across their daughter's bed. A luminous, spectral light pervaded the room, querying rather than affirming the sleeping form of Eileen, the clothes strewn on the floor, and the gallery of animals and pop stars that gazed down from the walls.

Joe hovered at the window, an indeterminate ghost caught between two worlds.

Time had slowed. The few cars in the street below glided by at ceremonial pace. Snowflakes drifted to earth, hesitated, were caught momentarily in an upward vortex, then resumed their wavering descent.

Birds dark against the rooftops.

The events of the last few hours looped round and round in Joe's brain as if seeking verification. The numbed drive back from the hospital to find the house lit up, the hallway swept clear of glass, a piece of cardboard in place of the broken pane in the door, and a fire burning in the grate. As if nothing at all had happened.

He had made tea while Eileen changed her clothes and then both of them had instinctively gone to Ciara's room and sat on the edge of the bed. Caught in a paradox of wanting to feel closer to their daughter yet needing to acknowledge her absence.

Where do you begin? Eileen had said.

They had sat there, in silence, lost for words, until quietly, almost imperceptibly, Eileen had begun to cry. He had put his arm round her, desperate to comfort her but knowing he could not. This was a new kind of futility.

Now, while Eileen slept, he went downstairs and telephoned his father and his parents-in-law. Woken from their bed so early on a Sunday morning they knew instinctively that something was wrong.

He set the front door ajar.

Fighting a powerful urge to leave everything exactly as it was, he began to tidy the house and to wash yesterday's dishes that were still sitting in the sink. In the hallway he attempted to remove the blood-marks from the carpet.

The dying embers of last night's fire hissed occasionally as snowflakes drifted down the chimney.

He heard the hall door being opened; it was his father. Hello, son, said Patsy. He put his arms around Joe. Son, I'm sorrier than I can ever say.

Setting aside his dripping overcoat he asked, How's Eileen coping?

She's asleep right now.

Why didn't you call me from the hospital?

To be honest, Da, it never even crossed my mind. I just couldn't think at all. Outside the house a car door slammed. That'll be Sheila and Don.

His parents-in-law were pale with shock. They stood lost in the centre of the room as if trying to find their way in a strange town.

How did it happen? said Sheila, there's no sense to this. She glanced about her. Where's Eileen?

Come and sit down, Sheila. Patsy guided her to the couch.

I mean, you prepare all your adult life for the death of your parents, it's the natural order of things, isn't it, but this . . . Jesus, Mary and Joseph, how could this ever happen?

You can't understand something like this, Sheila.

But I need to understand it, Patsy. It's my grandchild we're talking about here.

I'll make us some tea, said Joe. He caught his father's eye and Patsy followed him into the kitchen.

Listen, Da, will you hold the fort for half an hour? I have to get out of here.

Of course I will, son. Why don't you slip out the back door. I'll take care of things here.

He began to climb through the snow, leaving his home and the bulk of town beneath. Under the impress of cold air, his breathing was pained and shallow.

There were few people about; a bell pealed dully from afar.

He passed through Rosemount, the road dipping briefly before rising again, passed cows in a field enclosed by new housing, then turned on to Groarty Road which was no more than a country lane.

He stopped to catch his breath. A faint sun struggled low in the sky. Birds and bell-chimes drifted across the covered city. It was as if he had entered an earlier time, of Derry as a monastic settlement: a huddle of buildings on high ground, ambient nature, the crisp articulation of birds and below, far below, the reach of the River Foyle. Dark days of winter spent in the embrace of austerity, in study and contemplation, awaiting spring. Lodged firmly in the temporal yet always, resolutely, catching glimpses of the eternal.

The sky darkened, enclosing him in that soundless, transfixed moment before the snow falls. Then it began again. Within its fall he could see no-one and was himself unseen. He walked on blindly into the prevailing wind, knowing he would have to turn back soon. But the snow eased as suddenly as it had begun and, almost with disbelief, he watched the hills across the river, then the buildings, re-emerge, like the image on a photograph being processed, the morning becoming sluiced with light.

He stopped again and leaned upon a gate. A white sheet

had been pulled over the town, shrouding its slopes and hollows, imposing anonymity. There was no-one about, no sign of life beyond a few wisps of smoke rising from below. He tried to grasp what had happened. He repeated inwardly, Ciara is dead. The words simply floated on the surface of his mind. Ciara is dead. He could sense the terrible force that had wrenched his life out of shape, the violence wrought, but he could not feel it.

He set off back down the lane, his feet sinking with each step, while all around him as far as the eye could see, the snow stretched fresh and untrodden.

Later that same day the wind dropped and a freeze set in across the north-west of Ireland. Throughout the following week mist invariably hung above the city, trees stiffened into immobility, and on streetlamps and railings the angle of snow signified the direction from which that last wind had blown.

Like a ship trapped in polar ice, the city waited for the mercury to rise; each day the inhabitants going fitfully about their business, next morning rising to the same blear and illusive landscape. Sourceless sounds reached them, children's laughter where no children were visible, the rustle of voices in streets that appeared empty.

Apart from Ciara O'Kane there were eleven other deaths in Derry that week. Unknown to each other, the respective families shared similar rites of grief, conjoined only by the juxtaposed details of mourning and burial in the local papers.

In the front room of the O'Kanes' house the white coffin rested beside the far wall and for two days the mourners filled the house. Unsettled by the death of one so young they shifted continually from room to room, wary and hesitant, like a herd of wild animals scenting danger. The usual pieties wouldn't do; confronting Joe and Eileen they struggled to express their sense of dislocation, searching for words that never came.

At night Joe and Eileen, Patsy, Sheila and Don, Eileen's sisters Sinead and Anne and their husbands, along with one or two friends and relatives, took it in turns to sit with the body. Those keeping watch sat on upright, uncomfortable chairs or knelt to pray, perturbed, as they watched the candleflames skew in sudden draughts of wind, at having so much time on their hands to think, and startled on occasion by the outside world as late-night revellers crunched past the window. In the back kitchen the others chatted quietly over tea and toast.

In death, Ciara had relinquished all hold on the present day; indeed the more Joe gazed at her the more his daughter receded from him, slipping the generations until her shrouded body seemed, in its chill gravity, to belong to an earlier, pre-Christian age.

Eileen said little, to him or anyone else.

Why don't you lie down for a while, he had suggested to her on the second night.

The least I can do is be with her now.

Occasionally she would rise and stroke Ciara's cheek as if to reaffirm her continued presence, then resume her seat and her grip upon Sheila, Anne or Sinead.

Come the morning of the funeral the solitary voice of the priest shaped the opening words of the rosary; the response being taken up immediately by those in the room, a half-beat behind came the mourners in the hall and a half-beat behind them the men gathered in the icy front street who stubbed out their cigarettes and straightened into reverence.

The house filled with cold air.

Joe and Eileen kissed their daughter one last time. The undertaker moved towards the coffin.

No, said Eileen in a quiet voice, no, don't take her.

She gripped the coffin's edge. You have to listen to me, she begged the undertakers.

Come on, love, said Don, let her go.

He hugged Eileen to him and led her from the room. The undertakers quickly secured the lid in place and Joe and Patsy carried the coffin irrevocably from the house and began the walk to the church behind the slow-moving hearse.

Following mass, the cortège made its way back along Marlborough Terrace, past the O'Kanes' house, past the small park on whose swings and roundabouts she had regularly played, continued on to the Lone Moor Road and then finally turned in through the cemetery gates to begin the slow ascent through the banked rows of graves.

The sun was like a hole cut in the ice through which a faint glimmer of light escaped. A dog emerged from behind a headstone, studied the mourners briefly, then loped away in slow motion through the snow.

They halted beside a mound of fresh earth, the mourners huddling together for warmth. With brief and simple ceremony the white coffin was lowered into the snow-covered ground. Distinct in their dark attire, the mourners gazed at the great swell of river below and at a landscape that appeared determined to erase itself and start again. For a short time worldly thoughts fell away and they inhabited their own mortality.

Ceremony over, the mourners took it in turns to shake hands with Joe and Eileen before hesitantly dispersing, some drifting into the maze of pathways to search for the graves of relatives and friends. A reluctant Joe and Eileen were encouraged towards their waiting car. As it pulled away they gazed out the back window like two emigrants fixing in their mind a final image of home.

PART TWO

IN THE FOLLOWING days the cold spell broke. Normality returned to the town but for Joe and Eileen, left high and dry in a house that offered no succour or release, abnormality had become the order of their day. Like amputees, they felt the presence of what wasn't there.

They walked the house, moving from room to room, unable to settle anywhere for long, exchanging few words. Conscious of the eye falling casually on an item of furniture, on even the most mundane of household implements, and thereby detonating a memory of Ciara.

You know, said Eileen after returning from town one day, it's true what they say. At times like this it's simple acts of kindness from strangers that touch you the most.

More and more they sought their own personal forms of comfort, estranged from each other by guilt. Friends and family visited the house regularly but nevertheless Eileen took to spending time at her parents', sometimes staying overnight.

Joe sat up to all hours, keeping the radio on for company in the darkened back room. He thought often of Ciara in her grave. For the dark house brought him closer to her. Darkness removed the sense of time, all that was left were the wind through the trees and the lingering smell of his last cooked meal. Which could have been from any time and any place. His rational mind told him that in the great scheme of things her death was just another leaf falling from the tree but such a thought needed a perspective he did not possess. Again and again his daughter stepped light as a dancer into his mind. He contemplated the future they would never have. Life was usually revocable, lived on the premise that what was done today could always be undone; the thought that he could not see her again terrified him, like the infinity of space.

In the darkness he felt the generations draw closer together, the room filling with the shades of all those responsible for his presence on earth, come to comfort him.

Each morning he would start the day standing at the window and gazing into the back garden. He observed a bird walking there, unaware of his presence, as strange in its way as a landed UFO. Nothing was familiar any more; it was as if he saw objects and creatures for the first time. When he needed habit most it was denied him and he wondered if Eileen was experiencing the same dreadful acuity. When you live on your own, he realized, each day has to be an act of creation; whereas, with a partner, the burden is lifted somewhat, you let the desires and intentions of someone else be enough occasionally for the both of you. Eileen came and went now like a lodger, the timespan of her absences lengthening.

What few certainties he had he clung to. So that with the progression of each day he knew the light would fade and when it was entirely gone he knew it was night.

*

One afternoon he heard the key turn in the lock and Eileen entered, a carrier bag of groceries in each hand.

I thought I'd cook us a meal, she explained half-apologetically.

They chopped the vegetables together and while Eileen made the pasta sauce Joe prepared the garlic bread and grated the parmesan. He went out for a bottle of wine and when he returned the heady smell of a hot meal and the sight of Eileen at ease in front of the television shook his heart.

They sat side by side on the sofa, balanced the plates on their laps and ate with timid relish. The television stayed on as a third presence.

Being in this house is really hard for me at the moment, said Eileen. You have to try and understand that, Joe.

Do you want to sell the house? Would that help?

Eileen shook her head. The trouble is I can't bear the thought of anyone else living here either.

So where does that leave us? You can't live at your parents' for ever.

I know that. But right now it's a comfort of sorts to sleep in the same room I slept in as a child. It's almost like believing you can rewind time.

You seem to have it all worked out. And here's me sitting in an empty house not knowing which way to turn.

That's not fair. I'm just trying to get through this like you are.

I thought our way was to get through this together. After all, Eileen, I've hardly seen you since the funeral. For Christ's sake I have to ring your mother to find out how you are!

Don't give out to me, Joe. I'm in no mood for it.

They fell silent.

They could hear one of the O'Hagans from next door

out in their back yard; there was the creak of the coal-shed door, then the deep rasp and rattle of the coal scuttle being filled.

Have you ever known this house so quiet? said Eileen.

Unable to distract himself, persuaded that watching television or listening to music or the radio were but acts of evasion, Joe ended up finding comfort in all the sounds of life that infiltrated the house. When workmen began to dig up the road twenty yards from his front door, he even found himself heartened by this evidence of ordinary human activity.

But on the whole he was antagonistic to change. Change demonstrated a world moving forward and by implication a world moving further and further away from that known to his daughter. To participate in it, in his eyes, constituted an act of sacrilege. Instead he yearned for stasis. He kept the house exactly as it was, loath even, when the moment came, to flip the calendar on the wall to a new month. He threw out nothing but perishables. Any items that she had touched regularly, her favourite knife and fork in the cutlery drawer for instance, seemed to emanate a special aura, as if radioactive.

The odd night he would climb into Ciara's small bed so that, awaiting sleep, he could hear the same noises she had heard. He would lie in the dark and listen to the slight rattle of the window-frame, wind scouring the chimney-flue, the distant chimes of the Guildhall clock. Around this time of evening the O'Hagans' dog was let out for five minutes and he could hear the animal snuffling feverishly in their back yard, its little yelps of pleasure, barely able to contain itself with excitement.

In the morning when the central heating clicked on and warmth flooded through the pipes, the house would begin to creak and shift like an old sailing ship. Joe would lie on in Ciara's bed and moments of his own childhood would return to him. There he was aged three or four, slipping into his parents' bedroom on a Saturday morning, settling between them while they dozed, hearing a wood-pigeon call in the trees opposite. The first birdsong he had ever distinguished. Or a couple of years later, being allowed to stay up to welcome in the New Year, standing at the front door at midnight, the whole street seemingly out, and listening to the boats docked at the quay hooting in celebration. A neighbour walking back and forth offering whiskey to the grown-ups. People he barely knew shaking his hand and wishing him a happy New Year.

The images came thick and fast, without prompting. In its workings, his mind had turned cruel; he had an awed sense of all the memories folded in upon each other in his brain tissue, abiding, the vast majority never to be glimpsed. The dazzling excess of adulthood.

On Hallowe'en night, from a darkened bedroom, he watched people make their way into town, many of them in fancy dress. He had taken Ciara the year before, hoisted her on to his shoulders and carried her through the crowds.

A couple of hours later, the doorbell rang. He was tempted to leave it but after the second ring he went to the door. It was a neighbour, Eamon McDaid.

Joe, haven't you the spare key to Bridie Quigley's?

Aye, somewhere.

Her daughter's after ringing me from Belfast, she's been trying to get the mother all evening and there's no reply. She's worried so I said I'd take a look.

Wait'll I get the key and I'll come with you.

The house was in darkness; when they opened the front door there was no sound from within.

Bridie, called Eamon, it's Eamon McDaid.

Would she be a bit deaf? asked Joe.

Damned if I know.

They turned on the hall light, then stood listening for a moment.

Hallowe'en night, said Eamon, of all nights.

They opened the sitting-room door wide, turned on the light and leaning forward without entering, inspected the room. The same procedure for the living room. A clock somewhere in the house began to chime the hour. Further down the hall they checked the back kitchen.

Ah no! said Joe.

She was stretched out on the floor as if trying to peer under the cooker, her cheek pressed against the linoleum, the flowered housecoat up around her knees. Eamon leaned over and touched her.

Cold as ice, God rest her soul.

He straightened her clothing. She should never have been in this house on her own, he said quietly, she wasn't fit for it. But try telling her that.

It must've happened earlier in the day, said Joe, seeing as the lights weren't on.

They stood gazing at her as if to familiarize themselves with this new dimension to Bridie Quigley. The fireworks had begun in town, muffled explosions that lit up the world outside the kitchen window.

I suppose I'd better ring the daughter and break the news, said Eamon. Unless, of course . . .

No, I think it's better coming from you.

I thought you might say that.

Joe leaned against the sink. From down the hallway came Eamon's blurred voice. Before him the sky flared intermittently. The windowless room in the hospital came back to him; in death Bridie Quigley looked every bit as unnatural as his daughter. He surveyed the small kitchen, everything just so as though she'd been ready and waiting. On the wall was a Padre Pio calendar with notations against particular days of the month and a tacked photograph of a group of elderly men and women on what looked like an outing. A folded *Derry Journal* lay on the kitchen table alongside a packet of Silk Cuts, a lighter and an ashtray.

Bridie Quigley was stretched out on the bare lino like a parachutist free falling through space. Joe took a cushion from one of the chairs and placed it under her head. Some time during the morning or early afternoon she must have fallen, a heart attack or an embolism perhaps, or maybe she had slipped on a wet patch of lino and the fall had been too much for her. Had she lain there unable to move, too weak to call out, hearing the revellers passing the house on their way into town, their banter and laughter, the coarse vigour in their voices?

He got down on his hunkers beside her, wanting to offer closeness and some consolation, however belated it might be, and rested his hand on the worn housecoat.

He thought of his mother. He had been at her bedside that last morning but his father had put an arm round him, guided him away, and dropped him off at his aunt Kathleen's, from where, later that day, they had broken the news, though in truth he had known it from the moment his father led him from the hospital ward.

Eamon came back into the kitchen.

I hope to Christ I never have to do that again as long as I live, he said.

He dropped into a chair and hunched over, resting his forearms on his legs.

She knew the moment I opened my mouth. He ran a hand over his forehead. The sweat's running off me so it is.

He sucked the air into his lungs. I've aged ten years, he said, in the last five minutes.

The warm bread cradled in his arm gave off heat like a living thing as he walked to his parents-in-law's house on a sunny but chill winter's morning. The parked cars dusted with frost, in the sky a smudged thumbprint of moon. He passed shopgirls on their way into town for their Saturday day-jobs, thin and angular most of them, wearing in the name of fashion light, inadequate clothing. Pale, haunted creatures, uncomfortable in the light of day.

Sheila opened the door to him.

You're up and about early, she said, surprised.

I was out anyway so I thought I'd call round.

Come on in.

How's Eileen keeping?

She has her good days and her bad days. To tell you the truth, Joe, it's hard getting much out of her.

In the kitchen Don and Eileen were sitting side by side reading a newspaper spread on the table before them. The two heads rose as one.

We thought you were the postman, said Don as Eileen smiled uncertainly. Still in her pyjamas, she looked extraordinarily young, transformed into the girl he had never known.

Sorry to disappoint you.

Joe bent briefly to kiss his wife. Was she glad to see him? It was hard to tell. A sudden flare of anger seized him at the state of things; here she was sitting in her parents' home as if she had never left, as if her whole life, with all its attendant responsibilities, were still ahead of her.

How are you, she asked him, tugging at his sleeve until he looked her in the eye.

Not too bad.

Did you put the money in the credit union like I asked?

Yes.

And did you get someone to fix the broken gutter?

Leave the poor man alone, protested Sheila, he's only just walked in the door.

Yes, it's mended.

Good. Eileen tore a slim strip off the newspaper and began to fold and refold it. I think you must be telepathic because I was going to call round and see you today.

Is anything the matter?

No, it was just to let you know that I've taken a couple of days off work to visit Sinead in Brighton. I'm flying over tomorrow and I didn't want to go without telling you.

It'll do her the world of good, said Don, to spend a bit of time with her sister.

You don't mind, do you, Joe?

Through the kitchen window, he could see the thin covering of snow on Benevenagh and from a low winter sun there issued an austere, lemon sunlight that flooded the fields beneath the mountain.

No, why should I mind?

You know what you're like.

Sheila stood up. That's settled then. Will you have some breakfast, Joe?

Not for me, Sheila, thanks all the same. He straightened in his chair. Actually I've got a bit of news myself.

And what's that? asked Eileen.

I've got a job.

Holy God! said Sheila. That is news.

Where? asked Eileen.

At the Heritage Centre. I'm the new Research Officer.

No better man, said Don. If ever a job had your name on it, that's the one.

Congratulations, Joe. Eileen put her arms round him. It's wonderful news. And your father will be delighted. Mind you, he'll have to find something else to complain about now.

Never mind my father, Eileen, what about us, is it good news for us?

Of course it is, she said, how can you even ask that?

Sheila handed Joe a mug of tea. Why don't the pair of yous go into the front room, she suggested, you'll get a bit of peace in there.

The front room lay in darkness. It's a beautiful day, isn't it, said Eileen, almost sounding surprised as she pulled the heavy curtains open.

They perched forward on opposing armchairs. Joe gazed at the opening in his wife's pyjama top where her collar-bone was visible. He had never seen her appear so vulnerable and so diminished and he ached to look after her.

So when you do you start? she asked.

In a couple of weeks' time.

They're lucky to have you.

We'll see.

She pulled her feet up under her, rearranged her open dressing gown. And how's your da?

You know him, full of advice as usual. He's trying to persuade me to go to Galway with him for the weekend. Says it will do me good to get away.

Maybe he's right.

Eileen, he'll drive me to distraction. The two of us on our own for a weekend – it doesn't bear thinking about.

Well, you know best.

Her words seemed intent on bringing the conversation, or at least that part of it, to a close. She glanced out the window; as did he, wondering what had caught her eye.

Tell me this, he said, what do you do with yourself all day?

Oh, this and that. I don't sit around doing nothing, if that's what you think.

Don't you miss home?

Mmm, sometimes.

They sat in silence and Joe understood that now for Eileen silence and conversation were qualitatively little different, one was as serviceable as the other. Her words held no import. Like her parents she sounded pleased by the upturn in his fortunes but it was as if, like them, she did not expect his good fortune to materially affect her own in any way. She, it seemed, had her life and he had his, and yet not that long ago he had thought their lives and futures inextricably bound together, for good or ill. He felt powerless in the face of these changes, for this was not about him.

Hiding his distress he rose to go.

I'll be off. Give my love to Sinead when you see her. And ring me if you get a chance, will you do that?

Of course I will, promised Eileen. But do you have to go so soon?

As he pulled the front door behind him he was assaulted by loneliness, so physical he felt like retching. He and Eileen seemed to be drifting apart as inevitably as the galaxies. His life had lost all sense of familiarity. Where once there had been the ballast of responsibilities, now he was almost deranged by the freedom life offered. He could come and go as he pleased, a realization that deeply troubled him, as if in some way he was breaking the law or abroad without permission.

He had always yearned for an ordered life, to wake in the morning with some awareness of the shape of the day ahead. He liked things just so, a particularity more commonly associated with the elderly than with a man in his thirties. But Eileen humoured him, often more than he deserved; he was, he knew, a difficult man to live with. He thrived though on the pressures of marriage and fatherhood. To be needed, to be depended upon, gave him immense pleasure.

But all that had been taken from him. In his despair the click of the Sweeneys' front door seemed to foretell a future of doors closing, doors closing for ever on room after room – the same rooms that had once been full of possibilities. The future was now truly the future, awash with uncertainty. As if unwittingly he had been given another man's story and was now obliged to live it.

As the coach for Galway pulled out of the terminal and nosed its way into the traffic, Joe remarked with bad grace to his father, I can't believe I agreed to this.

Give over. Just getting out of this town for a couple of days will lift you.

What time will we get there?

About five o'clock.

The coach travelled through the Brandywell on to the Letterkenny Road, off the centre of which the rooks begrudgingly heaved themselves. To the left the Foyle gleamed like slack.

I used to go this road with my father, said Patsy. Every Christmas Day after our dinner we'd walk as far as Carrigan's and back again. No television in them days.

They journeyed into Donegal, from Letterkenny to Ballybofey, skirting the Blue Stack mountains to reach Donegal town, after which the magnetic pull of the Atlantic drew the road towards the coastline. From the oppression of narrow roads, overgrown hedges and looming mountains, they burst through into a wondrous sea-light, the landscape levelling, the eye, unimpeded, travelling as far as it desired. Their hearts lifted. Through the coach's ventilation came the first whiff of salty air to nudge them back to their respective childhoods.

We go through Bundoran, don't we? said Joe

We do. What of it?

Nothing, just that I remember we once took Ciara there in the car for the day. We'd no sooner crossed the border than she got carsick and Eileen and I hummed and haaed about turning back. But Ciara had her heart set on getting there. You couldn't argue with her. And in the end we had a wonderful day.

At Ballyshannon the coach picked up more passengers, who scurried to get on board as the rain began to slant in from the Atlantic. The day darkened. The driver switched on the headlights and, hunching over the wheel, pressed on.

I'm dying for a smoke, said Patsy. He shifted in his seat. Whoever designed these seats, he said, certainly didn't have the likes of me in mind.

Joe sat staring out the window, wanting to get the other side of Bundoran. He wondered what Eileen was doing at this very moment. He thought of the empty house in Derry, everything remaining exactly as it was until he returned: his trousers thrown over the back of a chair, the cups upturned on the draining board, just the occasional shudder of the fridge to disturb the silence. They passed a woman in her front garden struggling to get washing off the line; a white sheet flapping in the wind like a frantic, earthbound ghost.

Bundoran was awash from the fierce downpour, the gutters flowing free as mountain streams. The Christmas lights strung crisscross over the main street quivered in the vaporous air, iridescent, as illusory as their kindred that lay in the surface water of the pavement. Almost directly opposite them was the amusement arcade where he had lifted Ciara up so that she could drop her money into the fruit machine. Further down the street was the café where they had eaten fish and chips, sitting in old-fashioned high-backed booths, surrounded by Northern voices as if they had never left home. The walk along Tullan Strand, the two of them hoisting Ciara over the small waves of the shallows. Gazing out across Donegal Bay towards Slieve League. The engrossed, captivated look on Ciara's face as she combed the beach for shells to take home. Her skin turning brown virtually before their eyes. The old woman in the newsagent's giving her a pound to buy ice cream. Sailing back and forth in a banana boat at the amusements, Ciara laughing as she clung on to her mother like grim death.

There's O'Higgins's pub, his father informed him, a right Republican hole.

Along these wet pavements his daughter had walked in the height of summer. Her corporeal presence had moved in and out of the shops. Perhaps, infinitesimally, the town bore witness to her visit yet: a stone she had thrown on the beach still lying where it fell, two small greasy fingerprints marking the bright yellow wall of the café. Some of the coins she had used in the slot machines were probably still being recycled there, others dispersed as winnings throughout the length and breadth of Ireland.

There was a photograph somewhere, he remembered, of Ciara sitting on his knee at Bundoran beach.

The driver turned on the radio and tuned it into a country and western station. Steam rose from the newly boarded passengers. Joe wiped the misted window so he could continue to see the passing countryside. The weather was beginning to clear, the cloud cover breaking, and ahead, over Sligo, a blue sky awaited them.

'Welcome to Yeats Country', a sign announced.

You were forever reading as a boy, said Patsy. I'd come home from work, it didn't matter that it was a lovely summer's evening, you'd have your head stuck in a book.

I got that from you. You were always reading history books. And anything about Derry you could get your hands on.

Aye, I was always very interested in where I came from. You know, son, you're about to start a job that I would have given my eye-teeth to do.

Patsy straightened up in his seat.

I used to imagine, he went on, leaving the house and walking into town along Foyle Street. Whoever lived in my house a hundred years before me, someone now long dead and forgotten, would have done the same walk from the same place, his head probably full of the same trivial thoughts as me – would the rain hold off, where was the best place to buy this or that, would he call in for a drink. On his right the river, and if he looked across at the east bank it wouldn't be so very different from today. But Foyle Street itself, full of cheap hotels for the sailors and for emigrants waiting their passage, would be heaving. The far bank would be partially blocked from view by the clippers and steamships waiting at quayside. There'd be cattle bawling with fright in the sheds that ran alongside it. The smell of them would hit him and he'd smell the cargo from the various boats that were being unloaded, grain maybe or tar or tallow or corn. The same Foyle Street but a different world.

He paused, considering.

There was a powerful finality to that time which we've lost. When those people stepped on to the emigrant ships they knew that was it, they'd never be back, and everything they saw at dockside was a last glimpse in this life. Now everything's changeable.

Except death.

Except that, admittedly.

Benbulben loomed on their left, with what appeared to be miniature houses nestling on its enormous concave flank. Then the neat and proper Protestant church of Drumcliff, the Irish high cross guarding the entrance.

He had an operation, you know, said Joe, when he was in his late sixties. To rejuvenate his body.

Who did?

Yeats. To all intents and purposes it was a vasectomy but the idea was that it would rejuvenate the body by increasing the production of male hormones. It was daring of him to risk it.

And did it work?

He thought it did, which amounts to the same thing I suppose. He wrote some of his best poetry around that time.

They passed slowly through the narrow streets of Sligo town until they reached the bus station.

Twenty minutes, shouted the driver.

They got the last free table in a café just down from the station. Around them were groups of women taking a break from shopping, eating scones or pastries with their pots of tea. Carrier bags of groceries sprouted everywhere. The talk as animated as in a school canteen.

There are times, said Patsy, when I almost wish I'd been born a woman.

Back on the bus the pair of them dozed through the last stretch of journey, to be awakened finally by the movement of passengers in adjacent seats gathering their belongings. They stepped down into Eyre Square and Joe followed his father through the streets to their bed-and-breakfast, experiencing momentarily the sweet dependency of childhood when he had expected his father to know everything and had followed him everywhere, trustingly.

Later they made their way to McDonagh's for fish and chips. Despite the dark and the biting cold, they crossed the street to the weir and found a sheltered spot. They unwrapped the fish and chips and held them in their open palms like religious offerings while they ate.

I can't remember the last time we were together like this, said Patsy.

Probably not since we went on holiday as a family.

That's a brave while ago. We could never go further than Donegal because you were always carsick. I'd drive to the bottom of our street and you'd begin to turn green. That's where Ciara got it from.

I used to dread getting into a car.

A caravan at Kerrykeel and suchlike, that's where we'd go. I wasn't always as sympathetic, mind, as I should have been. After all, son, it was hardly your fault.

You must have been fed up with me though.

Not at all, far from it. I only wish I could have those days with you and your mother back again.

Patsy scrunched up his wrapper and rose to his feet.

I don't know about you but I'm done in. Let's have a quick pint and then call it a day.

In the dark Joe listened to his father in the twin bed snoring with a ferocity that threatened permanent damage. The crisp sheets smelled of summer. Just as his father had predicted, he felt relief at being away from Derry. But also an unexpected guilt that both he and Eileen were away at the same time. As if they had abandoned Ciara. Even though she was dead, even though she was buried in Creggan cemetery, he could not quell the idea that in some way his daughter still needed them. Sorrow was like love, the hub towards which everything radiated. And grieving was like being in love, its effortless centrality, so that out of the most unpromising facts and situations of everyday life you developed the ability to contrive connections to the lost or loved one.

At this remove from the numbing rituals of home, lying in the Galway dark, comforted by his father's snores, he saw how, with time, sorrow could become an arrogance and a self-indulgence, rendering other beauties in life peripheral. And worst of all, the threat of self-pity lurking round the corner, waiting to trip you up. For five years they had been parents only, with no time to be anything else; then suddenly this, the return to themselves, to the people they had been before Ciara, people whom they now barely recognized, whom they had thought never to meet again.

The following morning they were up early and, after breakfast, they walked along the main street. In Eason's they bought the *Irish News* and *Irish Times* and, while Patsy queued, Joe wandered over to the travel section, took down the *Rough Guide to England*, and looked up Brighton. 'The mid-eighteenth-century sea-bathing trend established the resort', he read. 'George IV, when Prince Regent, patronized the town in the company of his mistress. While Brighton has a Georgian charm, upmarket shops and classy restaurants, it is essentially bohemian in character with thousands of young foreign students and a thriving gay community.'

The narrow streets of Galway with their low, two-storeyed buildings were packed tight with pedestrians.

You feel you could reach up and touch the roofs of the houses, said Patsy, like what's-his-name.

Gulliver? said Joe.

That's the man.

In the afternoon they took the bus to Salthill then quickly wished they hadn't; wandering the seaside resort out of season – the majority of its entertainments closed, a bitter wind whipping in off the ocean, lines of Christmas lights swaying forlornly like they'd been up there for years – reduced them both to melancholy. They beat a hasty retreat.

That evening, hankering after some traditional music, they went to Naughton's. Patsy ordered the drinks while Joe took a seat at a corner table. He had to wait as Patsy struck up a conversation at the bar. Visited by those old familiars, irritation and envy, he watched his father. Watched him incline towards the woman beside him. Is that so . . . you don't say. His easy manner.

Do you have to talk to everyone in Galway before we go back? he asked on Patsy's return, hearing the petulance in his own voice.

The musicians wandered in singly and in pairs and leisurely proceeded to tune their instruments, tilting their heads to one side like birds as they sought a note. The bar began to fill and the seats around Patsy and Joe were taken, forcing them closer together, their knees touching beneath the table. The musicians eased themselves gently into a set of jigs, the fiddler drawing out the first few notes, then cranking up the tempo, the others joining in as if just at that moment recognizing the tune to be played. 'The Cat in the Corner' was followed by 'The Rakes of Westmeath'. A hum of conversation overlaid the music.

Another pint? asked Joe.

As he listened to the music he felt, as always, the homesick ache of the exile or the emigrant, despite the fact that he had never managed to leave Ireland. Laments for a girl, a place, a life left behind, an intimate naming of the familiar and the local, as if premised on departure being the natural order of things. A rendering of the world forsaken.

All that's missing now is a piano, said Patsy. I love the piano.

During the lulls in the music they heard the rain spatter

against the window. New customers entered the bar hastily, as if propelled through its doors by unseen hands. They would stand still for a second to get their bearings, then plunge into the vortex. The musicians, gathered unassumingly around a table like everyone else, were swallowed in the throng but from their general location came 'The Humours of Westport', 'Toss the Feathers' and 'Dogs among the Rushes'.

Another pint, said Patsy.

They fell into conversation with a young couple, Michael and Oona, who told them how they busked around the west during the summer while signing on in Galway.

It's getting hard though, said Michael, to tell the difference between the tourist season and the rest of the year. The place is coming down with foreigners. Travelling around the west of Ireland now is like taking a quick sprint through Europe.

You're not against it though, are you? asked Joe.

Not at all. Good luck to them. Anyway, if there's a problem with anyone it's with the locals. We're hospitable but we're not tolerant.

Look at racism in the States, said Oona, haven't the Irish-Americans always had a bad name for it.

I never saw a black man living in Derry until I was in my forties, said Patsy. Unless, of course, you count the Chinese.

'The Sweet Flowers of Milltown', 'Johnny Boyle's, 'I Lost My Love and I Care Not'.

Another pint, stated Joe, standing up.

Good man yourself, said a drunk at the next table.

The pub now seemed hermetically sealed, existing within its own tropical microclimate. The stagnant air heavy with low-lying smoke. All within conversed with great fervour, the men glad-handing each other, slapping and prodding and stroking their neighbours, huddled in conspiratorial groups or standing where they could find room to plant their feet, bawling out of them as if talking to the hard of hearing. The pints of Guinness lined up on the bar to settle roiled with a life of their own.

There was a call for quiet from one of the barmen, followed by a general sssshing. A young woman was standing alongside the musicians. Joe could just see her through the crowd, her dark, gypsy looks that were almost parodied by her large, hooped earrings and the scarf in her hair.

That's Cathy Jordan, whispered Michael, from Roscommon.

That's the same girl I was talking to earlier at the bar, said Patsy loudly, his eyes widening in delight, we had a great chat altogether.

Da, will you keep your voice down!

The bar became hushed, those who just a moment before had been roistering now turned their faces towards her in silent appreciation, and the outside world could be heard again as from the street beyond came a few isolated yells like war cries.

I'd like to dedicate this song to the two men who are down from Derry, she called, I hope you're enjoying Galway.

That's us! said Patsy, slapping Joe on the thigh, that's us she's talking about!

She began to sing 'The Maid of Culmore', her voice departing from and embellishing the slow air. It sounded newly minted, improvisatory, as if she and everyone present were still in the midst of the events described. Her voice rang clear as a bell and Joe could hear every word.

Leaving sweet lovely Derry for fair London town
There is no finer harbour all around can be found
Where the youngsters each evening go down to the shore
And the joy bells are ringing for the maid of Culmore.

The first time I saw her she passed me by
And the next time I saw her she bid me goodbye
But the last time I saw her it grieved my heart sore
For she sailed down Lough Foyle and away from Culmore.

If I had the power the storms for to rise
I would make the wind blow and I'd darken the skies
I would make the wind blow high and the salt seas to roar
And so stop my darling sail away from Culmore.

To the back parts of America my love I'll go and see
For it's there I know no-one and no-one knows me
And if I don't find her I'll return home no more
Like a pilgrim I'll wander for the maid of Culmore.

When she'd finished there was silence for an infinitesimal moment, then the applause erupted and she stepped into the crowd and vanished from sight.

Immediately the band struck up again – 'Farewell to Leitrim', 'The Mason's Apron', 'Music at the Gate'. The tapping of feet was like an army on the march. 'The Pleasures of Hope' and 'Hand me down the Tackle'. Patsy let a whoop out of him, jolted the table with his knee, and knocked his pint of Guinness over. It spread swiftly and effortlessly across the table like an oil slick as the others sprang from their chairs to avoid it.

Ah well, he said good-naturedly, no harm done. Another pint, everyone?

'The Garden of Butterflies', 'Marry When You're Young' 'The Maids of Castlebar'.

Last orders, shouted the head barman. The musicians steeled themselves for a final effort.

Joe made his way through the crowd to the toilet. Just inside the door a middle-aged man was studying his face intently in the mirror. A window above the urinals was open and the pure cold staggered Joe for a moment.

Jesus, I was fit to burst, said the man next to him.

They gazed out at the sky while they urinated, at the clouds streaming across it as if someone had their finger on the fast-forward button. Everything had quickened beyond the normal. The blood danced through Joe's body – his heart a rapidly ticking metronome – and the music thundered on at an equivalent tempo.

He took one last deep inhalation of fresh Atlantic air. For the first time in ages he was glad to be alive. Tomorrow would bring a more sober rendering of life but tonight, in his euphoria, he felt great warmth towards these men around him so that he wanted to touch them, to put his arm around a shoulder, to cup an elbow or rest a hand on the small of a back. Ever since Ciara's death, caught up in his world of mourning, the glance of every passer-by had seemed considered and icy with prejudice at his unforgivable failure to guide a child into adulthood. But now, as he walked back through the bar, the faces that turned to him were lit up and smiling, motivated solely by their own inner promptings; their eyes flicked over him indiscriminately, their disinterest was like a blessing upon him and he felt absolved. And when he finally reached his table, his father turned towards him, face flushed and triumphant.

Aren't you glad now you came to Galway, he cried. Be honest now, aren't you?

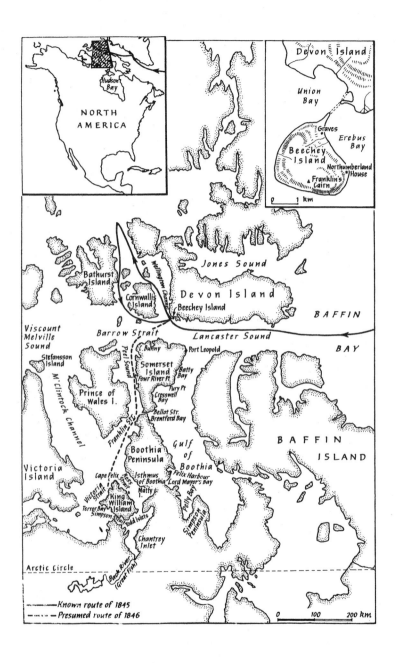

Inset (top left):

NORTH
AMERICA

Hudson
Bay

Inset (top right):

Devon Island

Union
Bay

Graves

Erebus
Bay

Beechey
Island

Northumberland
House

Franklin's
Cairn

1 km

Main map:

Jones Sound

Bathurst
Island

Cornwallis
Island

Wellington Channel

Devon Island

Beechey Island

BAFFIN

Viscount
Melville
Sound

Barrow Strait

Lancaster Sound

BAY

Stefansson
Island

C. Bunny

Port Leopold

Peel Sound

Somerset
Island

Batty
Bay

M'Clintock Channel

Prince of
Wales I.

Four River Pt.

Fury Pt.
Cresswell
Bay

Bellot Str.
Brentford Bay

Franklin Str.

Gulf
of
Boothia

BAFFIN

Victoria
Island

Boothia
Peninsula

ISLAND

Cape Felix

Isthmus
of Boothia

Felix Harbour
Lord Mayor's Bay

Matty
I.

Victoria
Strait

King
William
Island

Terror Bay
Simpson

Pelly Bay

Simpson
Peninsula

Montreal Islets

Chantrey
Inlet

Arctic Circle

Back River
(Great Fish)

—— Known route of 1845
– – – Presumed route of 1846

0   100   200 km

PART THREE

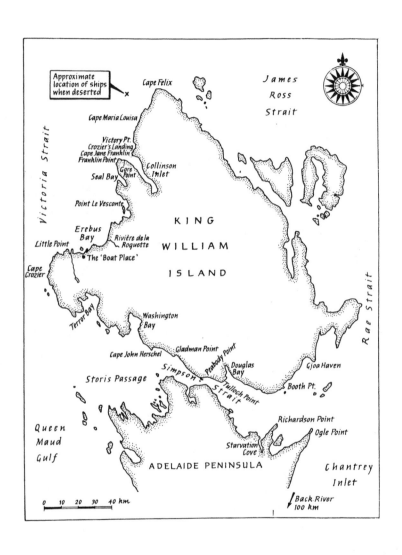

Approximate
location of ships
when deserted ———→ x

Cape Felix

*James
Ross
Strait*

Cape Maria Louisa

Victoria Strait

*Victory Pt.
Crozier's Landing
Cape Jane Franklin
Franklin Point*
*Gore
Point*
Seal Bay
*Collinson
Inlet*

Point Le Vesconte

KING

WILLIAM

ISLAND

*Erebus
Bay*
*Rivière de la
Roquette*
Little Point
The 'Boat Place'

*Cape
Crozier*

Rae Strait

Terror Bay

*Washington
Bay*

Cape John Herschel
Gladman Point
Peabody Point
*Douglas
Bay*
Gjoa Haven

Simpson
Storis Passage
Strait
Tulloch Point
Booth Pt.

Richardson Point

*Queen
Maud
Gulf*
Ogle Point

*Starvation
Cove*

ADELAIDE PENINSULA

*Chantrey
Inlet*

0 10 20 30 40 km

↙ *Back River*
100 km

HIS WORKPLACE WAS just off Ferryquay Street, within the city walls. Council workmen were stringing Christmas lights from building to building.

At the Heritage Centre his boss, Colm Casey, a short, burly, pugnacious man, led him swiftly round the various offices, introducing him to a blur of people.

C'mere now 'til I show you this, he said and took him into a room containing shelves filled with files, videos and cassettes.

What we have here are photographs, letters, interviews with local people dating back over the last fifty years, plus every scrap of footage of Derry we could get our hands on. We're building it up all the time. It's what you might call an unofficial history, created by the people who lived here. You can look up hiring fairs or life in the shirt factories or working at the American base during the war, it's all here.

Casey started back towards his office.

Next door's the genealogical records for the north-west, he said with a wave of the hand, we've collated them from the Public Records Office in Belfast.

How many people are working with us?

Well don't be thinking that everyone you met earlier is. This place houses a number of complementary organizations. Basically there's ourselves and Monica full time and we can use Lorraine sometimes as secretarial help. And, if we're very unlucky, every now and then they dump on us a couple of young fellas from the latest government scheme.

If you don't mind me asking, why'd you offer me the job?

Well, as I said to you on the phone, you knew a great deal about Derry already so you'd a head start over everyone else. You wouldn't believe some of the thickos that applied. Mind you, when we were interviewing you I couldn't work out whether you loved or hated this place –

– I'm not sure I know myself.

But you were passionate about it, Joe, which is what counts as far as I'm concerned. I don't want somebody who's going to sit around on his backside looking bored. You're going to be doing this work seven hours a day five days a week so you may as well be interested in what you're doing, for your own sake if nobody else's.

It means a lot to me, Colm. Especially working in a job like this.

Good. He held out his hand. We're glad to have you.

He walked along Spencer Road past the train station and past what was left of the old station beside it. The road rose steeply and at its crest he got a god's-eye view of the turns of the river, into one of which the initial settlement had been tucked. He recalled his history: 'A place in manner of an island,' Sir Henry Dowcra had written when he'd landed with the English expeditionary force in 1600, 'it lies in form of a bow bent, whereof the bog is the string and river the bow.'

Two causeways had been built across the treacherous ground but the combination of bog and river made it virtually impregnable. It was the Elizabethans who had been responsible for the first known map 'of the Iland and fort of the derry', sending it to London to delineate their progress. In it early Christian, medieval and Elizabethan Ireland inhabited the same small patch of ground, the different ages coexisting. Dowcra's men had built their main fort around the medieval Augustinian abbey whilst noting that the area also included a round tower, a church and a Dominican monastery.

Across the river he could see the putative site of that first habitation, dominated now by the Long Tower church, and below him, on this bank, the spot where he had stopped the car on his way to the hospital after Ciara's accident. The Foyle gleamed serenely, from this distance he could not distinguish the innumerable swirls and eddies of its surface. Small birds fluttered above mudbanks revealed by the outgoing tide. The wind hit him sideways as it blew in off the lough.

Dotted across the city, like songlines, were his markers, a building here, a street there, a void where once something had been, that spoke of a moment in his childhood or during schooldays, in the throes of a love affair or amidst marriage or fatherhood, moments sometimes buried in his subconscious awaiting recall. Occasionally his songline would crisscross another's by virtue of a shared experience although each would retain their own distinct memory of the event. He could walk through this city and sing his life; for good or bad it was all here.

Right now, though, even the most mundane experiences seemed peculiarly heightened, as though he had lost the ability to discriminate. Small, habitual acts of the everyday took on more significance than was perhaps wise. It had got to the point where he couldn't make himself a sandwich without it meaning something. He longed for the casual, the throwaway, the unimportant moment, for lightness and levity. Where previously Eileen would have bounced him out of these moods with a few well-chosen words now he pondered everything like a clairvoyant studying tea-leaves.

He settled into the new job. He sat at his desk, saying little at first. But it was wonderful to have people around him all day, he relished their comings and goings, the passing conversations. He caught the eye of Monica at the adjacent desk.

By any chance are you married to Eileen Sweeney that came from Creggan? she asked him tentatively.

I am.

And yous live on the Lone Moor?

That's right.

I went to school with Eileen.

Did you?

I did. I haven't seen her in years though.

Monica leaned forward and lowered her voice.

I hope you don't mind me bringing this up but I was wile sorry to hear about your wee girl.

Thank you.

I was going to call round at the time but I wasn't sure if Eileen would even remember me. Though I remember her from school as clear as day.

She turned her gaze from him as if an image of Eileen had suddenly appeared on the far wall.

Be sure and tell her I was thinking of her . . . Monica McFeely I was then.

I will of course, Monica.

She smiled gently. I imagine yous are a great comfort to each other.

During his lunch break he often slipped back home, switching on the television and turning up the sound so he could still hear it while he made himself a sandwich in the kitchen. In recent days, though, he sensed an indefinable difference between the house in the morning and at lunchtime. He sniffed the air. He walked around downstairs, not knowing what he expected to find. Then upstairs. He checked Ciara's room. The boxes into which he had packed her things still sat in the corner. The bed stripped, the walls displaying bright geometrical shapes where her posters had been.

Eileen had been horrified when he mentioned it.

You had no right to do it without asking me first, she'd said quietly. And now it can't be undone.

I'm not turning this room into a shrine, he had told her.

The following morning before he left for work he noted the exact position of the tea caddy and the sugar bowl on the tiles of the work surface. Come lunchtime they had shifted slightly.

That evening he rang Eileen.

Are you deliberately trying to avoid me?

What?

Why do you only come to the house when I'm not there?

It's not like that, Joe.

No?

If you must know –

If you must know! What sort of a phrase is that to use. I'm not some passing stranger you've bumped into on the street, in case you'd forgotten.

Thank you for reminding me, she said icily.

He hung up.

Fuck it, he said.

Every Friday at mid-morning they stopped work for tea and pastries, with everyone taking it in turns to go to the bakery.

Your best bet, said Monica to Joe when it came his turn, is the wee shop on Carlisle Road, they do lovely pastries.

When he gave his order to the woman behind the counter she looked up at him.

Are you working at the Heritage Centre?

That's right.

I thought so, I'd recognize that list anywhere. They never change from one week to the next. She picked up a flat pastry box, folded it into shape, and with a pair of tongs delicately settled the pastries within as if each were primed explosives. And you are?

Joe O'Kane, he said.

What's your father's name if you don't mind me asking?

Patsy O'Kane.

A big tall fella? From Tyrconnell Street?

He was originally. Why, do you know him?

I thought there was something familiar about your face. Sure of course I know your father, weren't he and I dancing partners way before you were born.

She sellotaped the box shut, wrapped a piece of string around it, and handed it over. I used to be quite a tall girl then, taller than I am now anyway, and him being the height he was and all, well it was only natural that we'd end up in each other's arms, so to speak. Not that I was complaining, I got the best of the deal. Oh, he was a great dancer, your father.

He was?

Patsy O'Kane! – don't be talking. A vision of grace he was and that's no exaggeration, and let me tell you, I wasn't the only girl who thought that way.

Are you sure we're thinking of the same man?

She laughed. Children know next to nothing about their parents, that's the trouble. When you see him next ask him about his dancing days with Mary Harkin.

He paused outside the shop, his mind working hard to shape an image of his father dancing. As the woman had said, how little he knew. His father's rendering of the past was always of the city he lived in and never of himself. Was there anyone to whom he spoke of his own life?

Crossing between the slow-moving cars, he started up the other side of Carlisle Road. Past the jeweller's, past the estate agent's, past the furniture store, and suddenly there in front of him in a shop window was his daughter.

He stopped in the middle of the pavement, fighting to hold back the tears that had risen inside him from nowhere.

She was smiling that shy, diffident smile she offered to strangers and she wore a dress that had been bought specially for the photograph, in which, he recalled, she had exultantly paraded up and down the living room the evening before. He and Eileen were sitting either side of her on a sofa and Ciara was tilted in against her mother's body.

That very photograph hung on their sitting-room wall and in his wallet he kept a small copy that he looked at almost every day. But there was something almost profane about having this image displayed in public so that anyone walking by could glance casually and without a second thought at their daughter.

He stepped into the photographer's.

Could I see Mr McCaul? he asked the girl behind the counter.

He's not here at the moment, she said, but I'm expecting him back shortly.

It's to do with the main photograph in your window –

They're not for sale, she said quickly, they're there for promotional purposes only.

I don't want to buy it. We already have it at home, it's of me and my family.

Is it? she said. Well I can assure you we wouldn't have displayed it without your permission, Mr McCaul's wile particular about that.

I'm sure he is, and I'm not criticizing you, but would you mind taking the photograph out of the window.

Oh I couldn't do that, I can't touch that window display. Mr McCaul does all the arranging. She looked perturbed that anyone would even contemplate asking her such a thing.

It's a lovely photo so it is, she added in a mollifying tone, as if this might change his mind.

Joe set the box of pastries on the counter. I'm afraid things have changed, he said, since that photograph was taken. We're now withdrawing our permission.

I don't think that's ever happened before.

Well it's happening now.

I don't want to sound like a broken record but you'll need to talk to Mr McCaul about it.

He said nothing for a moment, as if considering.

What's your name? he asked.

Mairead. Mairead Mullan.

Well, Mairead, the reason I'm asking you to take down the photo is because the girl in it was my daughter and she died not long after it was taken. And if my wife was to walk along here and see that photo, well it would probably kill her. It near enough killed me.

Why didn't you tell me that at the very start, she said, her voice rising, you only had to say.

It's not that easy to say.

I'll see to it now.

You don't think Mr McCaul will mind?

So what if he does?

She clambered into the window space and lifted the large frame off its hook. Glancing up and down the street as if she feared that Eileen might come along at any moment she slid the photograph back into the body of the shop.

There, she said, that's that done. I'll take it out the back in a minute where no-one will see it.

Thank you.

I'm wile sorry we've upset you like this.

You weren't to know.

She glanced down at the photograph. A wee girl that age dying, it doesn't bear thinking about.

No, he said, moving towards the door, it doesn't.

Back at the office they all looked up from their work as he came in.

I'm sure I know you, said Colm, didn't you used to work here?

Sorry for taking so long, Colm. Something came up.

That's the last time we'll send you out. We're all ready for our lunch now.

That night he lay in bed and listened to the wind whirling and wheeling outside. The shipping forecast had said force nine at Malin Head. There came to his ears the low, protesting moan of wood and metal under extreme pressure, punctuated by sudden loud cracks and reports. As if, amidst the great violence wrought outside, parts of the earth were being wrenched away and carried off for good. Handfuls of hail bounced off the window. The bedroom chimney sang.

Nights such as these were the worst. Unbidden, words first heard during his schooldays came back to him, 'a bare, forked animal'. He wanted to go up to the cemetery and drape a tarpaulin over the grave. He felt inconsolable.

The long night stretched ahead of him.

Have you ever heard of a man called William Coppin? Colm Casey leaned back in his chair and studied Joe.

The shipbuilder?

That's him.

Bits and pieces. My father told me about him.

He had a daughter, Louisa – Weesy for short – do you know about her?

Not a thing.

We're going to do a book on the pair of them, to be published locally, and I want you to do the research for it, maybe even write it if you think you're able.

Am I missing something, Colm? I know about Coppin but what's his daughter got to do with any of it?

Start with the newspaper records. You'll soon see why.

It was on his father's knee that Joe first began to learn the history of his birthplace, stories that were a mixture of fact and hearsay. As his father believed a good story repaid systematic retelling, over time Joe came to know them by heart. For a number of years that was all he knew but after initially choosing to take a job in the marketing department of a local newspaper rather than attend university he experienced an urgent need to know the history of Derry in much the same way as a prisoner needs to know the dimensions of his cell. He read everything he could get his hands on, from academic research to books and pamphlets, staggered by all that had happened in this tiny part of the world. Like a drop of seawater put under the microscope Derry seethed with activity. But the more knowledge he acquired the worse it got, all these newly acquired bits of information, insignificant in isolation, collectively held him to this part of the earth as the thousands of tiny pegs had restrained Gulliver in Lilliput. He felt as if he was being entrusted with the intimate details of someone's life, a trust that brought its own responsibilities, for after all, when such confidences are being whispered how can you turn away from the person concerned?

Starting as far back as it was possible to go Joe could canter through the highs and lows of the city's history with the practised ease of a guide on the top deck of a tourist bus. William Coppin's name certainly had its place in such a commentary but whatever his achievements as a shipbuilder,

Joe found it hard to believe that Coppin's story and that of his family merited the attention that he was now devoting to it.

He began to sift through the evidence, piecing together the known details of Coppin's life. He was born in Kinsale, County Cork, on 9 October 1805. At the time Kinsale boasted the chief dockyard in Ireland and, as William's uncles had served in the Royal Navy, the boy's fascination with the sea came as no surprise to his family. At the age of fifteen he saved a group of customs men from drowning when their boat overturned on the Shannon. His mother, her heart set on him joining the medical profession but recognizing her son's inflexible resolve, compromised and agreed that he could enter the trade of shipbuilding. A compromise, she hoped, that whilst allowing him proximity to the sea would keep him safely on dry land.

By the age of seventeen he had learned all that Ireland could teach him and so his parents sent him to Saint John, New Brunswick, to a relative there who owned a shipbuilding firm. He acquired further expertise and studied navigation every spare minute he was allowed. In a couple of years he was trading amongst the islands of the West Indies in vessels he had himself designed and built.

He met a group of merchants from Derry, one of whom wanted a ship built in Saint John to transport timber and deal back home to Derry. Coppin built the *Edward Reid*, then sailed it back himself, completing the voyage in just nineteen days and so impressing his employers that they offered him further work in Derry. For the next seven years he captained passenger ships to America and England.

These were the bare facts but behind them, Joe recognized, lay Coppin's driving ambition to build ships. He had his heart's desire though when he eventually managed to buy a local shipyard and foundry; now the ideas, sketches and innovations that for years had swarmed around his head could be shaped into wood and metal. He would launch his own ships on the Foyle.

A couple of years later in 1840 he designed and built Ivy House. It stood solitary and imposing on Strand Road and from its front windows you could look up the hill towards Gwyn's Institute, Richmond House and the Asylum. Of more importance to Coppin though were the back windows of his home; having deliberately sited Ivy House to overlook the slip dock of his shipyard (and with his bedroom and study both situated at the back of the house) he was able, like an anxious parent, to keep a watchful eye on his latest brainchild as it grew day by day.

Over the next few years, the *City of Derry*, the *Barbara* and the *Maiden City* left his slip in rapid succession. Ten thousand were reputed to have gathered at the river to witness the launch of the *Maiden City*. Stands were erected for the multitude, flags and pennants flew, and small craft bobbed impatiently on the water. And, in the words of a local newspaper, the *Sentinel*, all these festivities were presided over by a man 'whose talent and perseverance, under many difficulties, are only equalled by his urbanity and amiability of disposition'.

During his lifetime Joe had walked past Ivy House countless times but in the early 1990s it had been demolished to make way for a shopping complex. He could remember a fan-lighted doorway with a Doric column on either side and four windows on each floor that from the ground upwards gradually receded in size from rectilinear to square. He remembered the distinctive flat roof. Amongst the modest shops of Strand Road it had stood out as an imposing building. But until now he had never given any thought as to who had built it or who might once have lived there.

*

All day they kept coming, in ones and twos mostly, to stand at the quayside and stare at her. The *Great Northern* towered above them and above everything else in their world. When he had first picked up a pencil and begun to sketch her, William Coppin had known that ultimately she would be the largest ship ever constructed in Ireland but that realization had still not prepared him for the sight of the extraordinary vessel that stood before him. All of his skill and acumen had gone into the making of her, days spent working with his men, nights spent hunched over plans and designs in constant need of alteration.

This would, he promised himself, be a ship like no other. He'd fitted the *Great Northern* with a revolutionary new design, the Archimedean Screw Propeller. He believed this propeller to be the future and he wanted the *Great Northern* to be part of that future.

On the morning of the launch he woke early and watched the sun rise across the river. He walked up and down the deserted quayside, stepping in and out of the enormous shadow his ship cast. But he had little time to himself – in a matter of two hours the whole quayside was a crush of people. On the river upwards of seventy small boats hove back and forth, filled with ladies in their finery and their companions. The local brass band arrived and settled themselves, somewhat precariously, on the flat roof of Ivy House.

At eight o'clock the workmen began to drive the wedges with their hammers and at quarter to nine the last obstructions were removed and to a thunderous ovation from the crowd and a salvo from cannon on the wharf the *Great Northern* slid down into the Foyle. The impact sent a swell surging across the river and the small boats were each in turn lifted and plunged where they rode. From on high the band played as if their very lives depended on it.

In the evening Corporation Hall was the venue for a ball and supper for all the workmen and their families. Coppin ordinarily found such social occasions uncomfortable and in this instance was naturally shy of all the attention he received. He stood his ground though and accepted the plaudits with good grace.

A local businessman standing at his elbow informed him there were twenty thousand people at the launch and that, so great was the interest, the Donegal Grand Jury had been given special leave to attend.

Coppin left the hall the moment he thought his departure would not cause offence. Back home, he sat up for hours brooding over the future of his ship. She had been built for a possible government contract and, to that end, her upper deck contained forty-four gun portholes. But nothing was as yet signed and so he could not rest secure. Once the ship had been fitted out he would sail her to London and negotiate with the Admiralty. He had built a great ship, of that he was sure, and he felt equally certain that when the Admiralty saw her there would be no need for the usual sycophancy at which he was so inept; for once, he was in the position of strength and they would have to stoop to him.

In the early hours of the morning, when he was just about

to retire to bed, he heard music coming from the quayside. Looking out his window he could see them gathered alongside the *Great Northern*. They had lit a brazier and by its light their faces flared as if in the throes of great passion. He left the house and wandered over. As he approached, one of them was singing, accompanied by another on an accordion. He stood in the dark beyond their lit circle and listened. It was a song about emigration, about the harsh conditions that made leaving Ireland inevitable and of the sorrow of departure. 'Our ship at the present lies below Londonderry, To bear us away o'er the wide swelling sea.' Then the death of one life became rebirth elsewhere. 'The green fields of America are sweeter by far.'

Under the towering bulk of the *Great Northern*, with the Foyle lapping a few feet beneath them (the same waters from which so many had left), its words had the authority of fate. To his surprise Coppin was deeply moved. When the song ended he leaned towards the man nearest him and asked, What was that called?

'The Emigrant's Farewell', sir.

He stepped away from the circle, the song still echoing within him.

How easily might failure and penury steal upon you, he thought; the times required you to live by your wits or to suffer at your wits' end. The shadow of the workhouse or the emigrant ship always loomed. He could hardly imagine what it must be like for those who, having barely seen beyond the boundaries of their own parish, had to walk up the gangway of a ship, travel thousands of miles, then walk down the same gangway into a world where even the sun upon their faces felt unfamiliar.

And what of those left behind on the shoreline, forced

to confront this moment of finality. It was as if the departing emigrants were crossing the River Styx and America was the otherworld toward which they journeyed. 'Late of this parish' was the phrase used to describe one who had died, words that could apply equally well to the emigrant. As the ship receded from view those grieving friends and relatives knew they had only the unreliable play of memory to sustain them in the years ahead. Like the ground that they dug, they would sift through the rough clay of their minds again and again, hoping against hope that the light would fall on some image or scene previously unremembered with which they could feed themselves for a little while longer.

Five months later, after work on all the fittings for the *Great Northern* had been completed, they left Moville Bay, sailing for London by way of the Isle of Wight. They arrived in the capital on 10 January 1843. The *Illustrated London News* rhapsodized, 'This extraordinary steamer, now in the East India Docks, is the object of general astonishment. Her great length, breadth, and depth exceed, we believe, the dimensions of any steam vessel ever in existence. She was built at Londonderry by Captain Coppin, and is a remarkable monument of marine architecture . . . During this week, many persons entered the dockyard to gaze at this really wonderful object.'

Initial negotiations with the Admiralty were positive. Three trips were undertaken as a trial of the *Great Northern*'s ability and they expressed themselves highly satisfied with the outcome, tendering a verbal agreement to place her in commission between Calcutta and Hong Kong, transporting troops for the war with China. But then inexplicable delays occurred, meetings were postponed, and Coppin realized he had entered a world as full of sophistry and intrigue as any royal court, with its own laws and procedures of which he had no prior acquaintance. It was suggested to him that for things to move forward he might like, by whatever means he saw fit, to encourage certain individuals. When he refused to do so, it was as if his own pride and belief were now turned against him, as a wrestler might cunningly use his opponent's force to his advantage. What did it matter to them that he had built such a ship? Would not another vessel, even bigger and better, soon come along?

By all manner of subtle darts was he reminded of his nationality and of the fact that he was not an English gentleman. And Londonderry, where was it exactly? The more he argued and the more forthright he became, the more he realized the impropriety of his behaviour. Interest fell away and as one door slammed in his face it precipitated the slamming of half a dozen more, until no-one would speak to him.

The *Great Northern* languished in the East India Docks well beyond her appointed time and he languished in London, half believing that as long as he remained there his predicament was surmountable. But whilst he clung to this foolishness the harbour dues mounted up until eventually he was left with no choice, he had to sell the *Great Northern* to pay off his debts. The sum he accepted was thousands of pounds less than he'd hoped to receive from the Admiralty but, as they well knew, he was in no position to bargain.

He returned to Derry fuelled by a bitterness he had never known before. Amongst his workforce of over five hundred there were fearful murmurings of job losses, but he stood before them undaunted and told them that their livelihoods were safe and that they would immediately begin to build another ship to rival or even outdo the *Great Northern*. They had made history once, he told them, and they could do so again.

*

Inexorably Christmas approached. Joe walked through the crowds and through the false air of jollity. From shop doorways came ersatz music, carols which to his ears sounded like advertising jingles, while gaudy lights transformed windows into cheap shrines. Every charity under the sun seemed to shake a collecting tin beneath his nose.

Children stood fidgeting in the grip of resolute parents as they waited in line in the shopping centre for an introduction to Santa Claus.

Christmas can be a right pain in the arse, he overheard one man tell another, but you have to think of the weans.

Joe watched the starlings burst screaming from the trees in Shipquay Street and wheel out across the Foyle, heard their thin fading cries.

The festive season, he knew, was going to be a prison sentence this year, a slow dragging of ball and chain through a thousand spurious incarnations of happy families. Christmas cards had arrived at the house from distant acquaintances sending season's greetings to Joe, Eileen and Ciara. The simulacra of cosy wintry scenes that faced him everywhere – the robin on the branch, trees stooped beneath their burden of snow, a square of lamplight from a distant farmhouse window – only carried him back to the brutal, freak weather of early October and to his own stock of wintry images that would never leave him.

When the day of the office party arrived, he drank a few cans of beer at home in the morning, then walked to work, temporarily thinking the world a fine place. At lunchtime they all trooped out, ate their turkey dinner, wore paper hats, pulled crackers, threw streamers, yelled lustily at each other. The table piled with drinks. Their party merged with another further down the room and, having picked up one or two strays at the bar, they set off on a pub crawl around the town. As they progressed they gathered numbers like a peasant uprising. Occasionally a drunken Joe would spot a work colleague in the mêlée and think the face vaguely familiar.

Earlier in the evening he had become aware of one particular woman, always glimpsing her from afar, and now, in Jackie Mullan's, through a roll of the dice, he found himself next to her.

Have you ever been told you look like a woman in a Pre-Raphaelite painting? he asked her drunkenly.

All the time, she said. To the point of tedium.

Well, you do.

Joe wavered slightly on his feet. A man he didn't recognize placed a whiskey in his hand and moved on.

I noticed you at the start of the evening, he informed her.

I'm flattered.

He studied the curling abundance of hair and the alert, attractive face within it.

Is it my imagination or am I being mocked?

What else can you do to a drunk man, she said smiling, but mock him.

The bar swirled about him. He took a few deep breaths, steadied himself at the bar-counter, wanting to talk to her, wishing he had drunk less. His brain frighteningly opaque.

In that brief pause though a body suddenly interjected itself between them and a face he had never seen before smiled at him.

I'm going to kidnap her for a moment, the face said, and she was gone.

Briefly he watched her head bobbing some distance from him, saw her laugh, then he turned to speak to those nearest him, strangers all.

*

He woke to shouting and the repeated assault of a fist hammering on the front door. Captain Coppin! a voice called with mounting desperation. There were people running below the window, the clump of boots on the wooden quay. Coppin got out of bed, pulled on his dressing gown and stood in the centre of the room, adjusting to the presence of another sound that was constant and bewildering. It was as if a polar sea were thawing just outside his window, an extraordinary continuous crackling punctuated by sudden reports that might be icebergs breaking asunder.

He pulled the drapes aside and the noises he could not identify now made perfect and terrifying sense. Yet somehow he watched the spectacle with a detached calm, astonished at his own rationality, his mind analysing the few options that might now remain.

The fist kept hammering at the front door, the voice calling his name.

What's happening? said his wife, Dora, rising up in the bed.

Coppin never took his eyes from the window. The ship's on fire.

He heard her low moan as she scrambled towards him

but he turned without looking at her and walked down-stairs to open the front door. Francis Heaney, one of his workforce, stood petrified before him, his fist raised and a look of astonishment in his eye, as if the door opening was virtually the last thing he'd expected. He began to gibber and the fist unfurled and gestured towards the river. Without saying a word Coppin took hold of Heaney's coat, yanked him around, and together they strode along the side of the house to the quay.

The fire reared high above them, with the upper timbers wrapped in a sheet of flame. The heat was like an open furnace. A straggling line of men was passing buckets of water from hand to hand but the fire received each throw of water with a disdainful hiss.

Charles McCauley, Coppin's foreman, appeared at his side. There's fire engines on the way, sir, he shouted over the roar of the fire.

They may as well let her burn, said Coppin, the hull's beyond saving.

In the fire's radiance he recognized other members of his workforce, their faces racked by helplessness and despair. What they had worked so hard to build, what they had actually completed, was being reduced to ash before their eyes. He had always tried to instil in them a sense of history; reminding them that their work was not simply labour, that it should be viewed as of some moment, an achieve-ment that others would seek to surpass. But those words only served now to augment their sense of loss.

Three fire engines arrived and, as if tacitly acknowl-edging that the ship was indeed a lost cause, the crew prin-cipally concerned themselves with ensuring that the fire did not spread to the timber in the adjacent yard. Dora had come down to the quay, the children pressed close to her, and she stood mutely next to Coppin. In her arms she held the youngest, Louisa, who was unusually still, gazing enraptured at the conflagration as if this was the pinnacle of her young life to date.

Downriver, another fire burned as the sun rose piecemeal in its own blaze of colour. A true, constant light spread slowly over the river and over the growing crowd at quayside. Birds took up their song as if this was a day like any other. The flames began to recede slightly and the black outline of the burnt ship could be seen, still miraculously entire. Then in slow motion, almost imperceptible at first, she began to list to starboard. Hushed, all waited for her to topple over and crash into the slip dock but somehow she stopped, remaining perilously tilted, as if this was her chosen position until all was done.

No-one left the quayside. The crowd stretched away in both directions and Coppin was reminded of the launch of the *Great Northern*, the last time such numbers had gathered by the river. He knew now that his ambitions in shipbuilding would never be realized for there could be no recovery from this. For the past nine years he'd worked by the side of a river that the Vikings and the Elizabethans, great shipbuilders all, had once sailed upon. The Foyle had a history that added lustre to his own efforts. He had believed himself a man set apart but the life he so fervently desired did not seem to be his destiny. It terrified him to think that contentment rather than happiness was all he could hope for now. Contentment was a steady, low flame that never wavered. It was a life of small ambition. It was not what he had striven for.

Caught up in these thoughts, he did not at first realize

that a man stood in front of him, a man whom he recognized as one of his employees, though nameless like so many of them.

The man took off his cap and held out his hand. I'm very sorry, sir, he said.

Thank you, said Coppin. He was about to say something else but the man had already stepped away and behind him stood another man who in turn held out his hand and behind him a line was forming, the faces familiar, each man taking off his cap and waiting his moment with bowed head.

Of course the records, as Joe O'Kane was to discover, seldom revealed states of mind. The life story baldly stated that William Coppin built several smaller vessels, such as the schooner *Anne Coppin* and the paddle-steamers *Lady Franklin* and *Lion*, but that increasingly he turned towards salvage work as his livelihood, raising sunken ships with characteristic ingenuity and invention. But bitterness must have shadowed him. Local renown was no renown at all for a man who had built the *Great Northern*. Some days, looking out of his bedroom window, did the ghost of his great ship return to haunt him?

He was forty-one years of age, in his prime, ever curious, held rapt by problem solving. Like an implacable law of physics his mind surged to fill any vacuum of ignorance. But the great moment of his shipbuilding days had passed and the page with his name on it had been turned. In his heart he may have known at the time, or at least sensed, that the happenstance of life, cold and indifferent as it was, had worked irretrievably against him. He may have thought to settle for a quiet, workaday life. After all, there seemed little alternative. In his forty-one years he had packed in more experiences, more dramas, more victories and defeats than most men in their entire span. What else could life hope to surprise him with?

*

He rang Eileen to check she had no objections and when she offered none, he asked if she would like to help.

No, she said, I'd prefer you to do it.

So he climbed up into the loft and brought down the various Christmas presents they had bought for her item by item over the year. He collected them in a large bin-liner and next morning, five minutes before they opened, he left the bag outside the local St Vincent de Paul office.

On Christmas morning he rose very early in the winter dark. He made himself a cup of tea and sat listening to the radio. A farming programme reaffirmed that life went on regardless of the day. A cat, attracted by his kitchen light, mewled softly outside the window. He opened a tin of tuna, emptied some of the contents on to a saucer and set it on the window ledge.

He listened to the seven o'clock news. For half the world, he reminded himself, Christmas meant absolutely nothing at all. And those who had heard of it knew it only as a vague celebration in the Christian calendar, taking place on a date they could probably never remember.

The darkness gradually yielded. He observed the array of pots in the back yard, containing Eileen's plants and shrubs, as they took shape. All flecked by hoar-frost. Birds' nests visible in the bare trees. Chimneypots, leftovers from another age, as vestigial as the appendix in the human body. The moon slow to depart the scene. He within, watching.

On impulse he decided to go to early mass. He walked to it through a beautifully cold morning, his breath hallowing around him like cigar smoke. The ground crackled under his step.

The church was unusually full. A few children clutched dolls and sundry toys. One or two boys rolled trucks or fire engines up and down the seats, growling to themselves to signify locomotion, lost in their own world.

Joe paid little attention to the mass. He felt completely out of the Christmas loop, estranged; he had bought no presents, wanted none, and wished the day and festivities over as soon as decency permitted. And yet here, of all places, an unbeliever amongst the faithful, there was some comfort to be had. Not from the families, living fully in the moment and impatient to enter the whirl of the day, but rather from the old and infirm who attended this same mass every week and for whom this brief time in church might be all they could expect of human company today. For whom the next few hours offered only a procession of shades. For whom Christmas was a thing past.

On the pillars of the church were various watercolours of the birth of Jesus painted by local schoolchildren. Along the walls the Stations of the Cross illustrated the fate that ultimately awaited him. The bright winter sun lit the stained-glass window behind the altar. They prayed together for those who were away from home this Christmas, for those sick or in hospital, for the Church fathers, for peace in their own country, for peace across the world, for the sanctity of the family, for the dead. They prayed for their own intentions. When they were invited to offer each other a sign of peace, Joe turned to the old man next to him and shook his hand warmly.

During communion he stayed in his seat and watched the congregation file up to the altar. Thinking to himself that, like it or not, he would never feel so at ease anywhere else in the world.

In conclusion they were enjoined to bow their heads and pray for God's blessing. The priest raised his right hand and made a sign of the cross – the mass was over – whereupon they all stood to sing 'Adeste Fidelis'.

*

William Coppin travelled parallel to the river for the last few miles and reached Derry as dusk was falling. St Columb's Cathedral and Walker's Pillar were still just visible against the hillside. Sailing ships for the emigrants lined the quay, bound for Philadelphia, New York, St John and Quebec. The potato famine had turned emigration into an exodus; Derry was full of the poor wretches, bone-thin, wandering through the streets as if in a trance, their clothes flapping strange about them.

When he reached Ivy House he did not enter immediately but instead followed his usual custom and walked down to the quay. It was three months since he had last been home, his work as surveyor for the Board of Trade kept him incessantly busy, and after so much time away he loved to stand for a few moments and watch the riverwater coil and twist its way out into the lough and the deep Atlantic. As it had throughout every moment of his absence.

They had lit the oil lamps on the ground floor of Ivy House and the yellowing glow spilled out on to the dark ground. Within, unaware of his impending return, were Dora and his children, John, Anne, little Dora and William. Only four children now. During the last three months he had had to endure a voice within his head restating in dispassionate tones, as if informing a series of strangers, that in May his daughter Weesy had died from gastric fever just a few days short of her fourth birthday. He had heard the sentence again and again yet still he was not sure that he believed it. It was a stone that skipped across the surface of his brain and would not sink. When she was alive he had refused to use the children's pet name for her and instead he always addressed her as Louisa, her given name, maintaining as he saw it a father's necessary distance, but now that she was dead he too belatedly called her Weesy, as if to stress the fact that he had loved her truly all along.

During her final days he had sat alone in his study, the house silent, listening to the cries and laments coming from the quayside as relatives and friends said goodbye to the departing emigrants. Occasionally he could make out a name, but when it came time for the ship to cast off, the voices all merged into one great up-flung cry of sorrow. As he'd sat there, it was as if they were all mourning the imminent death of his child and he wondered if Weesy, immediately above him, could hear it too.

He took one last look now at the darkening waters on which so many had been carried away and then turned towards Ivy House.

Once he was inside they came running at the sound of his voice and after months of being alone his family were suddenly all about him. Only William, the youngest, shyly hung back. He distributed the small presents he had bought and they opened them with an almost frantic air. But as soon as this was done, Dora, amid much complaint, hustled them off to bed.

I need to talk to you, William, she said the moment they were gone.

What is it? His wife, such a calm woman, was unusually agitated.

I have not known what to do. You were away and there was no-one I felt I could truly confide in. It has been such a difficult time, William, and I have acted as I thought fit.

Just tell me, Dora, he said gently.

She raised her eyes, moist with distress, to him. The children claim that they can see Weesy.

What? What do you mean they see her?

It's been happening a great deal of the time you've been away. They say she is always about. That's the phrase they use, 'always about'.

But what do you actually see?

They've described it as a ball of bluish light yet they seem quite certain that it's her. She goes from room to room with them. At the children's insistence we've even had to set a place for her at table. Can you imagine that?

Coppin leaned over and took his wife's hand.

I'm truly sorry, Dora, that I haven't been here for you and the children when you needed me. They have all obviously been more affected by Weesy's death than either of us realized. I can only think that these visions must be a way of keeping her in their life, a fantasy world in which their sister participates.

Coppin squeezed his wife's hand and offered a reassuring smile. No doubt it is harmless but I am not sure we should encourage it.

He rose as if to bring the matter to an end.

But William, you don't understand, it's gone beyond that.

What do you mean?

Weesy now communicates with Anne. She talks to her.

Coppin sat down again quickly. They converse? Good God, Dora, what exactly is going on here!

I admit I was very sceptical at first, thinking that Anne sought attention for herself. But remember that Weesy was especially fond of Anne, so perhaps it is not so surprising after all.

Coppin looked at his wife in wonderment.

How can you speak so rationally of this?

You know Mr Mackay, don't you, William?

The banker? Yes, what of him?

Such a good man. On his way home from work he used to stop and talk to the children when they were playing in the garden. They were very fond of him.

But, Dora, what has Mr Mackay to do with anything?

Some weeks ago, after the children had gone to bed, I was sitting at the table about to begin a letter to my sister when Anne came back downstairs and told me that she had just woken up and that written on the wall opposite her bed were the words 'Mr Mackay is dead.' She was not in any way perturbed or upset by this except insofar as she cared for Mr Mackay. She did not for one moment doubt that it was true. I soothed her and led her back to bed – the writing, she told me, was there no more.

Next morning I went straight to Mr Mackay's bank, I felt I had to see him, to actually set eyes upon him. But the bank was closed and there was no notice or sign to explain why. Well, as it happens, I had some purchases to make in town and later that morning in William Graham's, where I was choosing some sheet music, I overheard two women talking and Mr Mackay's name was mentioned and when

I enquired further they told me he had died of a heart attack during the night.

Dora Coppin sat back in her chair and waited for her husband's response but William Coppin said nothing immediately, just stared at the floor unseeing.

I don't know how to explain it, Dora, he said at last, but such things do happen. Haven't I myself experienced them. We mustn't encourage the children though in any way, just go on about our lives as if nothing unusual was happening, and hopefully when they see this they will lose interest and there will be no more revelations.

But William, there has already been a further revelation.

Another? When?

Just a few days ago.

Dora Coppin raised a hand as if to ward off her husband's next words. Oh, I blame myself. But I had to know if these revelations truly came from somewhere beyond us, from a place where my dead daughter might be, and the only means I could think of was to ask a question that nobody in this world could answer. And so I told Anne to ask Weesy where in the Arctic Sir John Franklin could be found.

William Coppin reached forward in his seat.

You asked her what?

Where in the Arctic Sir John Franklin could be found.

And?

Dora Coppin smiled serenely. And she told me.

After a sleepless night William Coppin sat in his study next morning whilst his daughter Anne gazed at him expectantly from the other side of the desk. Still his mind swirled with thoughts of Franklin. Over the years he had followed with fascination the attempts to discover the Northwest Passage. To him this was more than mere adventure, for these men were charting a hitherto unknown world. The disappearance of Sir John Franklin, four years ago now, was a subject of much public debate; the newspapers reported with keen interest on the odysseys of the various relief ships sent by the Admiralty to scour the icy wastes of northern Canada and the Arctic in the hope of finding Franklin and his crew, or at least discovering some evidence of their fate.

But as yet nothing had been found. Wilder rumour suggested that, like flies in amber, Franklin's ships, the *Erebus* and the *Terror*, had become encased in giant icebergs, to drift in perpetuity among the ice packs, their dead crews still visible in the rigging and on deck, as though believing the ships still moved through their labours only.

Coppin had read every newspaper report he could find and had questioned during his work for the Board of Trade those whom he thought might have information not in the public domain. The one constant in this storm of rumour and conjecture was Franklin's wife, Lady Jane Franklin, who continued to lobby and fundraise assiduously, steadfast in her conviction that her husband was still alive. But even she, thought Coppin, must have entertained doubts. After all, it was known that the ships' stores were only sufficient for a three-year voyage, though Sir John Franklin had told the captain of a whaling ship in Baffin Bay, the last man to see the *Erebus* and *Terror* before they entered the ice, that he had provisions for five years and could 'make them spin out seven' if necessary.

Coppin raised his eyes from the desk and was startled to

see Anne sitting there, having completely forgotten about her. She smiled at him encouragingly.

Anne, he said, I have always thought you a clever girl and now that you're –

He paused.

Nine, she prompted.

– Now that you're nine, you are old enough to realize that the events happening in this house at present are most unusual. Your mother has told me that you and your brothers and sisters have seen Weesy during the time I have been away.

We see her all the time, Father.

And I believe she communicates with you particularly, Anne.

Yes. And I can ask her things.

Which you did a few days ago. You asked her about Sir John Franklin.

It was Mother's idea.

Now, Anne, I want you to describe to me exactly what you saw, but tell it slowly.

As Anne related her vision, of the Arctic scene that had appeared on the floor and of the words she had subsequently seen on the wall, words that she did not understand and had therefore spelled out to her mother, Coppin wrote it all down in a ledger. He already knew though what the writing on the wall spelled out. When she was done she sat patiently waiting for him to finish.

It was very cold in the room when I saw the ships, she announced. I was shivering so much I had to hold on to Mother's dress.

He looked across the desk and realized he barely knew the child sitting opposite. They had lived under the same roof all her life and yet he could not remember ever having asked her if she was happy or sad, who her friends were, what games she enjoyed playing. All he knew of her was second-hand, whatever Dora might choose to tell him of the children in their moments together. He had probably never attended to her like this before and now that he did she was determined not to let the moment pass without giving him a glimpse of her own inner life.

You have been a good girl, Anne, he said, and came round the desk to her. She stood up immediately as if dismissed but he put out a hand and drew her to him in a brief hug. He wasn't sure which of them was the more surprised.

I think I've remembered everything, she said.

I'm sure you have, he said. Go on now and play with the others.

When she was gone he sat again at his desk and looked at the words that his dead daughter had supposedly communicated to his living one. 'Erebus and Terror, Sir John Franklin, Lancaster Sound, Prince Regent Inlet, Point Victory, Victoria Channel.' He spread out before him a map of the Arctic. In the context of the search for Franklin the words made no sense. Point Victory was on King William Island and it was difficult to believe that Franklin would ever have gone so far south in search of a route. The considered opinion was that, as he had entered the Arctic through Lancaster Sound, any search should concentrate on this area. What was even more baffling was that there was no possible way of reaching King William Island from Prince Regent Inlet as the words implied; between the two lay the Boothia Peninsula. To reach King William Island you would have to travel down Peel Sound, not Prince Regent Inlet.

Coppin sat on in his study, gazing at the map. Afternoon became evening.

He wanted to believe, that much he knew. He wanted to believe that here in this house, tucked away in a disregarded part of the United Kingdom, lay the answer to a question that had puzzled the great minds of the day. He wanted to believe because of his own experiences with those great minds. He wanted to believe because he had been forced to sell the *Great Northern* for scrap metal and would never build such a ship again.

Anger whetted his memory. He did not yet know what he would do or who he would tell, if anyone. Did he hold in his hands a great answer or just the fantastical imaginings of his own children?

*

Why you had to buy a turkey I'll never know, said Joe.

It's Christmas.

Da, you bought an eighteen-pound bird! And in case you can't count, there's only two of us to eat it.

Joe opened the oven and slid the roasting-tray toward him. They leaned forward together and studied the bird.

How can you tell if it's ready? said Joe.

How would I know, these things were never my concern. Anyway, if you'd accepted Sheila's invitation in the first place . . .

She was only taking pity on us.

She could have pitied us all she liked while she was feeding us. Patsy prodded the turkey cautiously. There must be enough of it cooked by now for the pair of us.

We'll give it a wee while longer just to be safe.

They drank another gin and tonic and watched television, a seasonal programme in which the participants were reunited with friends and relatives they hadn't seen in years.

Not a dry eye in the house after that, said Patsy, blinking rapidly.

Finally they sat down at the table. Joe opened a bottle of wine for himself and set out a few bottles of Guinness for his father. Patsy raised his glass.

Here's to happier times ahead, son.

They bent to their task, neither of them feeling any necessity to talk when they ate. Then they pushed the empty plates away from them, sat back in their chairs.

That was a great feed, said Patsy. Didn't we do well, and not a woman in sight.

And what exactly did you do, said Joe, laughing, or did I miss something?

They settled themselves in front of the television again.

Didn't you used to wear glasses, son? said Patsy.

When I was younger I did but now I use contact lenses. God, Da, you can't have forgotten I wore glasses!

It's just that for a minute there I thought I'd imagined it.

Channel 4 was showing *Wild Strawberries*. They watched the first twenty minutes in complete silence.

Could someone explain to me, said Patsy, exactly what's going on here. If indeed anything is.

Memory, Da, it's about memory.

Is it too much to ask for something more traditional, and in English? Like *The Guns of Navarone* or *Lawrence of Arabia*. Or a good western?

Joe dropped the remote control into his father's lap.

See what you can find.

He went into the kitchen and began cutting up fruit for mulled wine. A rising wind spilled through the sycamores; somewhere in the darkness a cat was crying like an infant, a chilling, endless wail. The house seemed terribly empty, as if they were occupying a few rooms only in one wing of a vast mansion. It had become purely a place of habitation, a shelter, devoid of its history.

What's this? said Patsy, when Joe offered him a glass of mulled wine.

Try it.

With extreme reluctance Patsy took the glass, eyed it, sniffed it cautiously, then ventured an exploratory sip.

This, he said after a long pause, is lovely.

They set the bowl of mulled wine on the floor between them.

I remember the first time I ever wore glasses in public, said Joe. It was on a bus journey to Dublin. I was about sixteen and it was like seeing the world for the first time. I was on my own and I didn't pay any heed to the rest of them on the bus, just stared out the window, looking at animals in the fields, being able for the first time to read signposts for all the wee roads that led off somewhere.

At Strabane the bus made its first stop and there was a queue waiting. And then on climbed, one after another, the ugliest procession of people I've ever witnessed. I can see them still. There was nothing wrong with them but they all looked ill. And I realized then that on the whole that's what people looked like. I'd just been romanticizing the world for years because I couldn't see it properly.

You were unlucky though, son, said Patsy, that it was Strabane. That place would scare anyone.

Setting one toecap behind the other foot's heel, he pressured off each of his shoes.

While you were in the kitchen there I was just thinking about the old abattoir in the Little Diamond. I don't know if you would remember it, it was at the back of Celtic Park.

They'd let the animals graze in the field beforehand so that when the men were ready they could bring them straight in. They employed my da in a casual way, just to keep a count of the animals, mostly sheep and a few cows, to make sure none were stolen. But it became a bit of an obsession with him. At any hour of the day or night he'd take a notion and walk over to count the sheep. Three o'clock in the morning you'd hear the front door click shut and you'd know he was off. And it was very handy if he and my mother were having a row, he'd just put on his coat and say, 'I'm off to Celtic Park.' End of argument.

They finished the mulled wine and Joe produced a bottle of Jameson's. They filled their glasses, put their shoes back on, and stepped out into the back yard. Upturning a couple of plant pots they settled down on them.

Look at them stars, said Patsy, that's a great sky.

Some probably don't exist any more, said Joe, we're looking at the past.

That's all we do anyway, said Patsy, nothing odd there. He shivered and brought his knees together. It would founder you out here, son.

Joe went back inside and brought out their coats and the bottle of Jameson's.

Tell me something, Da, did you have many girlfriends?

Patsy laughed. What a question! I had a few, nothing serious though before your mother. I met her at a dance, that's how everyone met in them days.

And I hear you were a very good dancer.

I was, if I say so myself. And so was your mother. But who told you that?

I'll tell you later. Go on, how did yous get to know each other?

The pair of us used to go for long walks all the time. Up Sheriff's Mountain, for instance, or out the Letterkenny Road. In the summer we'd walk to Fahan, have a swim, go into Buncrana for fish and chips and then walk back to Derry. A good twenty-five mile round trip, I suppose, when you think of it, though it seemed to pass in a moment. I never, ever remember us struggling for something to say to each other.

He ran a hand over his face.

She's dead now these twenty-three years and yet sometimes when I wake in the morning I think she's lying there beside me and I turn to tell her something.

Patsy leaned forward and tapped his son on the knee.

I was on a bus the other day and this wee girl, she must have been in her early twenties, she was sitting there and then suddenly she just starts to cry. Out of nowhere. I suppose it was boyfriend trouble or somesuch. Well, that's how I feel sometimes. This terrible grief comes over me and I want to cry. And I very well might. And part of it, you know, is disbelief, which never leaves you.

I'd no idea it still hurt so much, Da.

Time, son, doesn't come into it. I'm afraid you'll learn that for yourself in the years ahead.

Joe leaned towards his father. Let's get ourselves indoors, Da.

They held hands and after one, two, three, pulled themselves off the plant pots. Heads suddenly reeling, they steadied each other.

We're fine, said Joe, we're fine. There's the back door over there.

God, said Patsy, but we're going to regret this in the morning.

*

Joe sat hunched over a map of the Arctic. He acquainted himself with place names – Barrow Strait, Viscount Melville Sound, McClintock Channel, Victoria Island – familiar British names appended to the ends of the earth. Like many before him, he traced with his finger the route that the Franklin expedition had taken.

The story of the search for the Northwest Passage, for a channel around the North American continent to the waters of the Pacific, thrilled him. A search that had haunted the English imagination since Elizabeth I. He read of early explorers like Martin Frobisher and John Davis setting out under the delusion that seawater only froze near to land and that there existed a perfect, calm, ice-free polar sea, could they but reach it. Of Henry Hudson being set adrift in a small boat by his rebellious crew in the bay that thereafter bore his name. Of Captain Cook attempting the Passage from west to east through the Bering Strait until the ice stopped him and of how, on turning back, he was attacked and killed by natives on Hawaii.

These were the adventure stories he had never read as a boy. Under their spell, he turned the central heating off in his house and, as the chill settled in around him, he read on.

As he reached the nineteenth century, he discovered that in a brief period before Franklin's final voyage, a matter of just forty years or so, the map of the known world was moved a thousand miles northwards. Fearful that a foreign nation would complete the Northwest Passage before them, the British Admiralty, in a fever of nationalistic zeal, sent forth one expedition after another.

Yet still the Arctic confounded its explorers. Travelling through Lancaster Sound in 1818, Captain John Ross saw 'the land, around the bottom of the bay, forming a connected chain of mountains' and so he turned back. But the Croker mountains, as Ross named them, were simply a mirage, for the truth was that clear water only lay ahead of him. It was a mistake that was to undermine his career, for fellow officers, once back in England, signally failed to corroborate his vision.

A year later, as the *Hecla* and the *Griper* under Edward Parry sailed through Lancaster Sound and beyond the illusory Croker mountains, the officers, as one of them noted in his journal, could not 'stifle inward pleasures' at seeing the open waters ahead. By September though, with winter closing in, they were safely anchored at Melville Island, ahead of them a wait of almost an entire year before the ice released them the following August. Nobody had ever wintered in such remote regions before, they were five hundred miles beyond the known world, two thousand miles from the nearest settlement. They stretched a canvas roof over the upper deck and waited it out. They had bread baked daily and freshly brewed beer. Parry grew mustard and cress to prevent scurvy. They put on farces and produced their own in-ship journal. They tamed a wild fox. They endured months of unending darkness until in February the sun rose for the first time. With the temperature at −55°, one of the crew poured water through a colander from forty feet up in the mast to see if it would freeze before hitting the deck. By May the men were wearing black crepe veils to prevent snow-blindness. Finally, in July, the ice began to break up around them. They had endured all with a quiet, undemonstrative heroism.

And what of Franklin at this time? Whilst Parry was ice-bound off Melville Island, Franklin was exploring the

Coppermine river in northern Canada, following it to its exit into Coronation Gulf, and then surveying eastwards along the Canadian coastline for over five hundred miles. Franklin hoped to find an Inuit settlement where they could winter but none being found they had no choice but to set off overland back towards their base camp at Fort Enterprise. With one hundred and fifty miles still to go, they were virtually out of food and only the killing of caribou and musk oxen saved them. Winter arrived suddenly. They tramped in single file through three feet of snow and survived by eating rock tripe, an edible lichen. On arrival at Fort Enterprise a note informed them that one of their party, who had been sent ahead, had gone to find their only allies in that wilderness, a group of Copper Indians. The only people who could save them. They ate boiled deerskin and a soup made from pulverized bone while they waited, aware that their lives were measured in days. Two of them died almost immediately and when the rescuers finally arrived they found an emaciated Franklin and his few companions on the verge of death.

When Parry and Franklin returned to England from their respective expeditions, it was Franklin's adventures that the public thrilled to. He was pointed out in the street as 'the man who ate his boots'. He had returned a hero. In private moments, did he think back to the long arguments he'd had with his parents before they'd reluctantly allowed him to enlist in the Royal Navy? Did he reflect on earlier brushes with death: surviving the battles of Copenhagen (aged just fourteen) and Trafalgar, or the weeks he had spent marooned on a sandbank on the Great Barrier Reef? All this had been preparatory to the main act of his life for, like a ship anchored to an iceberg, the Arctic now determined his future direction. Over the next twenty years he would return at every given opportunity until, in May 1845, the *Erebus* and the *Terror* left Woolwich on what Franklin confidently believed would be the completion of the Northwest Passage.

*

For months, William Coppin brooded over his dead daughter and over the vision of the lost Franklin that she had supposedly revealed. Though he considered himself a rational man, still he understood better than most the power of visions and the spell of the inexplicable. For on more than one occasion he himself had dreamed the future.

Over twenty years before, he had briefly returned to Ireland to visit his parents and was travelling back to New Brunswick on board the brig, *Levant*. For a week they were held off the Irish coast by contrary winds. Then, one night, he dreamed that in twenty-six days precisely they would reach Shelbourne Harbour in Nova Scotia. In the dream he climbed the mast and saw the harbour, a few fishing vessels at anchor and, on an island, guarding the harbour, a lighthouse. Through a telescope he saw the lighthouse keeper light the lamps. At breakfast next morning he'd related the dream to those assembled but the *Levant*'s captain had commented that to sail via Shelbourne Harbour would be out of his course. Teasingly the captain had written the dream out by hand on the white crossbeam of the cabin and dated it.

For the next three weeks they'd made good progress. Then thick fog descended, stopping the taking of observations and putting in some doubt their chart position. For days the fog smothered them. When finally it lifted he happened to be standing on deck and there before him growing ever clearer was the island with the lighthouse. He'd rushed down to the cabin immediately, checked the date the captain had written on the crossbeam and realized that twenty-six days had indeed passed. Climbing the mast, he waited and watched until finally he saw through his telescope the lamps in the lighthouse being lit, one by one.

So, if he could see across time and space, why not others? Why not the dead even?

A map of the Arctic lay spread permanently across his desk. He felt a strange elation, an excitement reminiscent of the time he'd worked on the *Great Northern*.

Sometimes at night, when everyone in the house was asleep, he would descend the stairs to the room where the children saw Weesy most frequently, in the hope that she would appear to him. He would sit in an armchair and wait patiently, listening to the heavy ticking of the clock. At high tide he could sense the Foyle surging beneath the house.

During these hours he felt closer to his daughter than he ever had when she was alive. After her death he had deliberately absented himself from the house, using work as an excuse to stay away for months at a time. But during those months he had wrestled with guilt, not loss, believing that Weesy's death was retribution for his ceaseless obsession with ships and shipbuilding and for the many ways in which his family had suffered as a result. When he did attend to his wife and children he loved them dearly, but his thoughts were usually elsewhere.

Often he would fall asleep in the chair and wake at dawn. Leaving the house by the back door, he would stand by the Foyle to take in the first stirrings of birds and animals. A small group of sanderlings, maybe, running at full pelt along the exposed shore, or an otter surfacing upriver. Behind him, the Presbyterian meeting-house and on the high ground further back, enclosed by high walls, the lunatic asylum. He had worked by and on this river for years yet, because of his obsession, he knew little of the detail of its history. He could have been anywhere. But this town had been good to him and had honoured him and he imagined that the rest of his life would be spent here and that here he would be buried.

Eventually one night, when his wife and children were asleep, he sat down and with a chart of the child's description before him he wrote a letter to Lady Franklin.

. . . I lost a beloved Child and in about six weeks after her death she appeared to her Brothers and Sisters – I must remark here that I have four Children at present living, the Eldest Boy John 14 years old, the second is a girl named Anne of 10 years, the third a girl called Dora of 6 years and the 4th is a Boy called William of 2 years – the deceased was a girl a little under 4 years and between the third and 4th child. The deceased Child Louisa appeared distinctly to the 3 Elder Children, and is constantly showing them scenes which I cannot now describe only so far as your interest is concerned the deceased speaks to her sister Anne by some chance the questions was put is Sir J. Franklin Alive when to the surprise of Anne, the room they were in appeared to be filled with Ice some Channels and a Ship in one narrow creek or harbour between two Mountains of Snow and Ice in a Sort of dilapidated State with Another in the distance and in a distinct Channel of water two Ships, the first had men on the deck and the second question put is Sir J. Franklin alive, if so make signal, in a few Moments she describes a round-faced Man ascends the Mast and waves his hat. The question being asked what part of the Arctic ocean is Sir

John Franklin in, the first scene completely disappears and on the wall are placed in large letters 'Erebus and Terror, Sir John Franklin, Lancaster Sound, Prince Regent Inlet, Point Victory, Victoria Channel', which would place Sir John and his crews on King William Island. I have written everything as described by the Child and perhaps you may believe them, as other circumstances which we have found borne out as predicted by this Child.

William Coppin reread everything he had written. On the page it looked like the ramblings of a lunatic. Doubtless Lady Franklin received such missives all the time, why would she choose to give credence to his? It was one thing for him to believe in private, it was another for him to risk his good name in the world at large.

He took the letter and placed it in his desk drawer, then locked it. The words of his dead daughter – if such they were – would stay within the family for the present time.

PART FOUR

JOE O'KANE WANDERED up and down the aisles of the supermarket. Since Ciara's death he hadn't paid much attention to what he ate, getting by on ready-made meals and takeaways. He might not eat all day then rise in the middle of the night and heat a meal in the microwave. Standing at the window, plate in hand, he would fix his attention on a window that was still lit and wonder what human drama was being played out behind it, comforted to see that there were others equally out of step with the world's timing.

Resolving to do something about his eating habits, he had turned to the shelf that held Eileen's cookery books and as a result was now searching the supermarket for items he knew by name only. As he hunted for a bottle of sherry vinegar amid a profusion of oils and vinegars a woman appeared alongside and he shifted over to give her more room.

You've forgotten me already, a female voice said mournfully.

Sorry? Joe turned to see by whom he was being addressed.

And after telling me I was one of the most beautiful

women you'd ever seen, a Pre-Raphaelite painting no less.

Oh, he said, it's you.

I suppose you're going to tell me now it was only the drink talking.

I must have made a right fool of myself.

No more than anyone else that night.

She inspected the contents of his shopping basket. I'm impressed, a man who can cook. You're an endangered species in this part of the world. You should invite me round for a meal.

He looked at her closely, trying to gauge if she was still teasing.

Just so you know, he said, I'm married.

That's all right, she answered brightly, so am I.

They walked through the aisles together, gathering their respective groceries.

I'm sorry if I was a bit sharp that night, she said. You just met me at a bad time.

No harm done. I didn't exactly distinguish myself.

Listen, I'm going to a party tomorrow night, why don't you and your wife come along.

I don't think Eileen would be too interested in a party.

Well come on your own then. You can escort me.

What about your husband?

He's not around.

I'm not sure I'm much company at the moment.

That doesn't matter. You can walk me there, hang around outside until I'm done, then walk me home.

He laughed. Put like that how can I refuse.

At the checkout they made arrangements to meet later.

Just one thing, he called after her as she walked away from him, I don't know your name.

Katie, she said, swinging round briefly as she walked away, I'm Katie. And you, if I remember correctly, are Joe.

They met at the corner of Clarendon Street and Strand Road, surrounded by the Saturday night crowd roaming from bar to bar, both feeling very old in the midst of it all. Young girls tottered past, as if walking was a skill they still sought to master. Birdlike cries rent the air. A group of teenage boys, hands in pockets and deep in conversation, stood gathered in a circle near him and every now and then one of the heads would swing outward to spit.

As they walked he told her a little about himself and she told him that she worked as a programme editor for the local BBC station, Radio Foyle. That she lived in Marlborough Road in Rosemount. That she was born in Southampton but had spent most of her adult life in London.

Is your husband English?

Yes.

And what does he think of Derry?

Insofar as he thinks about it at all, I imagine he hates the place. She caught Joe's eye. We're separated. He's still in London.

When they reached the house on Culmore Road she turned to him anxiously.

You are coming in, aren't you?

Of course I'm coming in! What do you take me for?

The hallway was full of people but they inched their way forward into the living room.

What's the occasion? asked Joe.

A colleague's birthday. She scanned the room doubtfully. But I don't imagine I'll know many here.

Stay put then 'til I get us a drink.

But when Joe returned Katie was gone. He spied her standing at the window with three men around her, she talking animatedly whilst they leaned in towards her in an exaggerated fashion.

He left her to it. As the evening progressed he slipped in and out of various conversations, met a man he had gone to school with, sat for a while on the stairs, and when the mood took him danced in the back room with whoever was on their feet at the time. Then the music slowed to love songs and he wandered out to the back door to look over the garden. A man was leaning against the jamb smoking. He offered Joe the open pack.

I don't usually, said Joe accepting.

He bent his head to the flame within the man's cupped hands.

I wish I could say the same, said the man. I smoke a pack a day regular as clockwork. In fact if you asked me I could probably tell you the actual time of day I'll smoke each one.

He took a long drag. Both the da and granda died of lung cancer and here's me – he raised his cigarette for emphasis – as if I hadn't a care in the world.

It's a hard habit to break.

Did you ever try Park Drive?

No.

That's what the pair of them smoked. Lethal. You might as well pour liquid tar down your throat. D'ye see if someone offered me da a filter cigarette, he'd snap the filter off before smoking it. Said he couldn't taste it otherwise. When I was living at home I'd be wakened every morning at seven on the dot by the sound of him coughing and spitting into the sink. And me mother shouting at him from the bed to stop it. By the time he'd finished I would be in the kitchen having me breakfast. In he'd come, make himself a cup of tea and light up. He'd stand by the window and look out at the morning, smiling away to himself. I think it was the best part of the day for him.

So this is where you are, Katie's voice said from behind them. I thought you'd deserted me.

They walked further up Culmore Road until they reached the Foyle Bridge. Halfway across they stopped and looked back towards Derry resting in the crook of the river. Distant and serene, it glowed in winter darkness like a mystic's dream. A spillage of light lay upon the water.

Katie gazed upriver. You forget how beautiful it is. I envy you being born somewhere beautiful, Southampton is such an ugly sprawl.

It's some recompense I suppose.

What does your wife think?

Like most people here my wife feels sorry for all those poor souls in the world who weren't born in Derry. But then, the inhabitants of this town see themselves as the chosen people.

You sound cynical. And I never took you for a cynical man.

And what kind of man did you take me for?

She paused, considering.

That's what I've been trying to work out. I'd say you're overly romantic, a touch unworldly. You feel things. That night in the pub when we first met I remember thinking you looked a lost soul.

He turned away from her and rested his arms on the bridge railing.

And then, before he knew what he was doing, he found himself telling her of Ciara's death. Once begun, it was as if another voice was speaking over which he had no control. He told her what he had told no-one before. Of all that had happened that last day: of the towel turning red before his eyes, of him standing by the river knowing something irrevocable had just occurred, of his desolation when the doctor removed the sheet and he saw that it was her. Of his guilt.

When he had finished Katie nodded gravely.

I knew there was something, Joe, I knew from the first day I met you there was something, but I didn't want to pry.

She stepped forward and put her arms around him, he hugged her back and they stood together for some time in silence.

It's been a while since anyone's hugged me, he said, somewhat sheepish.

We must do it again some time, she teased. She linked her arm in his and they began to walk back into town.

In the city centre the street cleaners were already out. They ghosted among the debris, systematically working their way behind a slow-moving bin lorry. In the half-dark a group of gulls swung low along Strand Road like bats out hunting.

Joe walked Katie to her front door.

Now you know where I live you must come round for dinner, she said.

I'd love to.

What about Wednesday then?

He nodded.

She leaned forward and kissed him on the cheek.

You've been the perfect escort, Mr O'Kane. I'm very grateful.

As he made his way home down Beechwood Avenue a thin wash of light on the horizon signalled the dawn. He found himself looking forward already to Wednesday. The evening just finished seemed almost illicit, a throwback, as if when he got back to the house his father would still be up, waiting to question him on where he'd been to this hour.

He thought of Eileen asleep at this moment, picturing her sprawled across the bed, the duvet kicked away, the long T-shirt riding up her legs. The hand beside her head balled into a fist. Sleeping alone in her parents' house as if he had never existed.

An occasional light burned in the houses he passed and as he looked in and saw the trappings of domesticity he felt as if he was living in an adjacent world, passing by along a dark street, unconnected, a ghost allowed to glimpse what would always be denied him.

*

A few days before the *Erebus* and *Terror* sailed from London in May 1845, John Franklin was recovering at home after a bout of flu. His wife Jane had just finished embroidering a silk Union Jack for him to take on the journey and as he lay resting on the couch, she covered his legs with the cloth. But Franklin sprang to his feet at once, admonishing her that you only placed the Union Jack over a corpse. It was a minor incident but one that Jane Franklin referred to in later years.

It may have been on her mind by the end of 1847 when the first stirrings of unease occurred at the absence of any news from Franklin; the Admiralty deciding therefore to send three relief expeditions to the Arctic. One entered via the Bering Strait, one travelled overland along the Mackenzie River and the third, under the command of Sir James Clark Ross, followed Franklin's original route through Lancaster Sound. Ross led an exploring party down the western coast of Somerset Island, alongside Peel Sound, but found no trace of Franklin and extreme conditions forced him to turn back toward his own ships.

Ross' return to England in November 1849 was final confirmation that Franklin had disappeared without trace. Prayers for his safe return were said in churches across the country. The usual hoaxes were perpetrated; bottles found along the English shoreline contained messages that purported to come from Franklin, there was even a message attached to a small balloon that came down near Gloucester.

On 4 April 1850 the *Toronto Globe* advertised a £20,000 reward to be given by 'Her Majesty's Government to any party or parties, of any country, who shall render efficient assistance to the crews of the discovery ships under the command of Sir John Franklin.' A further £10,000 was offered for information leading to their relief and another £10,000 to anyone who could ascertain the fate of the expedition.

The following month there was a knock at the door of 33 Spring Gardens, London, Lady Jane Franklin's temporary residence, and the maid retreated within to announce to Lady Jane that a Captain William Coppin of Derry in Ireland wished to speak to her.

Coppin had been in Liverpool on business when he read in *The Times* that the *Prince Albert*, a ship funded by Lady

Franklin, was shortly to depart from Aberdeen. Five expeditions had already left that year in search of Franklin but Coppin knew that if his daughter was to be believed they were all looking in the wrong place. They were attempting to explore the area around Lancaster Sound and Wellington Channel and none had thought to consider journeying as far south as King William Island. Doubtless, without his intervention, the *Prince Albert* would do the same.

He could no longer simply ignore the situation. He felt that he had a duty to tell Lady Franklin even if it left him subject to ridicule. He had carried this secret around with him for months now and deep within, if he was truly honest with himself, there was a growing compulsion to tell her, to tell everyone, of the extraordinary events that had come to pass in his own home. At times he felt heady with zeal, like a missionary going amongst the heathen, for whom, in his case, the writing on the wall had become as Holy Writ. He still feared losing his reputation but, as he reminded himself on occasion, his reputation sadly was not all he hoped it might be.

As he sat in Lady Franklin's drawing room awaiting her arrival, he composed in his head the sentences he hoped would persuade her she did not converse with a lunatic. When she swept into the room, accompanied by a young woman, he immediately sensed the force of her personality and saw the scepticism writ plain on her face. But she gathered herself and held out her hand.

Captain Coppin, she said, I'm Jane Franklin and this is my niece, Sophie Cracroft. My maid informs me you may have information regarding my husband.

That's right, Lady Franklin.

I have to tell you, Captain, that you are not the first such person to call at this house. Far from it. My husband's disappearance seems to have encouraged a – how shall I describe it – a mischievous disposition in a number of my fellow citizens.

They are nothing but charlatans, Aunt, said Sophie Cracroft with heat.

Quite. So you can understand, Captain, that whilst I do not wish to appear ungracious I will only sit with you for as long as I feel it to be of any value.

You are very candid, Lady Franklin.

I have become so. Now, tell me why you are here.

He told his story slowly, adopting a very deliberate voice, fearful that any impetuosity might be mistaken for a crank's ravings. Lady Franklin and Sophie Cracroft listened intently as if trying to discern the fatal flaw in his narrative that they knew to be there. In the spacious, high-ceilinged drawing room with a bustling, workaday London just the other side of the window, the unearthly particulars of his account seemed increasingly preposterous. He could not tell what the two women were thinking but they heard him through to the end.

A clock chimed as if to inform him his time was up.

Lady Franklin leaned forward in her seat. Captain Coppin, this may seem a foolish question considering you have come all this way to see me, but do you believe your own story?

I didn't at first, Lady Franklin, but the longer I have thought about it the more I believe. As you say I would not be here otherwise.

Quite. She turned to her niece. Ask Emma to bring us tea.

She stood up and gestured at him to do likewise.

I would like you to show me exactly where you believe my husband and his crew to be and mark the spot with an *x*.

She led him to an enormous map of the Arctic that hung on a far wall. Coppin studied it briefly, then drew a small *x* at Point Victory on the north-west of King William Island.

King William Island is very close to where Sir James Ross was last year, she said. Why did he not find any trace of the *Erebus* and *Terror*?

It may be that he did not travel far enough down Peel Sound.

She stared at the map intently. Yet according to you, a rescue ship should proceed down Prince Regent Inlet, not Peel Sound. But would I not be right in thinking that there is no channel by which a ship can travel from Prince Regent Inlet to King William Island? The crew would have to leave the ship and march across Boothia Peninsula. How do you explain this?

I can't. But that doesn't mean it can't be explained. One must remember that the Arctic is so new to us, to judge from the accounts we read in the newspapers it barely seems to be of this earth at all.

Coppin gestured toward the wall. You cannot look at this map as you would a map of England. The same certainties do not apply. In five years' time this map will have to be replaced and what comes after will be significantly different, new lines will be drawn, new names added. Our conclusions must be tempered accordingly.

I understand that. She hesitated, then spoke again. But what I don't profess to understand is why your dead child would choose to inform the world of the whereabouts of my husband.

Because we asked her, Lady Franklin. It's as simple as that.

You are aware though, are you not, that the British government has posted a reward for information leading to the rescue of the expedition.

Yes, I am aware of it.

And this has had no bearing on your decision to come and see me?

William Coppin smiled sadly. I think, Lady Franklin, you mistake me for a different man altogether.

She laid a hand on his arm. No, she said, I do not. Forgive me for provoking you but these are questions that I must ask. For my own peace of mind if nothing else.

She led him back to his seat and Sophie Cracroft rejoined them, shortly followed by the maid bearing the tea-tray. They made polite, non-committal conversation until the maid had served them and departed the room.

I have decided, Sophie, said Lady Franklin, turning towards her niece, to instruct Captain Forsythe to make for King William Island.

But, Aunt, do you not think you should consider this more carefully? With respect, Captain Coppin, every other ship that has set out this year is looking north of Barrow Strait. No-one believes that Uncle John could or would have travelled so far south.

Lady Franklin glanced fondly at her niece. You may find this hard to believe, Captain Coppin, but on the whole it's easier to persuade me than it is my niece.

I can understand her concern. I know you have invested a great deal of your own money in the *Prince Albert* and to accept my word – a man who has just walked in off the street – as to where that ship should go, well, it's a considerable risk.

Indeed it is. But it is not entirely groundless. I have always suspected that if my husband were to get into difficulties he would attempt to return by travelling down Back's Fish River into Canada. It's an area he has explored before and knows well. And of course, as you are aware, Back's Fish River is just south of King William Island. So I have my reasons for siding with your story. Whatever you may think of me I am not a capricious woman.

Coppin laughed. I would never call you that, Lady Franklin.

Good. She reached over and took her niece's hand. Now Sophie, there must be no differences between you and I. Whether or not this prophecy turns out to be true, I trust Captain Coppin and believe him to be a man of honour. It is a great consolation to be able to trust someone again, in some ways that is reward enough. But who knows, with the help of God the *Prince Albert* may find my husband and his crew alive and well on King William Island.

I hope so, Aunt.

Lady Franklin rose to her feet.

I take it you are returning to Ireland.

I go back tomorrow.

We must stay in close touch with each other. I will write to you of the *Prince Albert*'s departure and will keep you informed of further developments. And when next you are in London, you must come and visit us both.

I would be delighted to, Lady Franklin.

Please, call me Jane. And I, with your permission, will in future address you as William.

*

A trumpet was playing slow, mournful jazz as he followed her into the house.

Here, she said, handing him a bottle of chilled white wine and a corkscrew, make yourself useful.

He opened the bottle and filled two glasses whilst she busied herself in the kitchen. Miles Davis' *Sketches of Spain*, said the CD sleeve. He browsed through her bookshelves, took in the ceramic bowls, the candles, the stack of *Vanity Fair* magazines, the framed poster that dominated one wall, composed of a thick, jagged black mark upon a sand-coloured surface – *Antonio Tapies: Whitney Museum, New York*.

He walked into the kitchen. You've a lovely house.

She turned a flushed face towards him. Haven't I. It's the first time in years I've had a place of my own.

She swept open the oven door, lifted out a tray then slammed the door shut. Let's eat.

They sat at the table and ate tiny parcels of filo pastry filled with vegetables and chicken, dipping them first into bowls of thin, delicate sauces. For the first time in months Joe was caught up again in ritual, conscious once more of the rhythm of another's eating, of the tiny adjustments he thereby made, of their hands taking turns to dip the food.

If you don't mind me asking, he said, how come you're here and your husband's in England?

She stopped eating and laid an open hand against the edge of her plate, as if she considered pushing it away from her.

No, I don't mind you asking. You'd be surprised how few people actually do, though I know they want to. She took a couple of sips of wine. I'd only been seeing Phillip for a few months when we decided to get married. We had a simple, low-key ceremony, exactly what I wanted and I was very happy. After the honeymoon in Canada I moved into his flat. It was bigger than mine, though there still wasn't room for everything. So I gave a lot of my stuff away. I wasn't in the flat a week when I discovered he was sleeping with another woman. To be precise I moved in on the Tuesday and moved out on the Sunday.

Holy fuck!

That's more or less what I said at the time.

And what did he say?

Whatever men say at such times. I didn't really listen.

And where did you go?

I ended up with friends. But the practicalities – she flicked a hand dismissively – all of that didn't matter. What was truly dispiriting was to discover that I'd made the same mistake as thousands of other women. I'd become a statistic. You see, I had always believed myself a good judge of people, once that was taken away from me it was as if all my self-belief went with it.

You have to allow for mistakes in life.

I never did. But I've been suitably humbled.

She picked up the last filo pastry and dunked it in the sauce.

After London, Derry has taken some getting used to.

I can well believe it.

I remember on my first day at Radio Foyle I went round the corner to a bakery to buy some pastries. 'I'll have three ring doughnuts,' I said to the girl. She looked at me blankly. I pointed at the doughnuts. 'Gravy-rings,' she said, 'is that what you want?' I ask you, what sort of name is that for a pastry? And there were snowballs and Paris buns and God knows what else, every pastry seemed to have a different name from the one I knew. At the time it seemed worrying that I couldn't even buy a few buns without having to learn a new language.

And now?

Well, human beings are very adaptable, aren't they. It wasn't part of my life plan to live in this town but that's not to say I can't embrace the experience. I'll never belong here, it's such a closed community, but I must say, I do feel welcome.

They finished off the bottle of wine – Katie went into the kitchen and returned carrying a pot of Thai green curry – and they opened a second bottle. Miles Davis was replaced by Van Morrison.

There's almost a mythic Belfast out there now because of him, said Joe. And yet if you were to walk down Cyprus Avenue you'd be sorely disappointed, it's just like any other terraced street. My father always says that it's only reality that disappoints you, not the imagination. When you're looking at a building or a street, he says, always think of its past. It doesn't matter then if it's run down or dilapidated, suddenly it becomes full of possibilities. In fact, I'll give you an example. At one time there was a building on the Strand Road called Ivy House. The council demolished it in the early nineties. I walked past that building countless times over the years and never gave it a second glance. But in the last month or two I've begun to learn more and more about it, who lived there originally, why it was built on that exact spot, the part it played in this city's history. As a matter of fact the supermarket we met in was built on the site of where Ivy House used to stand.

Tell me more about it, said Katie.

So Joe told her of Coppin and the *Great Northern*, of the daughter Weesy, of Sir John and Lady Franklin, of the search for the Northwest Passage.

Is it any wonder, he said finally, that I find the past more captivating?

Later in the evening the talk moved to Katie's honeymoon in Canada.

I've always loved the cold, she said, and my dream was to go to Quebec City in winter. So we flew to Montreal and then took the train up to Quebec. The snow got deeper the further north we went. We sat in a lovely warm train, sipped coffee, and looked out at this brutal, implacable landscape. The St Lawrence came alongside us, with great blocks of ice floating on it.

It was −30 in Quebec City. I had never experienced cold like it. I stepped out of the train station and thought I was going to die. Nobody gives a damn what they look like, they just pile on enough clothes to keep themselves alive. They say that when someone is dying from extreme cold they can actually feel their internal organs beginning to freeze up. I kept thinking of tribes like the Mohicans who had first lived in that area, and of the fur trappers, and was full of wonder at them managing to survive in such a bleak, bleak world.

We had an attic room in a small hotel. We drank champagne every day and we'd fill the sink with snow from off the roof to chill the bottle. In the early morning I used to go out alone and climb up a hill behind the hotel to look out over the St Lawrence. Boats would be crossing back and forth, shouldering the ice floes aside. Everything white as far as the eye could see. I was able to stand there for about five minutes before the cold got too much for me. And yet, in those five minutes I have never felt more alive. I cried some days out of pure happiness. Something told me that life would never get any better.

She rose to her feet. And how right I was.

Standing at the window she pulled the curtain aside and gazed out at the street.

It's the middle of the night, you know.

Joe heaved himself out of the chair. I'd better go, I've got work in a few hours.

I wasn't trying to get rid of you. If you want to stay there's a spare room.

No, I'll head home.

At the door Katie kissed him on the cheek. You've no idea how much I enjoyed tonight, Joe.

When he reached his own house he paused for a moment, considering, then kept walking, turning down William Street and entering an all-night café. At the counter a young lad was pointing to a tray of pastries behind the woman serving.

Gone give us one of them there, he said.

One of these? said the woman.

Naw, there.

This?

Naw, over a bit.

Listen, son, it would be far easier if you just told me what you wanted rather than trying to point.

The youth grinned foolishly at Joe, then leaned forward and squinted at the tray.

One of them things with the pink icing.

Jesus, said the woman after he'd gone, we get some right ones in here.

Joe ordered a mug of tea and carried it to a seat by the window. Around him sat down-and-outs, clubbers, alcoholics, insomniacs, all whiling away the time, waiting for the dawn. The conversation was surprisingly hushed, as if they were afraid of disturbing all those in the city who slept. Gulls glided down from on high to squabble amongst the rubbish piled outside the fast-food outlets.

Joe stood outside the window and looked in at himself. At a man sitting alone at a café table nursing a mug of tea. At a quarter to five in the morning. When the spirit and body are at their lowest ebb, when the respectable world is abed.

He wondered what was going through the minds of those around him.

As for his own, it was filled with the image of Katie tramping up the snow-covered hill behind her hotel to gaze across an ice-filled St Lawrence. He could see her standing there in the early morning light, a resolute figure, determined, before the cold got too much for her, to take in all she could of this strange and wondrous new world.

*

The *Prince Albert* left Aberdeen on 5 June 1850. Having crossed the Atlantic and passed through Lancaster Sound Captain Forsythe and his civilian officer, William Parker Snow, stopped briefly at Sir James Ross' winter quarters at Port Leopold on the north-east tip of Somereset Island, and then proceeded down Prince Regent Inlet as instructed. But they had gone no further than seventy miles before they encountered ice off Fury Beach, ice that they took to be impenetrable. Instead of wintering over, as more experienced officers would have chosen to do, they made the tame decision to head for home.

The *Prince Albert* was back in England within four months of setting out.

But if their expedition was a story of incompetence and failure they did at least bring back news from one of the other ships involved in the search, and vital news at that; the first signs of the missing men had been found. On 23 August, Captain Erasmus Ommanney and officers of HMS *Assistance* had made a discovery at Cape Riley, on Devon Island. Ommanney recalled, 'I had the satisfaction of meeting with the first traces of Sir John Franklin's expedition, consisting of fragments of naval stores, ragged portions of clothing, preserved meat tins, &c . . . and the spot bore the appearance of an encampment.' Ommanney was convinced there was more to be found and continued searching. A large cairn was spotted on a nearby islet, Beechey Island; they took it apart, stone by stone, but there was no record from Franklin beneath it. To this day, this absence of any record is unexplained. It was the duty of every captain to leave details of his current state and his future plans whenever and wherever opportunity permitted; should disaster befall his ship, such a record might be their only hope of rescue.

The searching vessels now converged on Beechey Island and spread out to search it fully. Four days later, word of an incredible find travelled from ship to ship; the graves of three of Franklin's crew had been discovered. They were buried side by side on an isthmus facing Cape Riley. Two of the grave mounds were covered with limestone slabs.

On the headstones were chiselled the inscriptions:

Sacred to the memory of
John Hartnell, A.B. of H.M.S. Erebus,
Died January 4th, 1846
aged 25 years.
'Thus saith the Lord of Hosts, consider your ways.'
Haggai, i.7.

Sacred
to the
memory
of
William Braine, R.M.,
H.M.S. Erebus
Died April 3rd, 1846, aged 32 years.
'Choose ye this day whom ye will serve'.
Joshua, ch.xxiv, 15.

Sacred
to
the memory of
John Torrington
who departed
this
life 1st January,
A.D. 1846,
on board of H.M.S. Terror, aged 20 years.

One of the officers commented that in its stillness and seclusion the gravesite was like a village churchyard tucked away in a remote corner of England.

The searchers had found the camp where Franklin and his crew had spent upwards of ten months across the Arctic winter of 1845–46. There was a forge, a carpenter's shop, a storehouse, a tenting site; the minutiae of their time there still lay about, a pair of gloves set out to dry, a key, empty coal bags, fragments of clothing. A board painted with a black hand on a white background was found on both sides of the island, the hand pointing in the direction of the *Erebus* and *Terror* should any of Franklin's crewmembers ever become lost or disorientated during a snowstorm.

For the searchers, though, the most perplexing find was a pile of around seven hundred empty food tins that had once contained preserved meat. The number was far in excess of the amount that Franklin and his crew would have been expected to consume so early in their expedition. It prompted speculation that the meat had spoiled and that Franklin had had all the tins checked, casting away those deemed contaminated. Did this explain the fate of the missing men – had their food supplies run out? Why had three of the crew died only a few months after leaving England?

They considered exhuming the bodies. Dr Peter Sutherland, one of the surgeons on the rescue ships wrote later, 'It was suggested to have the graves opened, but as there seemed to be a feeling against this really very proper and most important step, the suggestion was not reiterated. It would have been very interesting to have examined into the cause of death; it is very probable there would be no difficulty in doing this, for the bodies would be found frozen as hard as possible, and in a high state of preservation in their icy casings.'

But at least they now knew where Franklin had first wintered in his search for the Northwest Passage. What they still did not know was the direction he had taken next.

In the summer of 1851 the rescue fleet found two separate pieces of wreckage that may well have come from

Franklin's ships. One was found to the north of Wellington Channel, the other on the shoreline of Victoria Island, hundreds of miles apart. The considered view was that Franklin could not have visited both places, it had to be one or the other. The Admiralty and the general public gave greater weight to the Wellington Channel find and it was henceforth assumed that somewhere in this vicinity lay the answer to the Franklin mystery, though increasingly it was conjectured that no answer at all would be forthcoming.

*

Throughout the five years of their daughter's life, Joe and Eileen, with camcorder and camera, had been diligently recording it, the results filling a stack of videos and several large photograph albums. Occasionally now Joe would flick through one of the albums or, just before going to bed, watch part of a video, leaning forward in his seat as if he couldn't quite believe what was passing before his eyes.

And in a sense he couldn't. Each scene in its particulars came back to him as he watched, he remembered where and when, a distillate of the emotion still lodged within. But just as the dream you have that moment awakened from can briefly seem more real than reality itself, so reality can sometimes take on all the disorientation of the dream. Joe O'Kane often contemplated the video evidence of his daughter's short life as though it was the product of his own fevered imaginings, as though he had always been childless. Yet there she was, a newborn in Eileen's arms on a summer's day in Brooke Park, or there, surrounded by friends and family at her baptism. The hullabaloo of birthday parties and of Christmas mornings, tottering along the beach at Fahan, picking up speed like a runaway train. Her first encounter with snow, hesitant at the back door, nothing previous in life having prepared her for this.

He heard her voice, by turns blithe and querulous. He could see the small mole on her left thigh. Her smile to the camcorder was really to him for she was too young to recognize its intermediary role. He did not understand how someone so extravagantly alive could be no more. This was no grey, insipid ghost, no half-glimpsed apparition, the child cavorting before him exhibited all the colours of the spectrum, emitted a high-voltage energy. Where had that life force gone? He could not believe that it had just flickered out and died.

Each time he watched the videos there was the renewed despair of what he had lost and yet he could not stop himself.

And when Eileen appeared with their daughter he had to remind himself that she was actually still alive. She had gone so fully from his life that her state of being seemed little different to Ciara's. In some ways her absence was even more baffling. She inhabited a limbo from which she could still be rescued, prayers and good works might yet bring her back to him.

Just a couple of miles from where he now sat she was going about her life, chatting with her parents, watching television, sitting down to an evening meal. He could walk those two miles to her parents' house, look in the window and see her miraculously before him.

As he moved about the house, influences reached him from beyond the grave. Photographs of dead relatives were dotted everywhere; he beheld them as regularly as he did his own face in the mirror. Whilst he watched himself age, studying his face for time's encroachments, his relatives remained the same, holding the same pose as if patiently waiting for him to catch up, secure in the knowledge that the day would finally arrive when life turned full circle and he would look at them and see himself.

*

Lady Franklin determined to send the *Prince Albert* back to the Arctic. She appointed a new captain, William Kennedy, a Canadian fur trader, and as his second-in-command, chose a young Frenchman, Joseph René Bellot. William Coppin was summoned to London.

All was as before. Sophie Cracroft was again present and they had afternoon tea. But in the intervening months Lady Franklin and William Coppin had corresponded and there had developed between them a mutual respect and a growing warmth. They now discussed the cost of the expedition and it soon became clear to Coppin that she was struggling to find sufficient funds.

I can help you, he said, at least in part.

I cannot ask you to do that.

You must let me. Would you jeopardize the *Prince Albert*'s departure?

She looked at him in some surprise. I did not realize this at first but it strikes me you are an impetuous man, William Coppin.

There are worse sins, Jane.

There certainly are. And I for one am very grateful for your impetuosity. She reached out and took both his hands. I accept your very kind offer. Thank you, you will always have my deepest gratitude.

There is no need to thank me, he said gruffly, it is only money after all.

She smiled and squeezed his hands as if in contradiction.

And the *Prince Albert*, he went on quickly, how are your plans progressing?

You know of course that everyone now advises me that to look anywhere but near Wellington Channel would be a waste of time and money.

That can hardly surprise you. Ever since they found the graves on Beechey Island it is assumed that the *Erebus* and *Terror* must be in the vicinity.

They also hint that you are having a deleterious effect on me, that I do not know my own mind any more.

Then they do not know you.

Quite. But I am a woman, William, and therefore, in their eyes, illogical and prone to whims and fancies. To my face they call me loyal and devoted but to each other they say, 'Poor Jane, she no longer knows what she is doing.'

You must not pay them any heed, Aunt, said Sophie Cracroft.

And yet not one of them, continued Lady Franklin, has the courage to counsel me that John might be dead. Do they consider me so naive, so foolish, that I could not think such a thought? Dear God, I think of nothing else.

She paused, then resumed in a voice that weighted each word she spoke.

What I require is honesty, and I see no point in having relations with anyone if they are not honest. My instinctive liking for you, William, was based on my conviction that you are an honest man. When we first met and I implied that it was only the financial reward you sought, the look on your face expressed openly your disappointment in me, you could not hide it. I knew then that I could trust you, and I have done so ever since.

She stood up and walked to the window. Her back turned to them, she gazed out at the chill street scene from which the light was fast fading.

Tell me, in your opinion is my husband dead?

I think it likely, Jane.

I think it likely too. But to my mind that is not sufficient reason to stop searching for him and his men. The dead should have our respect as much as the living.

She turned to face Coppin. I have a favour to ask of you. I should like Captain Kennedy to visit you in Derry, that he may speak with you in person and meet your daughter, Anne.

He would be most welcome.

Let me explain my reasons. I know that between now and his departure Captain Kennedy will be advised by virtually everyone he meets that he is going on a fool's errand. And no man wants to be considered a fool. My hope though is that when he hears word for word from Anne's lips what she has seen it will erase all his doubts about heading for King William Island. Otherwise I fear that when tested by an Arctic winter he will be found wanting.

If you think it will help, Jane, then we must arrange it as soon as possible.

So it was that a week later Captain Kennedy accompanied Coppin on the journey to Derry. He stayed for three days at Ivy House and during the course of his visit spoke several times with Anne. She repeated yet again all she had seen and heard and her artlessness seemed to impress Kennedy deeply. Coppin took him for walks about the city during which they conversed on the subject of ships and the sea, their talk though returning repeatedly to the fate of the *Erebus* and *Terror*.

There was much to admire in Kennedy. He had been

employed with the Hudson's Bay Company but felt such disgust at their treatment of the natives that he'd quit. When he arrived from Canada he told Lady Franklin that he was as happy to serve in a subordinate position in the expedition as he was to command. Coppin thought his lack of vanity a rare thing in a domain where men plotted and schemed for every advance in rank and status. But he worried that Kennedy might not have the single-mindedness, the obsessive drive necessary for the Arctic extreme.

When it came time for Kennedy to leave Derry the Coppin family gathered at the front door of Ivy House. The children had grown fond of him, charmed by his lively presence that was in such contrast to their father's intense, inward manner. Kennedy hugged and kissed each of them warmly.

Finally he turned to Anne. You have been very patient with me, he said bending towards her, considering the many questions that I have asked you. So now I will make you a promise. If I am fortunate enough to discover the whereabouts of Sir John Franklin, any reward that I may receive I will give to you and to your family. Let it be proof that I believe everything you have told me.

As he waved goodbye, the family wondered if they would ever see him again. All that is except Coppin, who had already arranged to go to Aberdeen from where the *Prince Albert* would set sail.

Inevitably this entailed neglecting his own business interests, and a workforce who needed his leadership. But he was seized with a drive and purpose that had eluded him since the days of the *Great Northern*. Responsibilities, he knew, would keep him on land but in his mind's eye he was sailing through the high icebergs of a world that reality would for ever deny him.

Once installed in a small hotel in Aberdeen he rose from his bed the moment he awoke, propelled into the new day by sheer excitement. But all around him, to his horror, he beheld disorder and confusion, men trooping off here and there as they saw fit, answerable to no-one. So he began instinctively to issue instructions in a voice used to being obeyed and by the end of the day men of their own volition were approaching him to ask what they might do next.

Although it was early summer a bitter wind blew in off the North Sea, a mild overture to the real drama that awaited them. If it should be this cold in Scotland now, a few of the novice crew speculated nervously, what must it be like in the midst of an Arctic winter? For at least a year, probably more, they'd live with the cold going deep into their bones, their breaths pluming in the open air with each exhalation, and above them, as if they were gazing from afar at their own predicament, a desolate white moon hanging perpetually in space.

Each evening in Aberdeen Coppin dined with Lady Franklin and Sophie Cracroft, both of whom had travelled up from London, and with them at table were Kennedy and Bellot. They talked of the spirit world; Kennedy described his few days in Derry and the strong impression Anne Coppin had made on him. Sophie Cracroft spoke of a visit that she and Lady Franklin had made two years ago to the clairvoyant Ellen Dawson.

Once she had put herself to sleep, said Sophie, Ellen Dawson chose to communicate with me rather than Aunt Jane. She told me that she had been on a long journey over sea and ice and that she could see a ship on the ice with a number of gentlemen aboard. One of them she described as rather old, short and stout, with a nice face, which of course I took to be my uncle. Is he ill? I asked. Oh no, she said, he is quite well. When I asked her which way the ship was moving she said that unfortunately she could not tell because there was a cloud before her.

She could see another ship near this one though, and another two ships not far away but, alas, she could not say if these two ships would reach the others because the cloud came down again. All the gentlemen, she said, had plenty of salt beef and biscuits to eat and they wore fur and smelt of brandy.

It was such poppycock, said Lady Franklin, she was simply telling us what we wanted to hear.

But we did credit it for a moment, Aunt, said Sophie.

Of course we did, we were frantic for good news. That is what I find most objectionable about the Ellen Dawsons of this world, they trade on people's pain and despair. Without the likes of us, yearning to believe, they could not earn a living.

As they spoke Coppin could not but wonder that they saw no comparison between him and Ellen Dawson. After all he himself at times felt like a charlatan, repeating the words from a vision to which a desperate woman clung. Was that why he had offered to help financially, as proof of good faith or because it might redeem him should they find no trace of Sir John Franklin on King William Island? Like everyone else round the table he was tense with waiting.

A few days later, on 3 June 1851, the *Prince Albert* set sail, passing the Old Man of Hoy on its way to the open sea.

To his right at the dinner party sat Sophie Cracroft, and beyond her sat Charles Dickens. When Coppin had been introduced to him earlier in the evening he had been surprised that the man who had written *David Copperfield, Dombey and Son, Martin Chuzzlewit* and *The Pickwick Papers* was of such youthful appearance.

I started early, sir, said Dickens dryly, after Coppin had framed this thought into a compliment. I had little choice in the matter.

Initially Dickens displayed a quiet, almost taciturn demeanour, but as they conversed it was as if someone had dropped a flame amongst kindling. His conversation crackled with acuity and wit, his face grew wondrously animated, and Coppin, sensing the force and assertion of his character, recognized that this was a man who would not be checked. Over dinner it transpired that Dickens had followed closely the various attempts to find and rescue Sir John Franklin. And it was also soon obvious, much to Coppin's astonishment and discomfiture, that Dickens was aware of Weesy Coppin's place in the chronology. He leaned forward, deaf to the other guests around the table, and questioned Coppin closely on the details of Weesy's appearances and on the descriptions given by Anne and the other children.

I find it difficult to believe in this spirit world, he said eventually, it is too whimsical for my taste. But I do not dismiss it entirely. Is it true that the *Prince Albert* is following the directions given in the vision?

That was their instructions.

Well, Captain Coppin, should they be successful and rescue Sir John and his men I may have to reconsider my position.

As if this were the final word on the subject Dickens then turned his attention to others about the table.

After dinner though, when the men were together over drinks, he took a seat next to Coppin. You may not be aware of it, he stated, but sadly we have in common the loss of a daughter. My own daughter, Dora, was taken just six months ago. She was but an infant.

I too have a daughter by that name.

Of course one should not be surprised at the occasion of a child's death, it is the way of our world. Children die in great numbers. But it is a terrible surprise nonetheless.

Where you there when it happened?

No, I was at a meeting that I had agreed to chair, and when word was brought it was my friend they informed first. He waited until I had finished speaking, then took me aside and told me. Dora had suffered convulsions, it seems, and had died quickly, there was nothing anyone could do.

There seldom is. You are reduced to having to stand and watch.

Yes, reduced is certainly the word. Dickens sipped at his drink. I take it, Captain, that you believe in the spirit world?

Not to believe would be to deny my own children.

Of course. But life though would be more bearable I think if we could only accept that when those we love die, that is an end to it. Did you ever ask yourself why your daughter has come back in this way?

I have asked myself little else. And the simple answer, I believe, is that she came back because she could not endure being parted from her brothers and sisters. Impelled by the injustice of such a short life, you might say. When I questioned my children about Weesy's presence they spoke of her going from room to room with them. As if she couldn't bear to miss a moment of their play. And they always insisted that a place be set for her at table that she might hear us talk and still feel part of the family.

Coppin smiled apologetically. All this is very fanciful, I know. You may think it beneath consideration.

But you yourself have never glimpsed anything untoward?

No, nor has my wife.

And the atmosphere of the house, did you detect any change when all this began?

I was not aware of any, though of course in such circumstances one's nerves are easily disturbed. My house sits beside the river and every play of light would unsettle me. I might be sitting in my study, a cloud would cover the sun, the room would darken, and I would look up, half expecting my dead daughter to be before me.

There was silence between them for a moment, both caught up in their own thoughts, then Dickens spoke.

What most intrigues me about your story is that it was only when challenged directly that Weesy imparted the information about Sir John. Had nobody ever asked, she would never, it seems, have conveyed it voluntarily.

It may not have been of any consequence to her. Worldly concerns, however important they may be, seldom matter to children.

And so it should be, do you not think? To introduce a child too early to the pitiless realities of pounds, shillings and pence is to impair them for the rest of their days. Childhood should be primarily about unreality if it is to be recalled with any pleasure in later life, it should be a time given over to the discovery and probing of one's imagination. That we permit children to work long hours in dreadful conditions is one of the great stains on our national life.

You speak as though you are trying to convince me, but I can assure you I am of like mind.

My apologies, it is a subject on which I feel very strongly and on which I am prone to sermonize given the least opportunity. It is pleasing to hear that you are of like mind for I must confess, Captain, that I was curious to meet you and wondered what sort of man you might be. On the one hand you are a shipbuilder, a most pragmatic profession – or so one would think, and yet you are also an inventor and therefore a visionary. It is a beguiling combination. A pillar of the community yet also a man with a secret life.

I'm not sure that I am all you take me to be.

Your achievements suggest otherwise. It is no surprise, perhaps, that a daughter of yours should return in spirit, or that your other children should see her. It is in the family, so to speak.

Do you really believe that such qualities can be inherited?

Why not? Is it so very different from inheriting a particular colour of eyes or hair? If a man or woman can pass on physical characteristics to their children, why not mental attributes as well. We are not a blank sheet of paper on which life begins to scribble the moment we are born, no, the writing has already begun.

A servant appeared before them to refill their glasses.

Lady Franklin tells me, Dickens continued, that Captain Kennedy visited you and your family in Londonderry and that he spoke in some detail with your daughter, Anne.

Yes indeed, he questioned her closely.

And did he seem convinced by what she had to tell him?

That was the impression he gave on his departure from us. He promised to give Anne any reward he might receive.

You are part of an extraordinary story, Captain. At the risk of sounding immodest, the public wait as impatiently for the next chapter of the Franklin mystery as they did for each serialization of *The Pickwick Papers* or *David Copperfield*. But of course in this instance with one principal difference, will we ever know how it ends?

The final chapter cannot be far away, said Coppin, we shall be reading it very soon I believe.

By the middle of July 1851, the *Prince Albert* was at the lower end of Melville Bay where they encountered ten whaling ships, tacking back and forth to avoid the heavier pack ice. They were joined by the American brigs, *Advance* and *Rescue*, and for almost a month the various captains and officers visited each other daily. But Kennedy kept his crew constantly striving to edge their way northwards and eventually in late August the *Prince Albert* reached the entrance to Lancaster Sound.

Kennedy's inexperience was now revealed for he wanted, despite the lateness of the season, to press on and attempt to sail down Prince Regent Inlet, instead of finding a safe harbour.

By this stage it seemed as if the Arctic was filled with ships searching for Franklin, for somewhere in this continent also there were ships under the command of Captains Austin and Penny. Kennedy, realizing it was vital to discover their whereabouts and progress, made for Port Leopold, which lay at the entrance to Prince Regent Inlet, hoping that they might have left a record there. The harbour was heavy with ice but Kennedy was convinced that a small boat could navigate the floes and he and a crew of four set out, taking only a few rockets and lanterns with them. As they neared the shore the wind changed and the ice closed in around the harbour, sealing them off from the *Prince Albert*. Bellot had no choice but to leave them, for the ship itself was now under threat, and so he made his way a good thirty miles down the coast until he found anchorage at Batty Bay.

Along with three members of the crew he tried to walk along the coast to Port Leopold but the weather was too severe and they were forced to turn back. For the next couple of months they had to wait. Bellot maintained the religious services that the devout Kennedy had introduced, the crew unsure as to whether it was their captain's well-being or departed soul they were praying for.

In October, before the complete dark of the Arctic night closed in upon them, Bellot made one last attempt to reach Port Leopold. This time they succeeded and there, within a boat roofed with canvas, were the waiting Kennedy and his men.

Once back on the ship they sat out the long dark winter and it was during this time that Kennedy came to a crucial decision. They would travel down the west coast of Boothia only as far as the magnetic north pole. To attempt to go further and reach King William Island would, he believed, be foolhardy and endanger his men.

In late March they were able to set off on foot, marching south across the frozen Cresswell Bay towards Boothia, which they intended to cross to reach its western shore and then continue on to King William Island. But early in their journey they stumbled across a cliff-lined channel leading westward which did not exist on any maps. They followed it and discovered that the channel separated North Somerset from Boothia Peninsula, which established the former as an island. Eventually they emerged at its western exit. Disorientated, they gazed north up Peel Sound and saw what Kennedy described as 'a continuous barrier of land' stretching from North Somerset to Prince of Wales Island. But in this chimerical world nothing was assured and like the unfortunate Sir John Ross thirty-four years earlier, who was convinced he saw a mountain range in what was the midst of Lancaster Sound, Kennedy and his men were deluded. There was clear water to the north, Peel Sound opening into Barrow Strait, but Kennedy, thinking otherwise, did what Jane Franklin had most feared and digressed from his orders. If Peel Sound was not navigable, went his thinking, then Franklin could not have come that way and therefore there was no point in proceeding further south towards King William Island. Instead he would keep going west, seeking open water suitable for the *Erebus* and *Terror* to have travelled through.

They crossed Peel Sound to Prince of Wales Island, Kennedy querying the wisdom of his decision – perhaps they should have gone south after all – Bellot chiding him that it was too late now to change his mind. Then across Prince of Wales Island, in quest of a western channel. Not realizing that they had already found what they were looking for. Luckless and low on provisions, badly afflicted by scurvy, they had no choice but to turn back, crossing the north end of Peel Sound towards Port Leopold. They reached the ship to find an anxious crew that was likewise suffering.

There was nothing for it but to set sail for home as soon as the ice permitted. Whilst they waited to be released, Kennedy pored over the maps in his possession, trying to ascertain the line of the march he had just undertaken, questioning the decisions he had made, riven by guilt at not following Lady Franklin's instructions. He knew that in all likelihood he would never again be given such a remarkable opportunity to write his name in maritime history.

*

During business visits to London, Coppin would often call on Lady Franklin, partly to discover if she had any word on Kennedy's progress and partly for the pleasure of her company. In these conversations they took the measure of each other, each privately determining how much of themselves they might be prepared to offer.

Do you think often of Weesy? she asked him.

She is in my thoughts now more than ever she was when alive – which causes me great shame. When it is all too late I have a desire to know her likes and dislikes, the particulars of her mind. More than anything I wish to know what she thought of me, though, in truth, I doubt it would make good listening.

We all have regrets, William. Sometimes I think life is composed of little else.

I had such a small amount of time to spend with the children that I ended up responding only to those who made demands of me, and Weesy was always the quiet child, the one who never sought attention. She would be on the periphery, watching. I remember the night that one of my ships burned down, when Dora brought all the children on to the dock. Weesy was only a baby then, her face unformed, and yet that night she had such a knowing look to her. She made no sound, nor did she move in Dora's arms, just gazed at the inferno as if something long known had finally come to pass and when she perceived that I watched her she held my eye. Perhaps I read too much into it, Jane, but I can see her face still and the flames flickering over it. To think that three years later she was dead.

Yet what hope we have of finding my husband lies with her. It may have been a short life but your daughter too had her purpose on this earth.

Coppin leaned back in his seat. Tell me something of Sir John if you will.

What is it you want to know?

Anything – how you first met, anything at all.

Well, let me see. We met twenty-eight years ago. I knew his first wife, Eleanor, and after she died John and I became close. Even then he was acquainted with fame, having already been to the Arctic. By the time we met I had already received a number of proposals of marriage but I was always very fastidious and no-one had quite matched my expectations of a husband. John was not a particularly handsome man – distinguished is probably the best word – and he could be unnecessarily rigid and formal at times but when he spoke it was with such animation and fire that you were completely drawn to him. And I can assure you that I was not the only woman who thought so.

When he first went to the Arctic, at which time we were still merely friends, he named part of the newly charted land Point Griffin, which was my maiden name. 'After the family,' he said at the time, but I knew it was really for me and I thought it wonderfully romantic. He would tell me stories of his adventures, though, typically, understating all the hazards and tribulations he had to endure. But those stories are a mixed blessing to me now because when I remind myself of the many obstacles he has overcome in the past I wonder if it is possible that he might do so again. Such thoughts do not rest easily with the rational conclusion that he has to be dead.

But until you know for certain it is only human to hope. Your husband is an extraordinary man, he and his crew may yet have found the means to survive.

You do not believe that any more than I do but it is kind of you to say it.

Lady Franklin paused as if considering her next words. I will tell you a terrible thing though, William. I have never been empathetic when it comes to general suffering. It is a failure of imagination, I grant you, but I can only relate to the individual. So the truth is I do not think of my husband's crew, I think only of him. And if I bring to mind a desolate landscape of ice and snow I see him standing there alone.

Perhaps the thought that your husband might be suffering is as much as you can bear?

Perhaps. She looked dubious. But you must agree that such an attitude hardly places me in a good light.

These are not normal circumstances.

The circumstances have nothing to do with it, I am what I am regardless. Now you must forgive me if what I am about to ask causes you distress but I wondered what effect Weesy's spirit returning has had on you?

Effect?

Yes, do you regard what has happened as salutary?

I have not really thought of it in such terms. If her communication helps to find Sir John then of course it will have been of enormous benefit.

But what of you, William, is it good for you?

Coppin shook his head. If I am honest I wish she had never come back. Apart from the awful guilt it induces in me I find myself wondering what place it is that Weesy now inhabits. If she is not truly dead and yet not truly alive, then she must be forever between the two. And I cannot imagine that to be a happy place, to be permitted glimpses of your former life, to see those you loved, and yet not to participate fully. She is becalmed between the living and the dead.

I feel the same about John. You mentioned earlier that I

should not give up hope but I have come to the conclusion that hope can be a terrible thing. It is a fire that feeds upon itself and will not be extinguished. And there are times when for sanity's sake it must be extinguished. I would not say this to anyone else, but a part of me, a large part of me, needs to believe that John is dead because certainty, in whatever form, is eventually more bearable than a world composed of maybe and perhaps. What I need is an answer, and at times I am not particular – any answer will do.

*

Joe O'Kane stood at the back entrance of the school amongst a clutch of parents and child minders, all waiting for the bell to ring and their charges to walk down the gravel path and through the corridor of beeches, towards them. He noticed how each glance in his direction was quickly averted, sensed the muted conversations going on around him, but he stood his ground while each parent drifted away with his or her offspring until, inevitably, there was no-one left waiting but him.

He recognized some of the children's faces, all grown a little older, all getting on with their lives. His daughter was barely lodged in their consciousness any more, five months being a long time in a child's perspective. He had no expectation that Ciara would appear amongst them but the revisiting of this scene, its familiarity, to know that he and she had been a part of this once, was strangely sufficient. It counterbalanced the time-lapse between death and departure that he had endured, the confused mind trying to come to terms with all that had happened, still seeing the world as it once was.

Just a week ago, when he'd woken in the early morning

dark, the bedsprings had given as if someone had climbed on to the bed. Lying on his back he had felt his body rise and fall slightly with the force, then a weight had suddenly settled across his midriff like someone sitting astride him. He had felt no fear for it was the familiar weight and pressure of a small child. And it sat astride him exactly as his daughter had on those early mornings when she wanted him to get up, leaning forward, her breath on his face, whispering that she wanted him to come downstairs *now*.

As she'd sat astride him that last day when she'd returned from town.

He had lain perfectly still, tantalized by his lost life coming back to him, the past rushing forward to fill the vacuum of the here and now. A strange emotion had taken hold of him, which he later identified as happiness. He didn't move a muscle for fear of breaking the spell. In this enchanted world Eileen lay beside him, his child straddled his waist, and for a moment it seemed possible that the darkness of the new day would lift to reveal him still living the life he had once known and loved.

*

Amongst the ships that had been sent out by the Admiralty in 1850 were the *Enterprise* (under Richard Collinson) and the *Investigator* (under Robert McClure) with orders to approach the Arctic from the west via the Bering Strait. Though the *Investigator* was the inferior ship, a daring decision by McClure meant that it reached the Arctic first. Between Hawaii and the Bering Strait lay the Aleutian Islands and whilst Collinson followed the prescribed course around them, McClure navigated through their midst. It was uncharted territory. They proceeded through heavy fog with the crew constantly on lookout. Above them the dull thump of sea birds crashing blindly into the sails.

They arrived in the Arctic weeks ahead of the *Enterprise* and travelled along the Alaskan coast. Trapped by ice in a strait that fed into a larger body of water, McClure led a sledging party up the strait until eventually they reached Point Russell. Before them lay what had to be Viscount Melville Sound. With the knowledge that had already been gleaned over the years by expeditions reaching this point from the east, it meant that McClure and his crew aboard the *Investigator* knew that they had actually completed the Northwest Passage.

At this point the wise option would have been to settle for these achievements and return home the way they had come, west through the Bering Strait. But McClure determined to press on and complete the Passage himself, envisaging the *Investigator* sailing triumphantly through Viscount Melville Sound, Barrow Strait and Lancaster Sound into the Atlantic Ocean. It was a terrible, almost fatal, mistake; the crew of the *Investigator* was to spend the next two winters trapped in the ice. By the spring of 1853 they were near death and preparing to desert the ship, set on a desperate march towards civilization that had no hope of success. Their lives were saved by the arrival of a party from the *Resolute*, a member of a new expedition that the Admiralty had sent in search of Franklin.

This expedition, under Sir Edward Belcher, was instructed to explore Wellington Channel following the general consensus that Franklin had to have travelled north, as Prince Regent Inlet to the south was considered impassable. Nobody ventured to suggest, as it seemed beyond the bounds of possibility, that Franklin might have journeyed both north *and* south.

Belcher found nothing around Wellington Channel. Like many before him, his expedition was a complete failure, though redeemed somewhat by the saving of the crew of the *Investigator* and by the fact that, in their explorations, they laid down hundred of miles of the Canadian Arctic coastline for future maps.

The failure of Kennedy in the *Prince Albert* had enraged William Coppin as much as it had disappointed him. Would no-one ever follow their orders and simply go where they were instructed? Did they not realize that under such conditions the evidence of their senses had to be treated with extreme circumspection? The doubts he had harboured about Kennedy were confirmed; the man had acted reasonably, and reasonableness sadly carried little weight in the Arctic.

And so, as the months passed, William Coppin, like everyone else, waited. But months became years and still the Franklin mystery remained unsolved. On 20 January 1854 the *London Gazette* carried a notice announcing that, unless there was information to the contrary, by the end of March the officers and crew of the *Erebus* and *Terror* would be considered to have died in Her Majesty's Service.

During this time the children's sightings of Weesy ended.

Have we done something to upset her, Father? Anne asked him.

I'm sure you haven't. Who can tell, Anne, why Weesy has had to leave us.

Now it was the turn of the children to wander from room to room, in search of her. They felt her absence all over again. They spoke of her, wondering why she did not visit them any more. He wondered the same. The more he wondered the more he began to doubt the veracity of the visions, viewing them increasingly as punishment for the absent-minded way in which he had loved his wife and family. Throughout his life, he had believed in the presence of a spirit-world – so what better way in which to beguile him? That Weesy would not appear to *him*, for so long her absent father, was cruelly appropriate. That he should dissipate so much time and money on a phantom search, to the detriment of his business, was a clever twist of the knife. That the lure glittering before him appeared to be the answer to the Franklin mystery showed an astute understanding of his temperament.

But three weeks after the deadline, by which time he was questioning everything, a breakthrough changed things irrevocably.

The scientist, Dr John Rae, was involved in surveying the Arctic coast of North America. Rae's work was strictly geographical, he gave little or no thought to finding Franklin, believing the chances of so doing were quite negligible. What happened next was explained by him in a letter sent subsequently to the Admiralty:

During my journey over the ice and snow this spring, with the view of completing the survey of the west shore of Boothia, I met with Esquimaux, in Pelly Bay, from one of whom I learned that a party of 'whitemen' (Kablounans) had perished from want of food some distance to the westward . . . Subsequently, further particulars were received, and a number of articles purchased, which place the fate of a portion, if not all, of the then survivors of Sir John Franklin's long-lost party beyond a doubt – a fate terrible as the imagination can conceive.

The articles purchased were unambiguous, they included Franklin's Order of Hanover and a silver spoon and fork, initialed F. R. M. C., which had belonged to Francis Crozier, Captain of the *Terror*. Rae wrote up the story that the Inuit had told him:

In the spring, four winters past (eighteen hundred and fifty), whilst some Esquimaux families were killing seals near the northern shore of a large island, named in Arrowsmith's charts King William's Land, about forty white men were seen travelling in company southward over the ice, and dragging a boat and sledges with them. They were passing along the west shore of the above-named island. None of the party could speak the Esquimaux language so well as to be understood; but by signs the natives were led to believe that the ship or ships had been crushed by ice, and that they were then going to where they expected to find deer to shoot. From the appearance of the men – all of whom, with the exception of an officer, were hauling on the drag-ropes of the sledge, and were looking thin – they were then supposed to be getting short of provisions; and they purchased a small seal, or piece of seal, from the natives.

The officer was described as being a tall, stout, middle-aged man. When their day's journey was terminated, they pitched tents to rest in.

At a later date, the same season, but previous to the disruption of the ice, the corpses of some thirty persons and some graves were discovered on the continent, and five dead bodies on an island near it, about a day's journey to the north-west of the mouth of a large stream, which can be no other than Back's Great Fish River (named by the Esquimaux Oot-koo-hi-ca-lik), as its description, and that of the low shore in the neighbourhood of Point Ogle and Montreal Island, agree exactly with that of Sir George Back. Some of the bodies were in a tent or tents; others were under the boat, which had been turned over to form a shelter; and some lay scattered about in different directions. Of those seen on the island; it was supposed that one was that of an officer (chief), as he had a telescope strapped over his shoulders, and his double-barrelled gun lay underneath him.

From the mutilated state of many of the bodies, and the contents of the kettles, it is evident that our wretched countrymen had been driven to the last dread alternative as a means of sustaining life.

Coppin read Rae's letter again and again, barely able to believe its evidence. All mistrust and prevarication fell away, to be replaced by guilt that he had ever doubted his daughter's veracity. The place where the Inuits claimed to have seen the party of white men – the northern shore of King William Island – was also the area foretold by his daughter. Four years earlier, when he had first contacted Lady Franklin, he had specified Point Victory near Felix Harbour on the western shore of King William Island as the place where the search should be concentrated and now Rae's evidence seemed to corroborate that view. Over the years expedition after expedition had combed the frozen Arctic, not always able to affirm if it was land or sea that lay beneath them, wintering over, surviving on the ice for months in crepuscular gloom. Yet throughout all this time King William Island had remained unexplored. In all the reports that Coppin had read, in all the discussions he'd taken part in, not once had it been suggested that King

William Island might hold the key to Franklin's disappearance. Only in the front room of Ivy House, as part of what seemed at first to be a children's fantasy, had the idea been proposed. The chilling words of Rae's statement though left little room for equivocation – King William Island was where they had died.

Surely also, thought Coppin, it demonstrated that Franklin must have travelled both north and south. Most likely he circled Cornwallis Island and then, after wintering at Beechey Island, went straight down Peel Sound only for his ships to become trapped in the ice there.

Your sister was correct about Captain Franklin, Coppin informed Anne as the family sat about the fire together.

But everything Weesy told us was true, said Anne simply, as if his remark was superfluous.

He realized now that he was the only one who had ever doubted, the only one for whom proof had been required.

Over the following days the newspapers reflected the general disbelief that Franklin and his men would ever have resorted to cannibalism. One of the most prominent figures to challenge Rae was Charles Dickens, who wrote a blazing rebuttal:

Some of the corpses, Dr Rae adds, in a letter to *The Times,* 'had been sadly mutilated, and had been stripped by those that had the misery to survive them, and who were found wrapped in two or three suits of clothes.' Had there been no bears thereabout, to mutilate the bodies; no wolves, no foxes? Lastly, no man can, with any show of reason, undertake to affirm that this sad remnant of Franklin's gallant band were not set upon and slain by the Esquimaux themselves. It is impossible to form an estimate of the character of any race of savage from their deferential behaviour to the white man while he is strong. The mistake has been made again and again; and the moment the white man has appeared in the new aspect of being weaker than the savage, the savage has changed and sprung upon him. There are pious persons, who, in their practice, with a strange inconsistency, claim for every child born to civilization all innate depravity, and for every savage born to the woods and wilds, all innate virtue. We believe every savage to be in his heart covetous, treacherous and cruel, and we have yet to learn what knowledge the white man – lost, houseless, shipless, apparently forgotten by his race, plainly famine-stricken, weak, frozen, helpless and dying – has of the gentleness of Esquimaux nature.

It is in reverence for the brave and enterprising, in admiration for the spirits who can endure even unto the end, in love for their names, and in tenderness for their memory, that we think of the specks, once ardent men, 'scattered about in different directions' on the waste of ice and snow, and plead for their lightest ashes. Our last claim in their behalf and honour, against the vague babble of savages, is that the instances in which this 'last resource' has been permitted to interpose between life and death, are few and exceptional, whereas the instances in which the sufferings of hunger have been borne until the pain was past, are very many. Also, and as the citadel of that position, that the better educated the man, the better disciplined the habits, the more reflective and religious the tone of thought, the more gigantically improbable the 'last resource' becomes.

The tone of this letter, thought Coppin, betrayed a man whose entire belief structure was being challenged. It was as if Dickens had temporarily lost the empathetic skills he demonstrated so wonderfully in his fiction, for who in truth could say what men might do in moments of great extremity? Better surely to look into your own heart and recognize, perhaps even attest to, the acts that you yourself might perform to stay alive. Something in Coppin recoiled at Dickens' all too easy opposition of English and Esquimaux, of civilized man and savage, as if the distinctions barely needed commenting upon. It was the same arrogance demonstrated a mere four or five years ago by English newspapers when famine had ruined most of Ireland; the Irish, they reported with more incredulity than pity, had been reduced to going down on their hands and knees and eating the very grass beneath them. Like the savages and beasts they really were, was the imputation. Yet what human being would not do likewise, for a slow death by starvation left little occasion for dignity. Unknown to each other, thousands of miles apart, had not Franklin's men and the Irish peasantry been linked by a shared sense of inevitability, by the terrifying realization that no-one could or would help them, that their past had become the totality of their lives. And had they not in their final days and hours, fallen back on the last thing to leave them, their cache of individual memories, all they had left to counter the horror of their imminent deaths and to remind them that life had been worthwhile after all. Memories whose significance they alone knew, markers of a life led, which they had never thought to share with another living soul and which they had now taken with them to the grave.

Other deaths now occupied the British public. With Britain's recent involvement in the Crimean War, engagements in such hitherto unknown places as Sebastopol and the Black Sea had begun to stir the general imagination. This shift was underlined by a moment of irony; in the same week that Rae's discoveries became common knowledge in England, Franklin's nephew, Alfred Lord Tennyson, began to write *The Charge of the Light Brigade*.

Whilst Rae's discoveries meant that the Admiralty could not entirely renege on their responsibilities, they chose not to fund another expedition and instead asked the Hudson's Bay Company to send a party down Back's Fish River. It was no more than a gesture. By the time the party had negotiated the river their canoes were too damaged to attempt a crossing in search of the beach where the bodies reputedly lay. What was needed, they stated, was a ship to approach from the north and from it a sledge-party could then reach King William Island.

Lady Franklin lobbied exhaustively for just such an expedition, to determine conclusively the fate of her husband and crew.

When Rae finally returned from the Arctic in 1856 he called upon Lady Franklin at home. He stood in front of a map on the wall, intent on marking the spot where a new expedition should search, but, to his astonishment, there before him he saw an *x* on the precise location, put there six years earlier by William Coppin. As Lady Franklin subsequently remarked to Coppin, 'Had you and I gone out together in 1850 we should have saved many of the lives.'

But the Admiralty continued to baulk at providing another ship and so Jane Franklin bought the schooner yacht *Fox* with her own money and had it refitted for the polar journey. She placed in command an Arctic veteran, Captain Leopold McClintock, and of its crew of twenty-five, seventeen had already taken part in the search for Franklin. When she watched the *Fox* sail from Aberdeen into the Pentland Firth on 1 July 1857, she was hesitant to believe that after so many disappointments and misadventures this departing ship might, in two or three years' time, bring back the truth she had virtually despaired of ever knowing.

*

On a Sunday afternoon Joe walked the short distance to his father's house in Elmwood Street. He knocked but there was no answer. Two doors away a man gazing idly up and down the street caught Joe's eye.

Are you looking for Patsy?

That's right.

He might be in the Bluebell.

His father was seated in the far corner of the Bluebell Bar eating a roast dinner, a Sunday paper propped in front of him. He looked astonished when he saw Joe.

Is something wrong?

No, I just thought I'd see how you were keeping.

How'd you know I was here?

A neighbour told me. Your whereabouts seem to be common knowledge.

And there's nothing wrong?

Does there have to be a national emergency before I can come and see my own father?

Joe sat down in the chair opposite and glanced around the bar. I didn't know they served meals at the Bluebell, he said.

They don't but Mary Feeney sometimes makes me a bite of dinner on a Sunday.

I can see I don't have to worry about you.

No, I'm well looked after. He glanced up from his dinner.

I hear tell you're going about with some English woman at the moment.

How do you know about her?

I have my spies.

She's a friend. We met at Christmas.

Well, it's not for me to tell you how to behave, son.

But you're going to anyway.

No, no, you're your own man. And I know things must be wile hard for you at the moment, what with all that's happened and Eileen still not back home.

Da, she's a friend, nothing more.

In my day a married man didn't have women friends.

Well now they do. And to be honest I'm very glad of her company, I've few enough friends as it is.

Patsy raised a hand. Fair enough, I'll say no more. But if Eileen or her mother ever get to hear about this I want a front row seat when you explain to them that you and this woman are just good friends.

The research files grew ever thicker. Joe copied everything he found: shipping records, birth certificates, street plans, maps, newspaper cuttings, period diaries, anything that might illuminate the life and times of William Coppin.

It seems to be going well, said Colm Casey when they met in his office to review progress.

I think so.

Where have you got to?

At the moment I'm reading McClintock's journal of his expedition.

Casey nodded. It never ceases to amaze me, he said, the sacrifices men were prepared to accept then. To go off into a terrifying unknown land for years at a time, imagine that. Imagine saying goodbye to your three-year-old daughter knowing she might be six or seven before you see her again –

Casey broke off in alarm and glanced at Joe.

It's all right, Colm, I know what you're thinking. Actually I've been meaning to ask if you knew about my daughter.

Casey nodded. I did, as it happens.

I thought so. So were you thinking that the Coppin story might be a help to me?

I wouldn't go that far. But I hoped that at the very least it would be a distraction. Look, Joe, if it makes any difference I didn't know about your daughter when we employed you, I heard about it later. And once I did my first thought was to keep you away from anything to do with death. But sure how could I? Most of the work we do here is about the past, and death's always there whether you like it or not. As for Coppin's story, maybe I hoped you'd find some comfort in it. But I knew it was risky.

Well, risky or not, it has helped. Up to now I've hardly spoken to a living soul about Ciara's death – one person to be exact – and it's taken a man from another century to remind me that I don't have a monopoly on grief. Don't ask me why, Colm, but William Coppin's story is just what I need right now.

It's crossed my mind that maybe you should write it then as well as research it.

Are you serious?

Well, you know more about it now than anyone else.

I'd love to give it a try.

Why don't you then?

*

At the beginning of June 1858 the *Fox* reached Beechey Island where they laid a marble slab in memory of Franklin and his men, then attempted to journey down Peel Sound but found it blocked by ice. The only other route to King William Island lay down Prince Regent Inlet and across Bellot Strait. 'We feel the crisis of our voyage is near at hand,' wrote McClintock in his journal. 'Does Bellot Strait really exist?'

In a deceptive world where through the years even the most experienced of seamen had suffered delusions, could they trust the word of two Arctic novices? The *Fox* ventured cautiously down Prince Regent Inlet and there, despite its concealment by islets, was the entrance to Bellot Strait. A powerful current swept them into the narrow channel. They passed pack ice being hurled about by the tide but when they reached their western exit they found their way blocked by more substantial ice. After several further attempts there was nothing for it but to concede defeat and so they sought winter quarters. Long months of darkness awaited them yet again.

In April they left the *Fox* and set off on sledge and on foot for King William Island. McClintock and his second-in-command, William Hobson, separated to scour the island. After some days apart, McClintock came across a small cairn and within it a note from his deputy Hobson, informing him that at Point Victory he had found a note from Franklin. It was a standard form giving details of their position.

28 May 1847. HM Ships *Erebus* and *Terror* wintered in the Ice in Lat. 70 5' N Long. 98 23'W. Having wintered in 1845–46 at Beechey Island, in lat 74 43' 28". Long. 91 39'15"W, after having ascended Wellington Channel to Lat. 77, and returned by the west side of Cornwallis Island. Sir John Franklin

commanding the Expedition. All well. Party consisting of 2 Officers and 6 Men left the ships on Monday 24 May 1847. Gm Gore, Lieut. Chas F. Des Voeux, mate.

The note proved categorically that Franklin had achieved what few thought possible, ascending Wellington Channel and descending Peel Sound in consecutive years. But a second message, scribbled around the note's margins almost a year later by Captain Fitzjames of the *Erebus*, described a transformation in their circumstances, the bare words hiding the dread and despair that Fitzjames must have been feeling.

25 April 1848 – HM's Ships *Terror* and *Erebus* were deserted on 22 April 5 leagues N.N.W. of this, having been beset since 12 September 1846. The Officers and crews, consisting of 105 souls, under the command of Captain F. R. M. Crozier, landed here in Lat. 69 37' 42" N, long. 98 41'W. This paper was found by Lt Irving under the cairn supposed to have been built by Sir James Ross in 1831, 4 miles to the northward, where it had been deposited by the late Commander Gore in June, 1847. Sir James Ross' pillar has not, however, been found, and the paper has been transferred to this position, which is that in which Sir James Ross' pillar was erected. Sir John Franklin died on 11 June 1847; and the total loss by deaths in the Expedition had been to this date 9 officers and 15 men.
James Fitzjames, Captain HMS *Erebus*.
F. R. M. Crozier, Captain and Senior Officer.
and start on tomorrow, 26th, for Back's Fish River.

The note was the only written record ever found of the Franklin expedition. And his would-be rescuers now realized that even before the first expedition had departed from England to seek him, Sir John Franklin was already dead. But what had happened to him and where his body lay, there seemed no way of knowing.

On further exploration of King William Island both Hobson and McClintock's parties came across a large boat, in which lay the skeletons of two of Franklin's men. One skeleton had been badly damaged by animals but the other lay wrapped in clothes and furs, the feet still encased in protective boots. McClintock's party were 'transfixed by awe' at the sight. The boat contained an astonishing variety of objects: silk handkerchiefs, soaps, sponges, slippers, toothbrushes, crested silver. There were half a dozen books, including the Bible, *Christian Melodies* and *The Vicar of Wakefield*. Amongst it all, the only useful objects were a pair of double-barrelled guns, the only provisions tea and chocolate. Why would men at the edge of death, they wondered, choose to load themselves down with such trivia; did they believe that as long as they continued to surround themselves with the trappings of civilization their situation could not be truly parlous? Or were these objects brought as a constant reminder of the life they sought to return to?

McClintock knew that the crews of the *Erebus* and *Terror* must, like Franklin, be long dead; the journey south towards Back's Fish River offered no deliverance for men in their condition. There was nothing more to be done in the Arctic. The *Fox* set sail for home. On the journey back McClintock sometimes took from his desk drawer the note they had found at Point Victory. He held it in front of him and gazed at the slightly smudged writing and tried to imagine what Fitzjames had been feeling at that moment. For death was at his elbow as he wrote. He and the men with him would have known that the walk to Back's Fish River was no more than a gesture, a fundamentally human gesture against the void.

And McClintock realized that some time in 1848, whilst walking along the shore of Simpson's Strait during their final days, the last living members of the Franklin expedition had had the comfortless distinction of actually completing the final section of the Northwest Passage.

Whilst McClintock searched King William Island for traces of Franklin, William Coppin was back home in Derry, where life was cruelly replaying itself. Harriet, his youngest daughter, who was only eighteen months old, took ill and in April, 1859, she died.

She was buried beside her older sister, Weesy, in St Augustine's churchyard. When the time came for the gravediggers to open the grave Coppin was with them and, despite their protests, he insisted that they dig sufficiently deep for him to see the lid of Weesy's coffin. It was soon evident though that his presence made them uncomfortable so whilst they dug he walked on to the city walls that adjoined the graveyard. Before him, perched on the edge of the walls, stood Walker's Pillar. The view from the top was supposed to be wonderful but until now he had had neither the time nor inclination to climb the pillar. He entered the dark portal and began ascending the curving stairs. He emerged on to a rail-enclosed platform, the centre of which was dominated by a larger than life statue of the Reverend George Walker, Governor of Derry during the siege of 1689. Walker's left arm was fully extended, pointing emphatically, and as Coppin followed the direction of his arm he realized that Walker was pointing downriver, towards where the supply ship, the *Mountjoy*, had first appeared to the starving inhabitants of the besieged city.

The city that now lay beneath Coppin's gaze had extended far beyond the original walls. And it was extending ever further, for these were days of rapid change. When he had first arrived in Derry all the land between the asylum and William Street had been meadow upon which goats and donkeys grazed, but now that land was covered with houses and new streets were springing up – Clarendon Street, Asylum Road, Queen Street, Princes Street, Edward Street – to accommodate the growing merchant class in the city. Further up the hill they had begun work on the site for a Catholic cathedral. And new industries were arriving, factories were being built.

He could not help but note, with as little self-pity as possible, that this prosperity and development had occurred twenty years too late for him. This was a high tide on which he would not sail.

He leaned over the edge of the railings. Directly below him was the line of cottages that comprised Nailor's Row. A few figures walked there, all alike, he could determine neither sex nor age. Gulls floated past, studiously ignoring him, and for a second he was made light-headed by their presence. He had lived and worked by the river, on low ground, from the moment he had come to Derry, frequenting an office filled with riverlight. Behind him, the city went about its business but the particulars of that business had never really interested him. What details he had gleaned had always been through others; he only knew the story of the siege of Derry because one of his children had related it to him. When he returned home from wherever his work for the Board of Trade might take him it was to a town still strange and unexplored. But did you need to know a place's history to call it home?

He crossed the parapet to look down upon the two gravediggers, dark figures almost indistinguishable from the heaped earth about them. They seemed though to have halted their work.

He began to descend. From the outer reaches of his mind he strove to recapture traces of the emotions he had felt as a young man upon his arrival in Derry from the West Indies. A faint afterglow from the fire that had once burned. Back then he had believed himself capable of changing the world! Buying the shipyard had been the first and most important step; from then on he would be beholden to no-one, he could direct his life as he wanted, his own hand on the tiller.

But that was before. Such hopes as he had once nursed were now buried as surely and as deeply as the dead in St Augustine's graveyard. His ships had years ago capitulated to disregard or to fire, his family, whom he had not loved enough, were being snatched from him one by one.

Fate was slowly stripping him bare.

The gravediggers were waiting patiently as if they had all the time in the world. He stepped to the edge of the grave, peered down into it and saw the lid of Weesy's coffin firmly in place. It seemed a long way down. The odour of dampness and mould reached him. His legs weakened momentarily and one of the gravediggers reached out a hand to steady him. Next month would be the tenth anniversary of her death. It was hard to believe that the body of his daughter lay within that rotting wooden box. And that very soon a tiny coffin containing her younger sister would be lowered down to lie beside her.

As he mourned the loss of Harriet, a child he had barely known, he grieved again for Weesy.

*

We don't see much of each other these days, said Patsy, as he concentrated on applying butter and jam to his scone. I'm glad you agreed to meet me.

Eileen took a sip of her tea and said nothing.

A young waitress set down a toasted sandwich on their table. Thank you, said Eileen to the waitress, and then to Patsy, I'm not trying to cut myself off, you know.

He glanced up at her, trying to detect her mood but her face told him nothing. He had always found her fairly inscrutable, she was much like Joe in that regard. For all he knew inscrutability could have been the quality that first attracted them to each other.

One of the consequences of a death in the family, Eileen, at least in my experience, is that a lot gets said that might not otherwise. Grief allows, maybe even encourages, a certain frankness. I say that because you and I need to stop worrying about offending each other. When you and Joe started going out together and he brought you round to the house I thought he was very lucky to have met you. And I still think that. You were the making of him. But for some reason or other you and I have never really hit it off. Maybe it's because I interfered too much in your lives, always offering advice when it wasn't asked for. And I know you think I'm too hard on him, and maybe I am, but it's well meant. If Marie was still alive I'm sure she'd have handled things differently but as it is . . .

As he spoke Eileen fingered her cup and looked anywhere but at Patsy.

Is this making you uncomfortable, he asked?

A bit, she said. But I like honesty, I'm all for that. It's just that I'm not used to you and me talking this way. She took a small bite from her sandwich and chewed it thoughtfully. I suppose what annoys me is that for as long as I've known Joe you've always been at him over something or other. He should be doing this, he should be doing that. Never just letting him be.

That's probably fair enough. But it's only because I worry about him so much, he's an only child, don't forget. In fact, I worry about the both of you, which is why I wanted to talk to you. And there's no need to look so worried, he added, noticing the sudden perturbation in her face, I'm not going to give off to you or anything.

I'm glad to hear it, she said. So what did you want to say to me?

I wanted to ask you to move back into the house with Joe. He held up a hand to pre-empt her speaking. Now I know what you're thinking – here he goes, interfering again – but I'm concerned about the both of you. Listen, Eileen, there's a hundred and one ways to deal with grief, everyone responds differently, and your way was to move back in with your parents. But I'm not sure that Joe's coping particularly well on his own. Nor for that matter, if I'm to be completely honest, do I think you're any the better for having moved out of the house.

How can you know how I'm feeling?

Patsy reached across the table and put his hand on her forearm. He spoke gently. Eileen, love, I know this much, you're not going to get over Ciara's death by pretending you're still a wee girl yourself. That might do for a while but eventually you've got to shoulder this situation you're in. I know marriage vows may not count for much these days but you both committed yourselves to helping each other through bad times as well as good. And what with Joe being stuck in the past – forever going on about this Coppin character – and you being trapped in your own childhood, well, right now the pair of you need each other.

D'you know when you come out of the cinema, said Eileen gravely, as if she hadn't heard a word he'd said, and some people immediately want to talk about the film they've just seen and others don't because they're still caught up in the spell of it?

Yes.

Well, that probably describes the difference between Joe and me at the moment: he wants to talk about Ciara all the time and I don't.

But Eileen, six months have passed –

Weren't you the one that told me there was no time limit on grieving.

Patsy shook his head in despair. It was probably stupid of me to think that I could talk you round. You must do whatever feels right.

He picked up his empty teacup and turned it in his hands, as if examining it for provenance. This might come as something of a surprise, he said, but I'm very fond of you, you know. I might not always show it but you're almost as much a daughter to me as Joe is my son.

And now you've made me blush, said Eileen, almost laughing in embarrassment. She rose to her feet. I really must get back to work.

They stood awkwardly on the pavement, then Patsy bent low and kissed Eileen on the cheek.

You can call round to my house for a cup of tea and a chat anytime, he said, you're always welcome.

Thank you, Patsy. And thank you for everything you said today.

As she turned to go he reached out a hand to stop her as if a thought had just occurred to him.

I don't want to go on about this but just imagine for a moment that it was Joe that had died. Think how you would have clung to Ciara, how she would have meant even more to you because she was the closest link you had to Joe on this earth. She would have been your only comfort. Well, if you'd let him, Joe could be a great comfort to you now. Whatever thoughts are going through your head, there isn't another human being better able to understand them. Eileen, love, you don't want to end up alone, there's nothing worse than that, believe me.

*

In the days that followed Harriet's funeral William Coppin was grateful to let the outside world re-enter his consciousness. He heard of McClintock's return and of the final proof of Franklin's death, quickly followed by a letter from Lady Franklin herself, giving details of McClintock's expedition.

McClintock's discoveries vindicated all his efforts. The Franklin expedition had after all travelled as far south as King William Island. And in all probability they had reached it by travelling down Peel Sound despite the fact that it was choked with ice for most of the year.

But McClintock had displayed shrewd judgement, realizing that Peel Sound was not a feasible option for him and instead he'd travelled down Prince Regent Inlet and across Bellot Strait, thereby avoiding the worst of the ice. But ten years ago, when Weesy had predicted such a route, Bellot

Strait did not exist on any maps. Was not this incontrovertible proof that what they had been told had come from beyond the grave?

As he turned over in his mind all that had happened, Coppin received a letter from William Kennedy, the former captain of the *Prince Albert*, whose thoughts were similarly preoccupied:

In particular, your child related that Sir John with his ships were to be found down Prince Regent Inlet, and that, about places named Victoria, exactly the name of the place where Sir John abandoned his ships, and deposited the only record that has been recovered from the Franklin expedition. How your child could have known these things is the more remarkable, because at the time, she not only had not the slightest intimation as to the whereabouts of poor Franklin, but Lady Franklin herself was so possessed with the matter that Sir John had gone up Wellington Channel, that most people were carried away with the same impression. I was among this number, and therefore did not attach the importance to these revelations that I ought to have done. Had I followed the route your little girl pointed out, I should have carried away from McClintock that honour, fame, and reward which he is now enjoying from the success that attended his expedition . . . and that by following the route pointed out by your child.

It was very remarkable that your child should have had these revelations, and I have often, since the return of McClintock, whilst struck at the literal truth of what your then little one must have seen, asked myself the question, how is it that such knowledge comes to us? and I have been sometimes disposed to think that intimations are, on rare occasions, made to mortals in the way that this must have been made known to your little one.

Coppin read the letter several times over the next few days and he kept coming back to one sentence in particular – *how is it that such knowledge comes to us?* He thought of all the premonitions he had had over the course of his own working life, premonitions that had on occasion saved lives. Had his daughter inherited this psychic ability, though in her case profoundly magnified, allowing her to inhabit the spaces between life and death? And what had happened to the energy behind the apparition, where had it gone?

What surprised him most was the ambivalence he'd experienced on receipt of the news of McClintock's findings. Whilst part of him had always wanted vindication, another voice deep within warned that once Franklin's fate was known Weesy would irrevocably rejoin the past. In a way it was the mystery of Franklin's whereabouts that had kept her alive. When McClintock and Hobson returned with the note they'd found at Point Victory they sounded the death knell not only for Franklin and his crew but for his daughter also.

He sat in his armchair and gazed out the window at the dusk sky over the Foyle, saddened beyond all expectation. For the first time in his life he felt old, his thoughts inclining towards the past rather than the future. It shocked him to realize that his best days could only be recollected now, not imagined. And what of his legacy, would he and his achievements be remembered at all, he wondered? Would his name endure? A hundred, a hundred and fifty years from now, would anyone speak of William Coppin?

PART FIVE

AS JOE STOOD at his front door he thought for a moment he could hear a heavenly choir singing within. He glanced up and down the street, seeking the source of it, then turned the key in the lock and stepped inside. A great wave of sound hit him, a classical chorus singing at full volume. Transfixed, he stood in the hallway as the voices swirled round the house.

Advancing forward, one careful step at a time, he peered into the living room. Eileen was leaning back in an armchair, gazing into space. On sight of him she clasped at her heart.

Jesus, you scared me! she cried. I didn't hear you come in.

Joe stared at her as if she were an apparition.

I scared you? he said in disbelief. I scared *you*? For your information, I'm surprised I haven't wet myself! What are you doing here?

I've moved back in.

Just like that? He sat down quickly in the nearest chair. You might have given me some warning.

I didn't realize it would be such a shock.

You know what I mean, Eileen. It's been so long.

Maybe I should have rung first, she conceded.

And what's all this? He waved a hand about in the air. You've never listened to classical music before in your life.

Well, things change, and I do now.

Not always, I hope, at this volume.

For the next few days they pretended to live as if they'd never been apart, falling back into their old routines, hoping against hope that habit might make all familiar again. They shared the same bed, but took intimacy no further. When Joe put his arm around Eileen's waist on their first night together he was shocked at how thin she had become. She lay rooted to the spot rather than snuggling back in against him as she would once have done. Come morning they each sprang out of bed the moment consciousness arrived.

And when they talked, that too was not as before. Gone was the tenor of the days when, with Ciara tucked up in bed, they would look back on their life together, on how the dice had fallen, how the cards had turned, conjecturing on the throws and hands that lay ahead. Both of them able to face the future with a light heart that bespoke happiness, for they were, after all, where they wanted to be.

Now, by contrast, conversation seemed to be no more than a plotting of coordinates – where each would be at any given moment – as if to come upon one another unawares was more than they could bear. Communication reduced to a form of air-traffic control.

Why did you come back, Eileen? Joe asked one day.

Would you rather I left again?

Of course not. I just wondered what happened to change your mind after so long away.

I was warned in no uncertain terms that I was risking

my marriage, that's what happened. My parents kept reminding me that if I weren't around, you just might find someone else. They went on and on about how hard it must be for you, all alone in the house, having to do all the cooking and cleaning and no-one to talk to. I tell you, you're well in there. I remember one wet night my mother standing at the window – Dad and I were watching television at the time – and out of nowhere in this sad voice she said 'I wonder how Joe's doing', as if you were some down-and-out wandering about in the downpour with nothing but a blanket round you. Honestly, it was like Chinese water torture listening to the pair of them, they just wouldn't give over. As far as they're concerned a woman's place is with her husband, end of story.

God, Eileen, I wish I'd never asked.

In the evenings, as a safe option, they would usually watch television. In their adopted positions, Eileen stretched out on the couch, Joe sprawled in the armchair, they looked as if they hadn't a care in the world. But they were neither alone nor together, each much too aware of the other, every insignificant twitch and murmur becoming freighted with meaning.

Occasionally, just before she left for work in the morning, Eileen would inform Joe that she was going out drinking that night with Karen from the surgery.

But I thought you and Karen had nothing in common, said Joe, the first time she mentioned it.

She's good craic, she doesn't take life too seriously.

That's hardly surprising at her age, sure what would she have to take seriously.

Around midnight he'd hear a prolonged metallic scratching at the front door as she tried to get the key in the lock. Then a heavy tread upon the stairs, punctuated by inexplicable pauses, before she resumed her climb. Eventually the bathroom door would close, there'd be the muffled sounds of water running, and a few minutes later she'd be in the bedroom where her clothes would drop item by item to the floor as she removed them.

That front door needs seeing to, she said, as she fell into bed like a stone, there's something wrong with the lock.

As for Joe, he made an effort to renew contact with some of the friends that he'd lost touch with since Ciara was born. But his heart wasn't in it. For him, life had changed fundamentally; they by contrast seemed determined to get back to a Shangri-La of their youth that apparently grew more and more intoxicating the further they moved away from it. Each week the same subjects were endlessly orbited.

He met Katie for lunch now and again but didn't mention this to Eileen. The ease he felt in Katie's company only accentuated the unease he felt with his wife, and with each meeting, with each casual revelation of their respective pasts, it became increasingly difficult for him to reveal this friendship to Eileen. More than that, he cherished the privacy of the relationship, its one-on-one nature.

Not that he had to make any effort to hide it from Eileen for she never questioned him about his day nor who he might have met in the course of it. Their most intimate moment was when they sat down together each Saturday morning to make out their weekly shopping list, a rare affirmation that they still shared each other's lives.

And so, in this manner, under the same roof and in the same bed, they passed their time. That the dark days of winter had ended scarcely warranted a mention; that the daffodils, appearing overnight and disappearing just as quickly, had come and gone, went unremarked. As new life flourished all around them, there seemed no limit to what they might choose to ignore.

Finally, as they lay in bed before sleep one night, Joe spoke.

There's no way we can go on like this, Eileen, or at least I can't. It's a mockery of how we once lived. I might as well be in some house in the next street for all the difference it makes to you.

That's not true, Joe.

Isn't it? Eileen love, I know you're lost without Ciara, but it's as if she never existed, we never talk about her.

I don't want to talk about her.

But if we don't, how are we ever going to come to terms with her death?

Eileen propped herself up on one elbow. You see, that's the difference between us, Joe. You have this belief that at some point, miraculously, there's going to be a return to normal service. In your world there's a solution to every problem. But from the moment we sat in that doctor's office at the hospital I've felt empty. And I expect to go on feeling empty. It's not self-pity so don't be thinking that, just a realization that life has changed, completely and utterly changed, and that for the rest of my days I'm going to carry this sadness around with me. Who says you get over loss? The fact is, we were meant to protect her from harm and we didn't do it.

D'ye think I don't realize that? I was the one at fault after all. What have you to condemn yourself for? You asked me enough times to get rid of that glass door and I didn't do it.

In some ways, Joe, I do blame you. I think that's one of the reasons I had to move out afterwards. Eileen gave a small laugh. You wouldn't believe the things I called you then.

Later that night Joe woke from a troubled sleep into a silence so intense and otherworldly he felt at that moment the only creature awake on the planet. Beside him, Eileen scarcely seemed to breathe, as if she too was implicated. His brain was working with fearful clarity. It was as if, only with the conscious mind numbed, when there was no drift towards sentimentality, only then could his brain properly assess the future possibilities. And what it showed him was laced with his worst fears. In the terrifying silence he watched a frieze of loveless scenes pan across his vision, he and Eileen going through the motions like two actors trapped in a touring play they had both long tired of. He felt powerless and alone. He prayed to hear the simplest of sounds, a dog bark, a stranger's steps on the street below, a taxi pulling up outside a house and sounding its horn, anything that might break the spell and comfort him. Frightened by Eileen's stillness he leaned over her and ever so gently placed a cupped hand beneath her nose that he might feel the reassurance of her breath upon his palm. As you might with your own child.

From their very first days in bed together he had gazed at her while she slept. In astonishment to begin with that she was actually there beside him; in frustration after an argument when too late the perfect riposte came into his head; in wonder during her pregnancy; and now in icy, middle-of-the-night terror at the realization that he might be denied experiencing those emotions ever again.

I can't just pretend it's there when it isn't, she had said to him earlier, I only wish I could.

He lay on his back in the dark bedroom. His head like an echo-box in which the silence thrummed. Nothing was decreed, he had to remember, no gods existed to determine your fate. He had not prayed when he'd stood at the front door waiting for the ambulance to arrive, when Eileen sat within cradling their daughter, and he would not pray now. The future was in his own hands, his and Eileen's, as it had always been.

I've been asked by Colm to go to London, to meet someone at the National Maritime Museum in Greenwich, he said to Eileen.

It was the first real lie he had ever told her.

How long will you be away for?

A couple of days. Will you be all right in the house on your own?

Of course I will, don't worry about me.

On the morning of his departure she offered to drive him to the airport but he insisted on ordering a taxi. You'll be late for work if you drive me, he said by way of explanation. As the taxi pulled away he turned in his seat to wave to her. She stood at the front door in her dressing gown, a small figure rapidly diminishing, her hand raised in farewell.

At the airport he met Katie in the departure lounge.

Did you tell Eileen the truth? she asked.

No.

I don't know why this has to be such a cloak and dagger business. It's not as if you're doing anything terribly wrong. I'm going to London to end what's left of my marriage and you want to look at the Franklin exhibits at Greenwich. We're friends, we're keeping each other company.

Joe eyed the other passengers in the lounge, worried that he might recognize someone.

I doubt Eileen would see it in those terms, he said

During the flight he said little, occupying himself with the morning paper, until, just before the plane began its descent into Stansted, he spoke to Katie as if oblivious to the last hour's passing, as if he was simply continuing an ongoing conversation.

To be perfectly honest with you, I was more scared that if I did tell Eileen the truth she wouldn't have been in the least put out. She would probably have agreed that it made perfect sense to come over to London with a female friend. That would have been far worse than any show of jealousy.

From Stansted they caught the express train to Liverpool Street station.

Well all I can say, said Katie as she settled herself in her seat, is that I'm appalled you've never even propositioned me. After all, when you think about it, everything's just right for an affair. I'm separated and you're having problems in your marriage. We should be at it like a pair of rutting animals.

You have a way of making it sound so attractive.

I'm a good-looking woman. She raised her voice in mock outrage. And you've never even tried to lay a finger on me! She prodded him playfully. What about my needs, you bastard!

Thank God that man's asleep, said Joe, indicating the passenger in the seat opposite, or I'd be mortified.

If indeed he is, said Katie.

At Liverpool Street underground station they parted.

You promise you'll come down to Southampton tomorrow?

I promise.

And you're a man of your word.

I am.

I'm glad to hear it. I'd offer to show you the sights but that would take all of five minutes. But we'll think of something to do. Anyway, it'll be such a relief for me to get away from my parents' questions, they are not going to be one bit happy when I break the news about me and Phillip.

At Greenwich, Joe wandered the streets, stepping in and out of specialist bookshops, checking their shelves for anything on polar exploration. Familiar names caught his eye. There were Cyriax and Neatby's books on the Franklin mystery, there was Farley Mowat and Vilhjalmur Stefansson. Within a glass case sat an 1854 edition in French of Bellot's journal aboard the *Prince Albert*, published posthumously.

He strolled amidst the grounds of the National Maritime Museum, circling the building again and again, reluctant to enter. Up to now the Franklin story had existed for him only on the purity of the printed page and he had sat in the Heritage Centre in Derry and let his imagination loose, rendering each scene in fine detail. To look upon the physical proof of the story seemed an act of betrayal.

Finally he entered the museum but, delaying the moment even further, he chose initially to visit a temporary exhibition on Scott and Shackleton. Within the display cases lay the protective clothing the explorers had worn, along with a selection of their possessions. There was film footage of them struggling to erect their tents, a scene that, according to the accompanying text, may well have been staged for the camera. On the walls, in enormous, blown-up photographs they approached the viewer, emerging out of blizzard and gale, their faces set and severe, their eyes glowing like those of medieval saints.

He bent over a glass case to inspect Scott's diary. Each night in his tent, in poor light just before sleep, Scott had scribbled the day's events, attempting to express the inexpressible, filling the pages with his tiny, cramped handwriting. Near the end, as death approached, he had written of one of his colleagues, 'He slept through the night . . . hoping not to wake.'

Eventually Joe made his way to the section marked 'Polar Explorers'. The Franklin exhibits consisted of just a few small fragments, all that remained of two ships and one hundred and twenty-nine men. A compass, buttons, a few items of cutlery, tin cans, a boot, and, there before him, the scrap of paper that had let the world know that Franklin was dead. Despite their evident age it was difficult to believe that these objects had actually resided with the men of the *Erebus* and *Terror*, that they had touched and used them every day. He peered closely at the official paper on which Captain Fitzjames of the *Erebus* had scribbled around the margins, the writing faint and water-stained in places. He read again the last sentence: 'Sir John Franklin died on 11 June 1847; and the total loss by deaths in the Expedition had been to this date 9 officers and 15 men'. He knew that as soon as Fitzjames had written those words they'd built a small cairn over the note and the next day, 26 April 1848, the remaining men had set off on the march for Back's Fish River, a destination that none of them would ever reach.

There was a small white card resting amongst the exhibits which, to Joe's astonishment, referred to Weesy Coppin of Londonderry and told of her involvement in solving the Franklin mystery. It listed the words seen on the wall of Ivy House: 'Erebus and Terror, Sir John Franklin, Lancaster Sound, Prince Regent Inlet, Point Victory', 'Victoria Channel.' The directions reading like an incantation. What he had considered no more than a local matter, a story unknown outside the town boundaries, had become part of the Franklin myth.

He left the museum and took a tube train to Canning Town station, from where he walked in the general direction of the Thames. Initially he came upon the Thames' offshoot, the River Lea, on whose far bank a huge industrial plant loomed, a coiling mass of pipes and funnels. A grey effluvium seeped into the rank air. The river edged past, slowly, diffidently, and at certain places the current seemed to turn back on itself, as if it too, all things considered, had had enough.

There were signposts for the East India Docks but following them seemed only to take him back to where he'd started. In growing frustration he studied his *A–Z* as he walked amidst a warren of streets that still retained something of the impersonal menace of their maritime heyday.

Eventually, walking to the top of a high overpass he was able to grasp the geography of the docklands. He saw how the Lea twisted and turned and doubled back on itself before finally entering the Thames. There was Canary Wharf to his right, London City Airport to his left. It was somewhere about here, amidst these wharves, that the *Great Northern* had ended her days. From her moment of arrival on 10 January 1843, she had prompted the newspapers to eulogy and for days afterwards the people flocked to her as to a monarch in state, all gazing up in astonishment at the sheer scale of her. But the weeks passed and the *Great Northern* still lay there, her appointed time past, her lustre slowly fading, more pretender now than legitimate.

Joe looked down upon ruined warehouses that had once been filled to bursting with exotica from the ends of the earth, but were now no more than a display site for the giant signs along their length advertising their conversion into loft-style apartments. The affluent of a new generation would soon be living here, the sea an irrelevance to them. Meanings and references, like artefacts of another day, would sink further and further into the silt.

He travelled back into the centre of London and from Charing Cross he walked across Trafalgar Square until he was standing outside what had once been 33 Spring Gardens. It was now the back entrance to a pub, but the steps ascending to the front door were still there and the basic shape of the house was unchanged. Just around the corner was the Admiralty, to which Lady Franklin was a regular and persistent visitor with her petitions and pleas.

As Joe stood there lost in thought, a group of office-workers, glasses in hand, gazed out from what had once been Lady Franklin's drawing room, eyeing him with faint curiosity. But to Joe the living seemed bleached, peripheral figures. Was it an illusion that the dead seemed full of purpose, striding through their days, knowing exactly why they were put on this earth? Or did any predetermined narrative assume the trappings of inevitability against the bewildering toings and froings of an uncompleted life?

He had come to London to affirm the story of William and Weesy Coppin and their link to the Franklin expedition and to reassure himself that all of this was no local shadow-world into which grief had lured him. And so he had stood at the East India Docks and he had stood in front of 33 Spring Gardens. He had walked into the National Maritime Museum and set eyes upon the few relics of Franklin's brought back from the North Pole.

And he had been filled with an emotion he barely recognized. It must be what the pilgrim feels upon visiting

Mecca or when standing and praying at the Western Wall or stepping within the portals of the church of the Holy Sepulchre in Bethlehem. As close to religion as he would ever get in this life, entering and being transformed by this force-field that surrounded certain buildings and objects.

Katie met him off the train.

You should really have come on a white horse, she said, because you've rescued me.

Is it that bad?

You would think, wouldn't you, that when a daughter tells her parents that her husband of one week has been cheating on her they might understand why she's getting a divorce. But not my parents, oh no. Do you not think you're being a bit hasty, Katie? Have you spoken to him properly, I'm sure he regrets what he did. Divorce is so final, you know. I finally lost it when my mother said with a straight face that all marriages go through difficult periods. Not in their first fucking week they don't! I shouted at her.

They probably just worry about you and don't know how else to express it. My father's the same.

But your father sounds lovely. He's interested in things, he travels around Ireland. At least you can have an intelligent conversation with him.

It's only recently I've been able to.

Recently's better than never.

Listen, I thought you were going to show me round Southampton. Isn't that why I came down here?

Well, she said doubtfully, I can show you what there is to see.

They wandered around the town centre – Just like everywhere else, isn't it? said Katie sourly – before stopping for a coffee at the main art gallery where a Craigie Aitchison retrospective was showing.

Shall we have a look? asked Joe.

As he moved through the rooms of the gallery, stepping from painting to painting Joe felt the emotion gather within him. He was held spellbound by a series of landscapes of Holy Isle painted from the slope on Arran, the island shimmering before a stupendous crimson sky as if at any moment it might ascend into the heavens. In some of these landscapes a small fishing boat would pass in front of the island, a thin wavy line of smoke angling from it, evidence of man's frail and temporary presence in this world.

There was also a series of paintings of the crucifixion. But Christ on his cross had been transposed to a Scottish terrain, a land of fields, rolling hills and whin bushes. With only animals present to bear witness to his death: a dog gazing up quizzically from beneath the cross, a bird perched on the cross-beam, sheep in the surrounding fields barely raising their heads from the grass. An ink-blue sky that suggested night had fallen and yet the earth strangely lit. Christ left to the equivocal comforts of nature.

When they stepped back out on to the street Joe said quietly, If we do nothing else today it was worth coming to Southampton just to see those paintings.

Lunching down at the docks, ordering steak and chips and a bottle of red wine, they watched the container ships gliding out along the Solent.

You know, it feels very strange being over here without Eileen.

I doubt it'll do either of you any harm.

No, we've been apart too much as it is. What we need now is time together.

Look on the bright side, at least you're back in the same house again.

Aye, for what that's worth. But if anything I'm lonelier now than I was when Eileen stayed at her parents. You have to remember that I was married to a woman who was wonderfully frank, even blunt at times, who always kept me on my toes because I never knew what she'd say next. Now you have to drag the words out of her.

Have you thought of going to counselling together?

Her mother suggested it but Eileen won't contemplate talking to a stranger about Ciara. She's far too private.

Does she talk to anyone about how she's feeling?

Not as far as I know. She keeps her thoughts to herself and if you ask her how she is she tells you she's fine. I look at her and externally she's the same woman, a bit thinner maybe, a bit more tired-looking, but it doesn't seem that long ago we were happy. God knows I can remember it easily enough.

Joe raised the empty wine bottle to attract the waiter's attention. Let's have another bottle, he said to Katie, and we can watch the ships go by.

For a few minutes they sat in silence as the Isle of Wight ferry slid out of port, its passengers leaning ruminatively against the deck rails in unwitting imitation of those who had left for ever on the great ocean liners.

I always thought, said Joe, it was far better to be waving from the deck than from the shore. Now I'm not so sure.

Have you travelled much?

No, though I've always wanted to. Even when I'm happy, I get restless. I keep thinking I'm missing something. And yet now that my life is completely fucked I want to be at home, even though home is a wretched place to be right now. Don't ask me to explain the logic of that one.

Katie sipped her wine, not venturing any comment, seeming content to let Joe do the talking.

Eileen doesn't make decisions any more, he continued, which is not like her at all. She was always the boss between us. If truth be told I just rubber-stamped the decisions she'd already made. It probably goes back to the first day we met, she asked me out and that set the tone for the rest of our lives together.

Not that it bothers me, far from it. You know the way some men see it as their place and their place only to change a fuse or a light bulb, as if it was some esoteric knowledge handed down from father to son. Or else they're forever doing bits and pieces about the house. Well, that was never me. I loved the fact that Eileen was so independent and so much her own person. It would never once have crossed her mind to ask me to mend a plug. You could drop Eileen on a desert island and not have to spend a minute worrying about her. When we first moved into our house, she built two bookcases to fit the recesses in the living room and if I'm completely honest my contribution was to hold the ladder and make the tea.

He paused.

I'm not sounding very masculine, am I? But then nothing changes if we just follow the old patterns. If Eileen has a more practical side than me then it makes sense to let her get on with it. When I was on the dole I used to pick Ciara up from school every day and make her a bit of dinner. My da was always giving off that it was no job for a man. But d'you know the high point of my day then? It was the moment the weans all came out of school together and I'd

214

be looking for Ciara amongst them and suddenly there she was. You get this rush of emotion when you see your own child, it's an extraordinary feeling. And she'd see me and come running over and take my hand.

He smiled a sad smile. And a lot of times I'd be gruff with her to hide my true feelings. Wasn't that the worst stupidity? Instead of just picking her up in my arms and telling her how much I loved her. That's what I should have done.

He looked up into Katie's face. I took such delight in her, you know.

She nodded. I can see that.

There can't be anything sadder in this life than describing what you should have done.

The lights had come on in the restaurant. Beyond, in a darkening blue haze, the ships still plied back and forth, ferrying between one shore and the next. Katie leaned in towards Joe as if she might offer some consoling words. Did I ever tell you, Joe, when we first met I thought you were a right pain in the arse?

She burst out laughing at the look on his face. Don't look so shocked. You've no idea how many drunken men I'd had to fend off by that stage of the day. One cocky little bastard after another, all thinking they were God's gift. You were just my next misfortune. If only men could realize how absolutely repulsive they are when they're drunk. And all that stuff about me looking like a Pre-Raphaelite painting, God almighty, was that supposed to be a chat-up line?

Actually I meant it.

Oh, don't get all prim. I'll only telling you this now because I'm so fond of you. To this day though I don't know why I spoke to you in the supermarket, every bone in my body told me not to.

I used to think honesty was one of your better qualities but I could be persuaded otherwise. God help the man who gets you.

No man is going to get me, thank you very much. I'll be doing the choosing. And after my recent disaster I'll be taking plenty of time at it.

But seriously, you must get lonely.

Of course I get lonely. My bed feels like it's the size of a football pitch these days. But as you can imagine I'm not very trusting of men right now. Come to think of it, I don't know how you sneaked in under my guard.

Considering the first impression I made, neither do I.

I'll never hear the end of that now. I'll bet you can hold a grudge with the best of them.

They took a taxi back into town and spent the next couple of hours shouting at each other in a succession of bars that all played loud music.

And to think, said Joe, gazing around him in bemusement, that people do this voluntarily, week in, week out.

You have to be young, which we're not.

You know, he said, covering one eye and then the other with the palm of his hand, I think I've lost a contact lens. That would explain why I can't see a bloody thing. I thought it was the drink. He handed Katie his glass. Hold that for a moment, will you, I'm going to the bathroom to take the other lens out.

At closing time the music was lowered, the lights flicked off and on, and they staggered out into the street.

Now, said Joe, somehow or other I've got to get to the station.

You don't have to go. You could always spend the night here.

What, at your parents'?

Actually I was thinking more of a hotel. Katie looked away and waited for Joe to speak.

There was a long silence.

Well for God's sake, Joe, say something!

I'm not sure what to say.

What about, 'I don't think that's a very good idea' or 'Have you thought what this might do to our friendship.' Either of those would be suitable clichés – if you can't think of anything else.

It probably isn't a good idea.

That goes without saying. But something beyond that, some insight into the deeper recesses of your mind would be helpful.

Why have you gone all sarcastic?

Because I'm embarrassed, why do you think? And you're not making it any easier.

I'm sorry, he said, putting his arms around her waist and pulling him towards her. Come on now, let's not fall out.

Katie linked her hands around his neck and they stood together, oblivious to the crowds milling about them.

His face was in the thick curl of her hair and her hands were a cool compress on the nape of his neck and he remembered back to Christmas when he'd met her that day on the pub crawl, standing there swaying in front of her, drunk then as now, and of how she had punctured his flushed bravado with a few mocking words. And he remembered the haunting, unexpected sadness that had swept over him when she was snatched away by another.

All right, he said finally, which way now?

*

The following evening on the flight to Derry she sat a few rows ahead of him. They had said little to each other in the departure lounge and she had told him she would prefer to sit on her own. As the plane climbed now over London he gazed down at the city thinning out, lights becoming further and further apart, until eventually there were only solitary cars travelling quiet back roads, their headlights like torches as they ventured cautiously through the dark.

When he entered the house on his return it was in darkness. He put on the kettle and went upstairs to see if Eileen had gone to bed early. As he passed the room that had been Ciara's bedroom, the door was ajar and he glimpsed the edge of a poster on the wall. Puzzled, he pushed opened the door and switched on the light.

The room looked exactly as it had been when Ciara was alive. Her favourite duvet cover was on the bed, the walls were covered with posters, the windowsill lined with small, furry toys, a stack of CDs sitting beside the music system they'd bought her on her last birthday, books and clothes everywhere. It was as if the last months had never happened, as if everything could be compressed into a bad dream of one night's duration.

Joe stared around the room in disbelief, a chill fear settling over him. The illuminated numbers of the clock radio on the bedside table pulsed on and off silently and upon the desk a book lay open as if someone had just stepped away for a moment.

He could smell his daughter in the room.

He sat down on the edge of the bed. Time passed. Eventually he heard the front door open, there was silence for a moment as if whoever had entered was standing in the hallway, then they started up the stairs.

He looked up to see Eileen leaning against the doorjamb. She studied his face. Are you angry? she said.

I don't know what I am. I got such a fright when I came in here.

I'm sorry, I suppose I should have been home but I didn't think you'd come into this room.

This isn't right, Eileen. A small part of me can understand why you've done it but it isn't right. You're going backwards rather than forwards.

She came into the room and sat on the bed beside him. I've been trying to think what I could say to make you see things in a different light. And I wondered if in some ways it isn't similar to your research – on Coppin and Franklin and all. I mean, you spend a lot of time dwelling on the past, trying to recreate it.

But not like this. I'm not interested in creating shrines to the past.

But how many times have you told me that the council should never have demolished Ivy House. Let's say they hadn't and Ivy House was still standing, wouldn't it have become a shrine to a dead man and his memory?

No, it would have been a public reminder of who he was, of everything he achieved.

Well this room is my public reminder. Ciara may not have made her mark in the world but I want to remember and acknowledge her.

When you speak it all sounds so reasonable. Joe gestured around the room. This isn't normal though, you can't pretend it is.

Normal? What's that got to do with anything? The word

means nothing to me any more. Life now is abnormal and the means of getting through it are abnormal and we have to face up to that. There's no 'getting back to normality', and more fool you if you think there is.

I realize that, Eileen, as well as you. But it's not being disloyal to Ciara to hope that we might find some peace in our lives, maybe even a bit of joy. Surely the way we live in the future is a testament to Ciara's existence, otherwise what's the point in her having lived at all?

That's a question I ask myself every day. If and when I find an answer to it, then I'm sure life will get easier for the both of us.

He woke in the night and realized that Eileen was not in bed beside him. Swaddled in their combined warmth he waited for her to return. Out of the darkness a low murmur reached him, a speaking voice, and he wondered who Eileen could be talking to in the dead of night?

He slipped out of bed and on the landing saw a light shining from beneath the door of Ciara's room. Eileen's voice was clearer now. It was not though the voice of someone in conversation, she did not seem to be listening and responding but instead spoke continuously in a level, narcotic tone.

He pushed open the door and immediately her voice stopped. She was sitting on the edge of the bed holding one of Ciara's storybooks and she looked up at him with a touch of exasperation in her face.

Eileen? he said, perplexed.

I'm all right, Joe.

But love, it's three o'clock in the morning.

I know.

Will you not come back to bed?

I will shortly. I just want to finish the story. She turned back to the book as if to emphasize her resolve.

Why are you sitting in here?

If I have to explain it, Joe, then you'll probably never understand.

Well at least try.

She laid her hands flat on the book as if to damp down her impatience. I like to read the stories I read to her, she said gently. And when I do I can see her lying there still. I'm sitting in the exact same place I always sat, I'm saying the same words, and there she is. Nothing has changed. It's as if the words bring her back, they summon her.

He went over to her and as he spoke he ran his hand through her hair, dark and cropped like a boy's.

Eileen, it's not that I don't want to understand or that I'm deliberately trying to oppose you in any way. I just wish we could share our grief as a couple, be close when it really matters. Don't you ever feel lonely? You must do, otherwise you wouldn't be sitting here in the middle of the night. It's wonderful that we're under the same roof again but what's the point if we don't help each other. The only thing I seem to do well with any regularity is annoy you.

It's not you personally, Joe, I just find it hard to be around people at the moment. What with having to spend my time at work around the sick, looking at them all and wondering how come they're alive and my daughter isn't. In the past I used to be so moved by the resilience of the older ones, the way they just kept going. But now, God forgive me, when one of them comes into the surgery I start thinking, if you had died, would Ciara still be alive, are you taking her place on this earth?

But Eileen, you can't relate every moment of your day to Ciara.

Oh but I can. What amazes me is that you can think of anything else.

Joe sat down on the bed beside Eileen and took her hand. The day we got back from the hospital, he said, remember how we came straight to this room. And we stayed here for ages and eventually you fell asleep. It was snowing outside and I stood at the window watching it fall and it felt like the snow was wiping out everything I had ever known in this life. I was terrified. My life was turning white before my eyes. And when I tried to think ahead, to the next few hours, that too was a blank. What future could there be? It was impossible to imagine leaving this room and continuing with all the daily bits and pieces of existence.

But you did.

What choice did I have? I was still a father, that hadn't ended, and I still had responsibilities. Ciara had to be mourned and buried, and there was you to think about. I couldn't walk away from that. And so I went down the stairs and I phoned my father and I phoned your parents and life went on.

I imagine a man has a different take on these things.

What do you mean?

Well I didn't think at all about mourning her or burying her – the arrangements. It didn't enter my head. As for the wake, I suppose if enough people tell you they're sorry about your child's death you might actually begin to realize it's happened.

Maybe that's why we have wakes, to help convince the family.

Everyone certainly tried their hardest to convince me.

She disengaged her hand from Joe's. Now go on back to bed, she said, giving him a gentle push, and I'll be in in a minute. And Joe, don't worry about me so much. I'm not going mad or anything.

As he closed the door behind him he heard her voice immediately pick up the story where she had left off.

*

When McClintock returned home, the news of his discovery at Victory Point induced a national mixture of sorrow and pride. Jane Franklin was acclaimed as an exemplar of fortitude, the *Daily Telegraph* going so far as to describe her as 'our English Penelope'. She had remained in England throughout all the years of her husband's absence, as if in the family home, waiting for the loved one to return. Now for the first time in many years she was not waiting impatiently for a ship to arrive back from the Arctic, her life no longer premised on events over which she had no control.

As though released, she felt an urge to travel. She had corresponded with Henry Grinnell, a benefactor in New York, for nearly ten years yet they had never met. Pressed by him she decided to visit America.

She was to be away from England for almost two years, travelling across America and visiting Canada, South America, the Sandwich Islands and Japan. On the boat to Japan she copied into her diary extracts from *Walden*, which had been published seven years previous. In particular she noted the passage in the conclusion, 'Is Franklin the only man who is lost, that his wife should be so earnest to find him? Does Mr Grinnell know where he himself is?' She assumed that Thoreau was suggesting that spiritual loss was all that really mattered, not surprising perhaps from a man who had chosen to remove himself from society.

With the departure of Jane Franklin abroad, William Coppin was in the unusual position for him of having to stay at home and miss someone. It was an unsettling condition. As he went about his day he sometimes wondered where Jane was at that particular moment. There would be an occasional letter from her, whereupon he would go immediately to his map to identify the exact spot she had last visited. It surprised him how much he missed their conversations. Having begun somewhat belatedly in life to communicate his innermost thoughts it was difficult to return to a life of introspection.

As ever it was work that brought release and, as ever, his mind teemed with ideas over which he had no control. They appeared from he knew not where, jostling for attention, and unless seized upon would disappear back again almost immediately. He could not fairly call it an attribute because he had no say in the matter. Except that amongst these sparks there were some that he chose to encourage, to fan into greater life until they glowed. And ultimately they became solutions to particularly difficult salvage operations he was in the midst of directing or they grew into inventions that he would patent in the hope that one day their utility would be recognized.

But such recognition did not guarantee attendant credit. Some years previously he had sent the Admiralty his design for an iron-plated steam-ram that could be incorporated into future British war ships. Not unexpectedly, considering his earlier dealings with them, the Admiralty had rejected the idea. Yet now it transpired they were intending to adapt his design without ever acknowledging his original concept. A terrible despair assailed him, that he could do nothing in the face of the Admiralty's disregard. Derry had never seemed further from the seat of power and influence. In this state, cast down, he received through the post an editorial from the *Liverpool Albion*:

The remark is a trite one which declares that in very numerous instances inventions of the highest value, and of the utmost importance, are forgotten and lost sight of soon after their first promulgation if nothing occurs to enforce on the public mind the necessity of their immediate adoption. In such case, also, it almost invariably happens, that after years have elapsed some emergency arises which at once directs attention, in one way or another, towards the past invention which would have met the now existing difficulty. When this occurs the resuscitated scheme is brought forward almost simultaneously by different claimants for the honour of the suggestion, while the original propounder is entirely ignored.

A peculiarly apt illustration of this may be found in connection with the invention of iron-plated steam-rams. In respect to priority in such a claim, Liverpool is entitled to a foremost place. So far as we are at present in possession of the facts, the first suggestion of steam-rams for the purposes of aggressive war was made in the columns of the *Albion* by Mr William Coppin, engineer and shipbuilder in Londonderry, who, in the beginning of February, 1853, recommended the construction of a vessel of 1000 tons, builders' measurement, so built and engined as to secure a speed of thirteen or fourteen knots an hour. The fore part of the vessel to be made solid for about fifty feet, and no part to be less in thickness, above light water line, than five feet, solid, and caulked inside and out. The stern and bow to be covered by a shield of malleable iron, containing in the centre a circular punch or cutter, capable of punching a piece out of the largest of our line-of-battles ships, of twelve square feet, at any distance below the surface of the water to seven feet, as opportunity may require. The inventor of this ram proceeds with the description of elaborate details for the construction and management of his invulnerable steam warship, including suggestions for increasing or diminishing her specific gravity, so as to make her have a greater or less draft of water. The cost of such a vessel as he suggests, he estimates at about £45,000.

He had entirely forgotten his letter to the *Albion*. That the paper should come to his defence, and he a stranger, touched him deeply.

He received no communication from Jane Franklin following her return to London from her travels. He wondered if their friendship had been of an intimacy and intensity that could only be sustained for a few short years. Perhaps he symbolized for her a time of uncertainty and protracted pain that she was now resolved to keep firmly in the past. Perhaps she was simply trying to live for the future, the waters of which she did not want to muddy with old emotions. Whatever the reasons, he missed her as the person to whom he had revealed so much of his inner being.

But work, habit, constant travelling, dulled the sharp edge of loss. The pursuit of salvage took him across Europe. His methods were often unorthodox and at such times there would be expressions of polite dubiety to his face and barely restrained ridicule behind his back. But what no-one could gainsay was that hushed, transcendent moment, when all waited with different degrees of faith to see if the ship would actually rise from the sea floor.

At Cherbourg he had attempted to raise the *Iowa*, which had sunk with a cargo of coal. But pumping had proved ineffective, water continuing to pour in through the broken portholes. So, to much initial laughter, he determined they would use different-sized corks which, one by one, were attached to an iron rod and forced through twenty feet of coal until they blocked a porthole. Forty-two portholes he sealed this way and then to everyone's astonishment but his, the ship was refloated with cargo intact. It was a miracle of sorts but then, that was the way of it, he went now from place to place like an itinerant journeyman performing miracles.

*

What am I to do about her?

Joe sat in the back room of his father's house, into which little natural light fell.

Son, you just have to be patient and hope that things take a turn for the better.

I've tried suggesting counselling again but she won't hear of it.

It's not everyone's cup of tea.

Well she needs to talk to somebody.

And I'm sure she will, in her own good time. You can't rush these things.

It's all very well you saying that, Da, but you're not seeing her every day. Most of the time she lives in some fantasy in her head where Ciara's still alive; she's not in the real world at all.

Well, I can understand that. It took me a long time to even acknowledge that your mother was dead. And after all these years I'm still getting over it. When it comes to grief there's no time scale, it's as if everyone has a different clock in their head going at a different speed.

You make it sound perfectly rational.

Oh, it's anything but that, believe you me. Patsy met Joe's worried gaze. Listen, son, have you ever asked yourself why I'm always going off to someplace or other? Does it not strike you as a bit odd at my age?

I've never really given it much thought. You always said it was because you wanted to see more of your own country.

That's what I said, right enough. But it isn't always that simple. If I'm honest it's more to do with feeling lonely. Some memory of Marie will trigger things and then I can't sit still, I have to get out of Derry. So off I go. This town is full of memories for me, there's hardly a street that doesn't have some story attached to it.

I never knew you were so lonely, Da, said Joe, looking at his father wonderingly.

There's no reason why you should, said Patsy. He leaned forward and took a cigarette from the pack lying on the coffee table. Anyhow, I'm only telling you this so you'll not worry so much about Eileen. You might feel you're slowly coming to terms with Ciara's death but don't assume the same thing of Eileen. Be there for her but at the same time leave her be, if that makes any sense.

Her birthday's coming up. I want to do something special but for the life of me I can't think what.

Between the pair of us we should be able to come up with a few ideas.

I want it to be something that'll take her out of herself, an experience more than anything.

Yous could go away for a few days.

I don't think Eileen would want to spend that long away from the house. Or with me for that matter.

You're not taking a very positive view of this.

I'm being realistic, Da. All I want to do is give her spirits a bit of a lift.

Patsy leaned back and closed his eyes. He took a drag from his cigarette and blew a long coil of smoke towards the ceiling. They sat in silence for a minute or two.

What would Eileen like? mused Patsy to himself, repeating the phrase like a mantra. What would Eileen like?

He opened his eyes. What about a trip on the river, he said. On one of those boats that takes you downriver and back again.

Jesus, Da, that's a great idea. She'd love it, she's never been on the river in her life. Neither have I for that matter.

They have a bar on the boat, said Patsy, warming to his idea, and live music sometimes. If I remember rightly the whole thing lasts about a couple of hours. Surely to God Eileen can put up with you for that long.

She'll probably be having such a good time she won't even realize I'm there. Joe got to his feet. I'll book it first thing in the morning.

Patsy walked with him to the front door.

I know you're only joking, son, he said, but still and all it's sad to hear you talking about your marriage that way. I'd never seen a happier couple than the pair of ye.

Joe stood on the pavement beneath the weak orange street-light. That's how it used to be right enough, he said, as if describing something in the long ago. And who knows, maybe we will be again. He patted his father's arm.

I'll see you soon, Da, he said, and thanks.

Patsy stood at the door and watched his son trudge up the street. He felt old and helpless, knowing he could do nothing for him. At the corner Joe turned and gave him a brief wave before disappearing from sight.

Amongst all the books that Joe O'Kane had read concerning the search for the Northwest Passage and the speculations on the disappearance of the *Erebus* and *Terror*, the voices of the Inuit were only ever encountered at second-hand and often in poor translation at that. He understood that nineteenth-century explorers felt that the Inuit narratives they transcribed had to be regarded with some caution, believing the Inuit would modify the facts if they thought it more likely to make their inquisitors happy. Yet this did not accord with their willingness to describe in chilling and graphic detail the occasions in which they had discovered the dead bodies of white men and the evidence of cannibalism they had also found.

A more likely explanation for any discrepancies was the Inuits' disinterest in the past; for them, caught up in a life where existence is often parlous, the present was more than enough. When the European explorers first interrogated them in the years following Franklin's disappearance, the Inuit could not understand this obsession with past events. It was an indulgence their culture could not permit. Death, stalking their lives as it did, held little mystery for them.

The exchanges between the two cultures offered rich opportunities for mutual incomprehension. The Europeans, each of them driven through life by the promptings of a powerful ego, at first assumed similar motivation in their interlocutors. But eventually they began to realize that an Inuit would sit and listen politely to a particular story being told by one of his fellows as if hearing it for the first time, without ever venturing to remark that he too had been present. Such reticence was beyond the comprehension of the Europeans. They had come face to face with a people for whom civility was a practised virtue rather than a casual aspiration.

The main chronicler of the Inuit view of events concerning the Franklin disaster was Charles Francis Hall, an American who had, like William Coppin, followed with fascination all attempts to find Franklin. Hall was convinced that some of the crew were still alive and when he arrived in the Arctic in July 1864 he was determined to follow in the footsteps of Dr John Rae and reach King William Island. For the next five years Hall lived with the Inuit, gathering stories and evidence. A combination of circumstances – poor weather, ill health, and Inuit prevarication – delayed his departure for King William Island but eventually his wish was granted and the Inuit escorted him across Boothia Peninsula to Rae Strait. On arrival he met with In-nook-poo-zhe-jook, the Inuit who fifteen years earlier had told Rae of the dead white men on King William Island. In-nook-poo-zhe-jook revealed to him that he had subsequently returned to King William Island to claim some of the sailors' possessions and had found a tent full of dead men and a boat surrounded by skeletons. Hall also met with two natives who claimed to have encountered a group of white men dragging a sledge along the shoreline of Washington Bay. For a week Hall interviewed them, noting down all they could remember.

Hall had intended to spend the entire summer on King William Island, exploring it thoroughly, but the Inuit would not countenance such a plan, declaring that the island was poor for hunting and that they must return before the thaw set in. Hall had one week only.

After years of waiting, years spent dreaming of this moment, Hall was left with seven days in which to search. It was an impossible task. He believed from conversations with the Inuit that the Franklin records were in a vault near Victory Point but if this were true it could be verified only when the snow had fully melted. Near the Peffer River they found a skeleton, later identified by a gold filling as Lieutenant Henry Le Vesconte of the *Erebus*. It was the only discovery that Hall would make in the short time allowed him.

He departed the Arctic an embittered man, his view of the Inuit warped beyond repair. Two months previously he had written of In-nook-poo-zhe-jook, '(he) has a noble bearing. His whole face is an index that he has a heart kind and true. I delight in his companionship.' But now his thoughts had darkened, 'I believe In-nook-poo-zhe-jook like the other Inuit of Neitchille will lie and *he* without any regard to consequences. He speaks truth and falsehood all intermingled so that it is impossible to tell which is which unless it be of matter that one questioning him knows himself the facts. And yet he is a man apparently of honest face . . . It is a very great pity that the Neitchille Inuit are such consummate liars.'

When word reached him he immediately began the long journey home. He had to cross the European mainland, catch a boat to England, cross England, catch another boat, before finally travelling the road to Derry, of which he knew every twist and turn.

By the time he arrived at Ivy House she was in the final stages of pneumonia. Her pale damp face lay among the pillows of their bed. He whispered her name but if she heard him she gave no sign.

When the doctor called to check on her condition Coppin led him into his study where they could talk in private. He asked the doctor to be candid with him and was told that nothing further could be done and that at most she had days left. He thanked him and went upstairs to resume his seat by the bed.

The hours passed and still she did not wake. At times she desperately sucked air back into her lungs. Other times she rested calmly on her back with her arms held out from her like someone expecting to become airborne at any moment.

By late evening Coppin, worn out from travelling, fell asleep in the chair and no-one in the family had the heart to disturb him. He woke in the early morning with the dawn light edging towards him across the bedroom floor. He leaned over his wife, lifting the hair away from her face.

She opened her eyes. William, she whispered, you're back.

Of course I am, Dora. I came the moment I heard you were unwell.

She slid a hand across the bed for him to take. What would I do without you, she said.

He lifted her hand and kissed it. I will stay here beside you now and you must try to regain your strength.

I fear, she smiled, that that may be beyond me.

His heart full, he said nothing in reply, just bent over and kissed her hand again. She closed her eyes and drifted back into sleep. There was a gentle tap on the door and Ellen, Dora's sister, stepped into the room.

How is she? she asked.

The same. He stood up and stretched.

You should go outside for a while, William, it's a beautiful morning. I will stay with Dora.

As always, he walked down to the river. The sun rested on the rim of the world and a few clouds, unique as fingerprints, idled in the sky, as if in no hurry to leave the vicinity. It was, as Ellen had said, a beautiful morning. He sat on a bollard and tried to contemplate the inevitable darkness that lay ahead.

For the next few days he came down to the quayside in the early morning, the rest of the day being spent sitting with Dora or talking with the children, an experience he had seldom had time for over the preceding years. They were all adults now and Anne was still an enigma to him; she displayed the same grave air of self-containment she'd had as a child. She spoke only when spoken to and her answers were as precise as if she were repeating word for word what she'd been told by someone else.

Can you remember when you used to see Weesy? he asked her as they sat alone at breakfast.

Of course, father, very clearly.

And do you still miss her?

Yes, I think of her sometimes. She was my best friend as well as my sister.

I remember when Captain Kennedy came to visit us, how you took his hand and walked him round the house, showing him all the places where Weesy appeared to you.

I felt very important then. She lowered her gaze to her

hands resting on the table. Nothing since has ever made me feel the same.

Those were extraordinary days, Anne. I could not at first believe what was happening in my own house, to think that my children might have the answer to the Franklin mystery.

You had never paid us such attention before.

I have not been a good father, I admit it. Nor husband, for that matter. When I first met your dear mother I was obsessed with shipbuilding, it was all I thought of. But she was very patient and understanding and one day I realized I could not be without her. She has been a far better wife than I ever deserved.

He stood up. I must go sit with her, he said. He went upstairs and took his seat by the bed.

He was there two days later when, as the doctor had predicted, she died. He could do nothing but sit and watch her die. Once again the Derry ground was opened for one of his family and once again he stood in St Augustine's churchyard as they were lowered into it.

During her life with William, Dora Coppin had always exhibited a modest nature, never seeking praise or attention for her achievements nor over the years had she ever turned to her husband for sympathy when misfortune struck, as it inevitably did. She had spent more nights alone in the marital bed than she had ever anticipated but then she had always known that marriage to William Coppin would be neither safe nor predictable. His absences from home forced her though to develop a self-sufficiency not part of her original nature and so she seldom waited until his return to ask his advice on this or that matter but instead went straight ahead and did as she saw fit. It was a liberating experience and to her surprise William did not object. To her further surprise she discovered she possessed an aptitude for financial matters that managed to circumvent the irregularity of William's income. By degrees she found herself assisting him in his business affairs, for her husband had little or no grasp of bookkeeping. He could not sit still in front of a ledger; it was like trying to teach lessons to a child impatient to be outside playing in the open air.

Why must I learn all this, he had complained to her one day, when you already understand it so well?

And so it was that she took over the running of the financial side of the business and strove to curb her husband's spendthrift tendencies as best she could. At first he behaved much as before, shaking hands on deals the particulars of which he informed her of belatedly. I will not have this, William, she'd told him, either the agreement is tendered in writing or I will no longer oversee your finances. Horrified at such a prospect, he had acquiesced at once. Thus she bought herself the time required to examine the details of each contract before it was signed and to suggest alterations where necessary. Whatever you think best, Dora, William would concede with barely a quibble.

That her brilliant husband was so inept with money gave her considerable pleasure, though of course she knew better than to tell him so. As time passed William Coppin increasingly came to depend on his wife, more than once wondering how he had ever managed before her.

Her death changed everything irrevocably. The disarray in his heart was mirrored by the extent to which his business affairs foundered. He could not cope. The ledgers filled with her careful handwriting remained closed and he returned to conducting his business in the haphazard fashion with which he had begun his working life. He was in his sixties now, his children had all drifted away from home, yet he continued to take financial risks that were all the more perilous for the lack of the safety net that had been his wife. It was almost as if he sought dissolution. His children did their best to advise him but he had done with prudence and thrift and would not be told. The money that Dora had so assiduously salted away was soon dissipated. His debts mounted. There could only be one conclusion and eventually and inevitably, seven years after his wife's death, he sold the foundry and the shipyard and, worst of all, he sold Ivy House.

Had he been a younger man he might have signed on with one of the ships that lined Derry quay and worked his passage to another part of the world from where he could start a new chapter in his life. But such acts were not for him any more. When all his debts had been cleared there was very little money left for the rest of his days. He was at the mercy of the world; the poorhouse beckoned. Or it would have but for his eldest son, John, who stepped in and offered to pay the lease on a small house for him. He found what he was looking for in Sackville Street, in a row of terraced council houses, and John immediately signed a twenty-year lease on the property. It was no more than fifty yards from the river, just around the corner from Ivy House. He could not imagine living in another part of the city; this was where he had worked and dreamed and like the ghost of the man he had once been he would haunt these streets by the river. For years to come the citizens of Derry would continue to see him pass back and forward, a simulacrum, in mock imitation of his prior eminence. They pointed him out to their children and grandchildren, a once-famous man fallen on hard times. There he went, returning again and again to the scene of his former glory, thinner now and frailer, as if death were claiming him piecemeal.

But though reduced in figure and in circumstance he remained undaunted, convinced that his mind would fail him last of all. Each day his body offered fresh evidence of decline, each day another small task proved beyond his capabilities, but never once did his mind let him down, remaining a true and doughty friend to him as all else fell away.

For years after Hall, rumours persisted of white men being encountered amongst the Arctic wastes. Whalers passed on stories from the Inuit of cairns and records just waiting to be discovered. It prompted an American cavalry officer, Lieutenant Frederick Schwatka to lead a tiny expedition to King William Island. His was to be the last expedition of the nineteenth century and the last to speak to the actual participants of the drama.

Schwatka spent the summer of 1879 following the line of march that Franklin's crew had most probably taken. Near Point Victory they came upon an open grave that, according to Schwatka, had been 'despoiled by the natives some years before'. In his journal he wrote, 'In the grave was found the object-glass of a marine telescope, and a few officer's gilt-buttons stamped with an anchor and surrounded by a crown. Under the head was a coloured silk handkerchief, still in a fair state of preservation, and many pieces of coarsely stitched canvas, showing that this had been used as a receptacle of the body when interred.'

A skull and other bones were scattered around the site; a medal bearing the name John Irving was found. Because of the care and attention that had gone into the interment,

Schwatka believed that Irving had been buried from the ships. He and his men gathered the bones together, intending to return them to Irving's home.

They also came across the large boat that McClintock had discovered nineteen years earlier which had then contained the intact skeletons of two of Franklin's men and an array of items from the ships. But here too the bones were now scattered as far as the eye could see.

Before Schwatka left the Arctic, he had a conversation with an old Inuit woman and her son, the details of which still provoke speculation and debate today. The son told Schwatka that he had come across one of the lifeboats that Franklin's crew had been dragging with them on their last march. Around the boat he saw a number of skulls plus the bones of arms and legs that appeared to have been sawed off. Inside the boat there were two boxes, one filled with books, the other filled with bones.

It has been conjectured ever since that the contents of one box were the logbooks of the *Erebus* and *Terror* whilst the other contained the bones of Sir John Franklin. Neither box has ever been found.

*

Each time he travelled this road as an adult it brought back to him emotions of twenty-five years earlier. Trapped then within the hot car, his cheek pressed against the cool glass of the back-seat window, he had awaited with weary fatalism the first stirrings of nausea. A journey of just fourteen miles that seemed to go on for ever. His mother would chat away, asking him question after question in an attempt to distract him, which only made matters worse, whilst his father sat silently behind the wheel, lost in thought.

The shop that had always marked the halfway point of the journey was still operating; its shop-front, with its display of beachballs, fishing nets and buckets and spades, the first intimation of the impending coastline. And then the dark green tunnel of overhanging trees, like a deep plunge into seawater, and soon after his mother would say, Any second now you'll see it, any second now, and sure enough there it was, far off to the left, the glitter of the ocean.

The car filled with light. His father would roll down the window and engage in an exaggerated display of deep breathing. The last houses were behind them and from the elevated road they looked down on the packed strand at Fahan. Invariably the tide was well out and invariably a few intrepid children, nothing daunted, clutching their buckets and spades, could be seen in the distance resolutely making their way across the gleaming sand as if intending to reach Rathmullan on the other side of the lough.

And now, a quarter of a century later, the tide was still well out and a spring sun lit Fahan but the beach was empty save for a few people walking their dogs. Beside him Katie was looking everywhere but at the road, having eased down to thirty to enjoy the view.

You've gone very quiet, she said.

I was remembering my childhood here.

Oh I can just picture you, a skinny little thing probably, wandering about on your own, staring into rockpools, collecting shells. Ready to run into the sea if any girl tried to speak to you.

Some things never change.

As if! Don't give me that butter wouldn't melt in your mouth routine, it doesn't fool me for a second. You're nowhere near as innocent as you'd like to think you are.

That's a shame.

Can I just remind you that it was you who first spoke to me.

And haven't I been regretting it ever since.

Many a true word.

She glanced down at the map spread open on her lap.

I don't know why you keep looking at that map, said Joe. We're not crossing the Kalahari Desert. You couldn't get lost here if you tried.

I'm just acquainting myself with the area. After all, if I like the look of this house then Buncrana will be my new home.

Are you sure you know what you're doing? This place will be as quiet as the grave in winter.

That'll suit me nicely.

They drove into Buncrana and located the house. The estate agent was already there, sitting patiently in his car, smoking and listening to the radio. It was a small two-up-two-down cottage on the end of a row of six and from the rear windows you had a view of the lough back towards Derry.

We don't get many buying a house like this to live in all year, said the estate agent, it's summer homes is all the rage now. He took Katie round each of the rooms whilst Joe stood at an upstairs window and watched a powerboat perform figures of eight on the lough.

That's the one, said Katie firmly the moment they were back in the car.

Would you not be as well to take a look at a few others before you decide?

There's no need. And anyway, I've put in an offer.

In town they had fish and chips in an old-fashioned café, sitting in high-backed wooden booths, followed by a stroll up one side of the long high street and back down the other.

There you have it, said Joe, that to all intents and purposes is Buncrana in its entirety, one main street.

It's enough for me.

Mind you, come summer you'll think you've never left Derry for they all flock here. Our version of the Hamptons you might call Buncrana.

Why are you being so sarcastic about this?

Because I think you're mad. I have as fond memories of this place as anyone but Buncrana in winter?

Have you ever actually stayed here in winter?

No. But then I haven't wrestled a grizzly bear either and I've no desire to try.

Oh, be like that then.

They walked along the strand in the failing spring light. Every now and then Katie bent to inspect a particular stone or shell, turning it in her hand before casting it away. Pinpricks of light were beginning to appear along the coastline as darkness came in off the sea. A few seabirds wandered the tide-line, picking at the damp sand disconsolately.

Eventually they arrived at the far end of the beach and turned to begin the long walk back.

How are you and Eileen getting on at the moment? asked Katie.

Not too well, to be honest. It's so hard to talk to her.

And how hard do you try?

I've tried everything to get her to open up. Why, do you not believe me?

It's not that. I just think you're happier reacting to situations rather than instigating them. Like most men, anything for an easy life.

I don't know where this is coming from, Katie, but believe

me I'm not exactly sitting back counting my blessings.

Katie turned to face him. My divorce will be through soon, Joe, and it's forced me to think about where my life's going. I have to start making some decisions rather than just drifting unhappily along. In fact I've already started because I don't think we should see each other any more.

What? You're not serious.

I'm entirely serious. We've become far too close. Look at what nearly happened in Southampton. I'm not going to put Eileen through the same things I suffered.

Is this why you're moving to Buncrana?

It has something to do with it. But I've also had enough of cities for a while. I love the thought of driving back here at the end of the day, of going to sleep to the sound of the sea and of waking up to it again. This might sound a bit pompous but my life needs to become more honourable than it is at present.

Joe could barely see Katie's face as she spoke. On the horizon a long thin aperture of grey light was slowly closing.

So that's it, he said, we just stop seeing each other.

Maybe one day we can be friends again.

I think that very unlikely.

If you say so. She veered off into the darkness.

He had known all along, without ever truly acknowledging it, that their closeness was perilous. She had blown into his life at a time when he desperately needed someone new to talk to, someone unacquainted with his history, and now, after all their conversations, there wasn't another living soul bar Eileen who knew more about his mortal fears. For a fleeting moment in time, born out of loss, they had become voluble, two normally guarded individuals not worrying for once about loss of face or embarrassment.

But now she was stepping out of his life as suddenly as she had entered it. She would carry his secrets around with her, as he would carry hers, and they would talk of them no more. She would cross his path occasionally and they would say hello and engage in a brief, strained conversation as if they barely knew each other. That was their future. And already he felt nostalgia for what hadn't yet passed.

Katie, he called into the darkness, Katie, but no voice answered above the hiss and fizz of the tide. He trudged on, expecting at any moment that she would materialize alongside him and pass some facetious remark about his gruff manner. Out on the lough a single flickering light indicated a fishing boat making its way towards the open sea.

He turned up the beach toward the dunes. Somewhere on the other side her car was parked. He pushed his way through the marram grass until he found the small car park and, in the weak illumination from its single light, he saw that her car had gone. For an instant he regressed to a child-like state – abandoned, in the dark, far from home – before pulling himself together and walking the few hundred yards along the main road to the Drift Inn, within whose net-covered walls he drank a couple of pints of Guinness and considered his situation.

He decided that, rather than catch a bus or order a taxi, he would walk back to Derry. It would be the middle of the night before he got there but he relished the thought of the walk, his ultimate exhaustion and the deep sleep that hopefully would ensue. And along the road he would have time to think. He put down his glass, gestured a farewell to the barman, and stepped out into the Donegal night.

He set off at a relaxed pace, his hands in his coat pockets, like a man sauntering towards nowhere in particular. The sea whispered in his right ear before eventually fading away, the night sky darkened further, and, as he passed the occasional house, the inhabitants seemed to move behind their lit windows in a dream of his own imagining.

A car tooted its horn as it passed him and pulled in ahead. The window descended to reveal a large, grey-haired man who turned a friendly face towards him.

Can I give you a lift, son?

Thanks all the same but I'm fine.

Where is it you're heading anyway?

Derry.

My God, d'you know how far you have to walk?

I do. Don't worry, it's my own choice.

Well, you're a better man than me. If I had to walk to Derry, I'd be in intensive care for a week. He studied Joe closely. You're sure you're all right now?

I am.

Fair enough. I'll leave you to it. He raised a hand in farewell.

On the crest of the hill solitary windows were lit like beacons.

On this very road over thirty years ago his father and mother had walked in the early days of their courtship. At a time when they barely knew each other, when there were always more questions to ask, more discoveries to be made, sending a plumbline down into each other's depths. What had they talked about? The wind blew through the trees beneath which he passed like conversations of long ago, the very same trees that had sheltered his parents. The light of summer had glazed their world and the future must have seemed indistinguishable from the quiet euphoria of the present moment. He felt very close to the both of them, walking in their footsteps, his dead mother whom he'd barely known and his father who, after years of confusion, he was finally beginning to understand.

A low crescent moon scythed through the trees, moving parallel to him. The houses he passed were now in total darkness. At certain moments he felt as if he were walking through a world over which the sun had never risen. After six miles he sat on a low wall for a brief rest and in the field behind him an animal let out a deep, heartfelt sigh as if sorely troubled. He heard it rearrange itself on the ground, moaning softly all the while. Joe sat very still, not wanting to reveal his presence, and gradually his ear tuned to the ceaseless rustle of the surrounding nightworld, to the susurrus of birds stealing from tree to tree, and he sensed the swirl of activity, small armies on the march, about his stationary feet.

Our presence on this earth, he thought, is proved as much by the acknowledgement of others, be they human or animal, as by our own actions.

An occasional car swooped down the dip in the road and picked out for a fraction of a second his white, crinkled face in its headlights. Then all was darkness again. He lowered himself from the wall and continued walking. He tried to empty his mind, to concentrate only on the rhythm his feet made. But he could not do it. He looked back down the tunnel of his mind to happier times and wondered if happiness was only ever retrospective. Could he recall an instance from his own past when he had truly known, in that very moment, that he was happy? He thought of Eileen and he thought of Ciara and he knew, with a kind of terror, that happiness for him was indissolubly linked to the both of them.

Tomorrow was his wife's thirtieth birthday. Acting on Patsy's suggestion, he had booked the boat trip on the Foyle for her. But, things being as they were between them, he had no idea how she'd respond to this surprise, if she'd even agree to get on the boat. He had given up trying to understand how her mind worked. And yet still, more than anything else in the world, he wanted to please her.

The moon rose up the sky, the stars shifted, turned a few, almost imperceptible, degrees.

The further he walked the more light-headed he became. He imagined himself one of the emigrants that in a past century, in the dead of night as now, had passed this way. Leaving their own beds for the last time, walking through the only world they had ever known to Derry and to the emigrant ships that awaited them. Coming from all quarters of the villages and towns of the north-west, mesmerized as sleepwalkers, drawn inexorably towards a future that nothing in their past had thought to prepare them for. Pity the poor emigrant, as the song said. Yes indeed.

In the pulsing darkness nothing seemed real and all seemed possible if you imagined it hard enough. And so it was that suddenly Ciara was there, walking beside him. As if all night she'd been waiting patiently on this road for him to appear. Now her small hand was in his. Swinging along confidently because she felt safe and protected. His daughter. She wore a summer dress, despite it being a cold April night, her hair pulled back into a ponytail. He slowed his pace to accommodate her. He thought of days walking back from school with her, just the pair of them, talking about this and that, he not fully realizing what he held in his hand, what she meant to him. The cruel ration of days that had been apportioned to her. And to him.

At a crossroads the signpost informed him he was five miles from Derry.

Not far now, he told her.

A boat waiting. The three of them setting off down the Foyle to a new life together, past the old landmarks, past the scurry of everyday affairs. The town tilted upward on both banks as if to display all that they were leaving behind. Don't look back. This is that rare thing, a second chance. The wind freshening as they move beyond Culmore. From mid-river the familiar world looked astonishingly different, as it should, as if they had been given new eyes with which to see. Ahead, the pure white light of the open sea.

And he almost believed it, that he could will a new existence into being. But when he reached the outskirts of Derry, where the streetlights began, he felt her fade from his side and he was alone again and nothing had changed except for that brief, buoyant moment, lifted on a single wave of happiness. The dark walk from Buncrana had been but a moment out of time.

With his body belatedly realizing that it had just walked nearly fourteen miles, tiredness penetrated every muscle, and he plodded the last stage home, passing other lost souls who drifted past as if condemned to do so for perpetuity.

The light in the front room was on when he reached the house and in the hallway stood Eileen, and behind her his father, who both stared as if they couldn't quite believe it was him.

Happy birthday, he said.

What? said Eileen. What did you say?

Happy birthday. Well, it is your birthday now, isn't it?

Do you know what time it is?

He looked at his watch. Five past four.

I know what time it is, thank you, she said in an even voice. What I really want to know is where you've been to this time of night and why you never thought to give me a call.

Buncrana, that's where I've been. And since when did you care what time I came in at?

Joe, I've been worried sick about you. I've left I don't know how many messages on your mobile. If it hadn't been for Patsy stopping me, I'd have rung the police by now as well.

Best not to get them involved, said Patsy, who hadn't moved from behind his daughter-in-law.

Eileen opened her mouth to say something, then thought better of it. I could slap you, she said, I really could. But you're here now and that's all that matters.

Later, after they'd packed Patsy off in a taxi amid protestations that he was perfectly able to walk, they finally made it up to bed. Lying on his back, overcome with a sweet exhaustion, Joe was astonished when Eileen slid across and snuggled in against him.

Don't ever do that again, she said.

I won't, he promised.

I thought something had happened to you.

I wasn't thinking, Eileen. You know what I'm like.

She pulled herself closer. The house felt so empty, that was why I had to get your father round.

Still in a state of shock, he placed his fingers on the small of her back, cautiously, ready to withdraw them the instant she spoke. But Eileen said nothing.

He cradled her. The two of them in the bed together, the rest of the world without.

The room began to lighten. Birds struck up their first song and he remembered someone once telling him that they did this to reassure each other that all had survived the night.

Eileen's voice came muffled from beneath the duvet.

What's that? he asked fondly, planting a kiss on the crown of her head.

She tilted her head back so that he could hear her properly. And what, might I ask, were you doing in Buncrana anyway?

With his research completed Joe tried to piece together from the bewildering mix of facts and speculation the story of the fate of Sir John Franklin and his crew. He started from the day in September of 1846 when the *Erebus* and *Terror* departed Beechey Island, on which they had buried three of their number, John Torrington, John Hartnell and William Braine, and travelled down Peel Sound in search of the Northwest Passage. It was surprisingly free of ice and they progressed unhindered, pleased with their good fortune. What they could not know was that the ice would form behind them and that for the next decade Peel Sound would be impassable, cutting off any possibility of retreat by that route.

In his cabin Sir John Franklin read the narratives of his predecessors. From their observations he believed there was open sea to the west of King William Island that would lead to their eventual completion of the Northwest Passage. But when they reached Victoria Strait it was ice-filled, the short summer season was almost over, and he had no choice but to winter to the north of King William Island. It is not known precisely where Franklin found shelter for his ships but in May of the following year he sent Lieutenant Gore, Des Voeux, and six men from the *Erebus* to King William Island to investigate the island's west coast. Four miles north of Victory Point they left in a cairn their record:

HM Ships *Erebus* and *Terror* Wintered in the Ice in May 1847

Lat. 70 5' N. Long. 98 23' W.

Having wintered in 1846–7 at Beechey Island in Lat. 74 43' N. Long. 91 39' 15" W.,

after having ascended Wellington Channel to Lat. 77, and returned by the West side of Cornwallis Island.

Sir John Franklin commanding the Expedition.

All well.

Party consisting of 2 officers and 6 men left the Ships on Monday 24th May, 1847 Gm. Gore, Lieut.

Chas. F. Des Voeux. Mate.

The reference to 'All Well' may subsequently have haunted them, for when they made it back to the ships Sir John Franklin was either dead or dying. He was sixty-one. What they did with Franklin's body remains a mystery to the present day; it is assumed that his men would have transported his body to land for burial but no trace has ever been found. An Inuit rumour exists that Franklin was buried on one of two small islets to the north of King William Island but no serious attempt has ever been made to investigate this claim.

Between September 1846 and April 1848 the *Erebus* and *Terror* drifted a mere nineteen miles. Beset by ice and with no fresh meat left on board, the crew began to succumb to scurvy. On 22 April, with twenty-four men having died in the past year, including Gore and Des Voeux, they abandoned the ships. The command had now passed to Captain Crozier and the final decision on which direction they would take fell to him. Crozier was an Arctic veteran and rather than travelling north to seek help, a journey his weakening men might never survive, he decided they would travel south along the western shore of King William Island towards Back's Fish River which held the prospect of plentiful game to hunt. Considering their dire situation Crozier may well have taken the most rational choice but as they turned their faces southward, unbeknownst to them, miles to the north, James Clark Ross was on his way with a relief and search party towards Prince Regent Inlet.

The men of the *Erebus* and *Terror* now had to traverse the bleak west coast of King William Island, dragging three boats with them that were positioned on improvised sledges.

Eleven years later Leopold McClintock walked the same route as he sought to discover their fate. He wrote of it:

> The coast we marched along was extremely low – a mere series of ridges of limestone shingle, almost destitute of fossils . . . The prospect to seaward was not less forbidding – a rugged surface of crushed-up pack, including much heavy ice. In these shallow ice-covered seas, seals are but seldom found: and it is highly probably that all animal life in them is as scarce as upon the land.
>
> Nothing can exceed the gloom and desolation of the western coast of King William Island . . . It is not by any means the 'land abounding with reindeer and musk oxen' which we expected to find: the natives told us there were none of the latter and very few of the former upon it.

At Victory Point Commander Fitzjames opened the tin can containing the record left the previous year by Lieutenant Gore. In temperatures so low the ink had to be thawed he added further information in the margins, the same note, now on display in the National Maritime Museum, that subsequently told the world of the death of Franklin and of their decision to make for Back's Fish river.

25 April 1848 – HM's Ships *Terror* and *Erebus* were deserted on 22 April 5 leagues N.N.W. of this, having been beset since 12 September 1846. The Officers and crews, consisting of 105 souls, under the command of Captain F. R. M. Crozier, landed here in Lat. 69 37' 42" N, long. 98 41' W. This paper was found by Lt Irving under the cairn supposed to have been built by Sir James Ross in 1831, 4 miles to the northward, where it had been deposited by the late Commander Gore in June, 1847. Sir James Ross' pillar has not, however, been found, and the paper has been transferred to this position, which is that in which Sir James Ross' pillar was erected. Sir John Franklin died on 11 June 1847; and the total loss by deaths in the Expedition had been to this date 9 officers and 15 men.
James Fitzjames, Captain HMS *Erebus*.
F. R. M. Crozier, Captain and Senior Officer.
and start on tomorrow, 26th, for Back's Fish River.

This note is the last written evidence of the actions of Franklin's men; from Victory Point onwards their story is as much speculation as fact.

They had taken a considerable number of items off the ships with them, possibly because they feared the ships might break up in the ice, but many of these items were left behind at Victory Point, protected from the elements by standing tents, as if they considered the possibility of return. Years later they were still there when McClintock passed; amongst them a pile of clothing four feet high that the crew had discarded.

Fourteen officers and ninety men set off from Victory Point but the trek was slow and painful; with many debilitated by scurvy, the whole party was slowed down and they were able to manage only a few miles a day. At Terror Bay a large tent was pitched and it was decided that the weakest would remain there, along with a few of their healthier colleagues, and two of their three boats. The remainder would keep going in search of help.

Those who managed to carry on had their first encounter with the Inuit on the east coast of Washington Bay. In 1869 two eyewitnesses, Tukketa and Owwer, recounted that meeting with Charles Hall and his field notes record their reactions:

Tukketa and Owwer now tell that they, with Tooshooarttharu and Monger, were on the west shore of King William Island with their families sealing, and this a long time ago. They were getting ready to move – the time in the morning and the sun high – when Tukketa saw something in the distance on the smooth ice that looked white and thought it was a bear. The company had got all ready to start travelling on the land. Soon as Tukketa saw this something white, he told his companions of it, when all waited, hoping it was a bear. As they watched, the white object grew larger, for it was coming down towards them. They saw the white thing moving along, in the direction of the coast, turning in a kind of circling way just as the little bay turned. At length they began to see many black objects moving along with what they had first espied as white in the distance. The object that they first had seen as white proved to be a sail raised on the boat and as this got nearer saw this sail shake in the wind. On seeing what they did, the object grew plainer and they thought of white men and began to be afraid.

Two of Franklin's party approached the Inuit and attempted to communicate with them, describing how their ships were being crushed in the ice. They both bore the unmistakable signs of scurvy, their mouths hard and dry and black. The Inuit sold them seal-meat but would not delay, for to delay with these strangers was to endanger their own families; they could not secure food for both themselves and the white men. Days later though the Inuit did wait at Gladman Point for Franklin's party to catch up with them but they never arrived and the Inuit moved on.

After the Inuit departed, the surviving crew only managed to travel fifteen miles east of Washington Bay before the first of them died. McClintock subsequently discovered the body: the fact that it was not buried suggests the man wandered off on his own and became lost in a blizzard.

Shortly after midnight of the 24th May, when slowly walking along a gravel ridge near the beach, which the winds kept partially bare of snow, I came upon a human skeleton, partly exposed, with here and there a few fragments of clothing appearing through the snow. The skeleton – now perfectly bleached – was lying upon its face, the limbs and smaller bones either dissevered or gnawed away by small animals . . . A pocket-book afforded strong grounds of hope that some information might be subsequently obtained respecting the unfortunate owner and the calamitous march of the lost crews, but at the time it was frozen hard . . . This poor man seems to have selected the bare ridgetop, as affording the least tiresome walking, and to have fallen upon his face in the position in which we found him.

If Franklin's men were journeying towards Back's Fish River, as stated in the record at Victory Point, they should have left King William Island at the spot where Simpson Strait was at its narrowest, but instead they kept going east, following the coastline. At some point on the march therefore they must have changed their minds and decided to make for Repulse Bay where they knew the Inuit gathered in large numbers. From there, with Inuit help, they could travel north to the whalers on Baffin Island and their deliverance.

But as they walked along the King William Island coastline they continued to die. One of their last camps was at Douglas Bay where seven perished and from where, over the next few years, their bones would be swept out to sea; the remainder abandoned the boat they had been dragging with them and continued on.

Further along the coast the Inuit told Hall of finding the graves of two men. Hall noted their description:

The bodies buried by placing stones around and over them – the remains facing upwards and the hands had been folded in a very precise manner across the breasts of both. Clothes all on and flesh all on the bones. On back of each a suspended knife found. The bodies perfect when found but the Innuits having left the remains unburied after unearthing them, the foxes have eaten most sinews all off the bones.

When Hall returned with them to the spot, they discovered one complete skeleton beneath the snow. The skeleton was returned to England where it was identified as that of Henry Le Vesconte, a lieutenant on the *Erebus*.

Eventually the remaining men, a half dozen or so, crossed

from King William Island on to the Todd Islands. They would go no further. They had undertaken an extraordinary walk of almost two hundred miles from their icebound ships, burying their comrades as they fell, demonstrating a moving affection for each other by the care and attention they invested in each burial, but now emaciated and reduced, any further travelling or exertions were beyond them.

And what of those left behind at Terror Bay, what had become of them? The following spring, in search of Franklin's men, the Inuit retraced their steps along King William Island and at Terror Bay they discovered a tent. An Inuit woman present described the scene to Schwatka:

> There were dead bodies in the tent, and outside some were covered over with sand. There was no flesh on them – nothing but the bones and clothes. There were a great many; she had forgotten how many . . . The bones had the chords [*sic*] or sinews still attached to them. One of the bodies had the flesh on, but this one's stomach was gone. There were one or two graves outside. They did not open the graves at this time; saw a great many things lying around. There were knives, forks, spoons, watches, many books, clothing, blankets, and such things.

Many of these items were taken by the Inuit.

Unlike those who had marched across King William Island, the men left behind at Terror Bay had abandoned the deeply ingrained discipline of their working lives. Some chose to return to the ships where a quantity of food still remained; the others, many too weak to move, stayed put and eventually resorted to cannibalism. *In extremis* these dying men dismembered their dead companions outside the tent, sawing through bones and boring a hole in each skull so that the brains could be removed.

Of the crew-members struggling back towards the *Erebus* and *Terror*, most managed only a day's march before exhaustion and illness meant they had to make camp at Erebus Bay. This enforced decision sealed their fate; survival depended on the strength to keep going. The first discovery of their bodies was made by an Inuit, Pooyetta, a year later, skulls and bones scattered about a boat, many of the arms and legs having been sawed off. It would be another nine years before McClintock and Hobson found a second boat nearby, two skeletons lying within, the sight of which had left them 'transfixed with awe'.

And there was further Inuit evidence of cannibalism amongst Franklin's men, descriptions of bones 'broken up for the marrow in them' and piled 'close to the cooking place', of 'long boots' which 'came up high as the knees and that in some was cooked human flesh – that is human flesh that had been boiled'.

For those who made it back to the *Erebus* and *Terror* their situation, after so much wasted effort, must have seemed hopeless. They had no way of knowing if their companions had ever made it to safety and even if they had done, a rescue party would surely not reach them in time. Confined to the *Terror*, for the *Erebus* lay on its side crushed by the ice, they waited, striving to stay alive. They were desperately ill, emaciated, reduced to a dull lethargy Each time one of their number died, the body was taken to the *Erebus* and placed in a sleeping bunk, for it was beyond the survivors to dig a grave in the ice.

As they awaited their end, with all hope virtually extinguished, the ice, miraculously, began to break up and the

Terror floated free for the first time in years. Rousing themselves, they decided on one last undertaking; they would sail the *Terror* to the south coast of King William Island and through Simpson Strait in the hope of encountering the Inuit.

They managed to negotiate the various reefs that initially littered their route but were unable to find the narrow entrance to Simpson Strait. They anchored the *Terror* near Kirkwall Island to the west of the Adelaide Peninsula whilst they set out in a small boat to search for the entrance. But the ice closed in and the *Terror* was trapped yet again.

The next indication of what happened came once more from the Inuit. In late May or early June they discovered the *Terror* far from shore and, after having watched it for some time, believed it to be deserted. One of them told Hall of their first visit:

> Then all the Innuits went to the ship and stole a good deal – broke into a place that was fastened up and there found a very large white man who was dead, very tall man. There was flesh about this dead man, that is, his remains quite perfect – it took 5 men to lift him. The place smelt very bad. His clothes all on. Found dead on the floor – not in a sleeping place or berth . . .

Determined to ransack the ship but finding the hatchways locked, they smashed an entry through the hull and took everything they could find. The abandoned *Terror* was now truly helpless; in the coming months, when the ice melted, the water would pour through her hull and she would sink into the Arctic sea.

But the Inuit also told Hall of footprints in the snow, marks left by the very last survivors of the combined crews of the *Erebus* and the *Terror*. Having abandoned their ice-bound ship, this final group, upwards of ten in number, used their small boat to navigate through Simpson Strait, intending ultimately to veer southwards to find the mouth of the Back River. They were not to make it. The Inuit found their upturned boat at Starvation Cove on the north coast of the Adelaide Peninsula; when they righted it, the bodies lay beneath. The boat had been the men's last refuge; unable to go on, with death hovering, they had lain together in the sheltered dark and heard the wind scream about them, heard their laboured breathing, past words now, each of them concentrating on their own final moments of life.

All except one. Five miles to the south-east of the boat a solitary body was found face down in the snow. The will to survive had taken him beyond his companions at Starvation Cove, stumbling off alone into the white mist in search of Back's Fish River. The last man – unidentified, a name on a roster only – alone as few are alone in this life, arms out-stretched, sleepwalking through the Arctic as if it were simply a bad dream whilst behind him, spread out across King William Island, lay the bodies of those with whom he had set out from Greenhithe on a May morning four years pre-vious. A morning that had been filled with high hopes and with a conviction that they would journey through the Northwest Passage and return to England triumphant. Even the portents seemed in their favour. As Eleanor, Franklin's daughter from his first marriage, wrote to her aunt:

Just as they were setting sail, a dove settled on one of the masts, and remained there for some time. Every one was pleased with the good omen, and if it be an omen of peace and harmony, I think there is every reason of its being true.

PART SIX

HE ROSE VERY early, as was his wont, out of a thin sleep that never seemed far from consciousness. Easing aside the curtain, he studied the deserted street, the first light of a new June day. He seldom ventured out now, for to leave the house brought with it the risk that he would not make it back again. His health, like everything else, was deserting him. But then, at eighty-nine years of age, what else could he expect; he had lived far beyond the natural life span. At the bathroom mirror, he pulled back his lower lip and peered at the few teeth that remained, long, discoloured, the gums receding. Only wisps of hair left too, the dome of skull more or less fully visible. Hard to believe that he had once been a fleshy man, his bones amply cushioned. To think that he had once attacked his food with gusto, great plate-fuls set in front of him and devoured with the same energy he'd devoted then to everything, to life itself. That earlier incarnation he recalled now as one might a long-forgotten friend unexpectedly alluded to, one memory prompting another. Yes, he had known that man once, had shared good times with him, but it had been so long ago and life had changed so irrevocably in the intervening years. Now, should he deign to eat, he could manage only tea and bread, everything else was too much effort, indigestible, or wasted on his failing senses. The man who had champed merrily on whatever piece of red meat came his way was now reduced to the inglorious feel of bread softening and crumbling in his mouth. His appetite had truly gone.

And yet his mind had not. Whilst it might lack its original sharpness and whilst the timespan between deciding to do something and forgetting what that something was might grow ever shorter (he seemed to be forever poised in the various rooms of his house trying to remember what had brought him there), his mind could still be roused into a state of animation. How that was possible, he could not say. It was as if his body and mind had different expectations of their tenure on this earth, his body about to give up the ghost, his mind assuming it had good years ahead. He kept a sheaf of blank paper near at hand and from somewhere or other an idea, as fresh as a fish just pulled from the ocean, would come to him, rendered on to the page in jottings and sketches, the same process by which all his inventions had started. A mere eight years ago, at the age of eighty-one and with an enthusiasm bordering on the naive he had still been patenting these inventions. But all that was beyond him now, financial reward or acclaim were but empty promises repeated once too often. He gave them no further credence at this late stage in life.

Once again, he stepped over to the window and peered out. He lived now in constant terror; it was only a matter of time before the men from the Corporation arrived, broke down his front door and threw him on to the street. They had given him notice of eviction and the date had passed; they would surely act soon. He had believed himself without friend or advocate in this ordeal and had been greatly heartened and gratified that the *Derry Journal*, without solicitation, thought to write an editorial earlier this month on his behalf. It lay open on the table before him, a constant reminder that he was not entirely forgotten in this world:

1 June 1894
EVICTING CAPTAIN COPPIN
The Corporation, in their majority, are determined to have an odious distinction in accomplishing – if they be allowed to defy the ratepayers by accomplishing it – their Baths and Wash-houses scheme. They are to play the part of evictors; and, if we be not greatly misinformed, the conditions under which they move to their purpose give evidence of a cleverness and, we fear, a callousness, that will be fully appreciated, if not very much admired in Derry. They have made arrangements to evict Captain Coppin. How have they placed themselves in the position of doing so? They have, we are informed, served on him a notice of ejectment for the 20th of June, and in this have shown no regard for the fact that this venerable and valuable citizen is enfeebled by the decay of age and seriously ill as well. Is not this a pretty performance to be done in the name of the people of Derry whose welfare Captain Coppin had at heart, and whose genius did honour to our city in days agone? Captain Coppin, as we all know, was a man of genius and many enterprises. He was a great employer of skilled labour and a good employer, aiming, above all else, to make the works he engaged in benefit Derry and Derry tradesmen. He won applause and made a name. But he was a bad financier and a worst diplomatist; and thus, with one remarkable touch of misfortune in a brilliant career added – a misfortune not of his making –

he became poor. He lost his property. He who had made the banks of the Foyle sing merrily to the tune of the ship-wrights' industry sank into privacy a broken man. In this critical moment a relation of his family – so it is stated – purchased the leased interest in the premises now occupied by him. There was, it seems, an implied understanding that at its expiry the lease would be renewed. This purchased interest was obviously and in fact for the one purpose – to give Captain Coppin a home secure for his life. The Derry Corporation majority now step in to play Claricarde – a worthy, a noble enterprise! Now a plain question or two are here presented. Did Captain Coppin hold under lease by purchase, and on the understanding that he was to enjoy its continuance? Was the renewal sought on the part of Captain Coppin, and is it not the fact that with this know-ledge procurable, if not actually ascertained, the majority of the Corporation set about grabbing the property? What have the Hon. the Irish Society to say to this? The Visitation is to be here in July. What a nice discovery it will be for them to find full across their path – radiant as usual with festivities – the scene of an eviction painful and offensive to the public eye to a peculiar degree. We do not believe that the Hon. body are in full possession of the informa-tion we now place before them; but when they come to know the nature of the thing that is to be done, we venture to tell them that they owe it to the honour of a great life now near its close to interpose, if they yet can, for the cause of justice and public decency. The citizens are deeply moved over this matter, and would stay the hand of the evictor if it can be done, or at least they desire that Captain Coppin be fairly, nay, generously treated.

It was unsettling to have another sum up your life in this fashion; even worse, the editorial in tone and content was close to an obituary. But the fact that every breath he drew acted as an impediment to progress gave him immense satisfaction; he did not want a single brick of this city to change, let it stay as he had known it, as his wife and children had known it. The future was nothing to him, he had no part to play in it. Would he be alive this time next year – in June 1895? He doubted it, the very thought of the winter ahead was almost sufficient to kill him.

But the newspaper had most certainly been accurate in describing him as 'a bad financier'. It was his great undoing, the reason he was at the mercy of strangers now. Once Dora had died all those years ago, he had lost any semblance of thrift, frittering away his money on vain and madcap enterprises that he'd hoped would restore a surface gleam to his life. Despite a voice within counselling that this was folly, he had continued regardless, ignoring the natural arc of his own life which, having already reached its apex, was now engaged in concomitant decline. And it could all be traced back to that moment at quayside when the ship that he hoped would be even more remarkable than the *Great Northern* had been consumed by fire in the slip dock. For the first time in his life he'd felt the weight of gravity pressing upon him. Not only did the fire occasion serious concerns about his finances and his family responsibilities but more than that, it produced a sense of doubt from which he had never recovered. Previously he had thought himself chosen, blessed, able to wish into existence whatever his mind conceived worthy. Dream and reality had fed off each other. But on that terrible morning, with the sun not yet risen, his faith had deserted him. Brought down to earth, chastened by a shiver of mortality, he saw reflected in the faces of his workmen a despair they had borne all their lives but with which he was only then becoming acquainted.

Who can say why we hide the truth from ourselves? Since that moment by the river he had spent the remainder of his life waiting, still hoping himself special, waiting patiently. All his life he had sought to transcend the normal, through shipbuilding, through invention; why else had Weesy's reappearance meant so much to him but as an opportunity to shape the known world by processes he could not begin to understand. Mystery had always transfixed him. How was it that a dead child knew where a group of English explorers had drawn their last breath and could then communicate the correct route for finding them? And his child at that. As the years had passed he had yearned for Weesy to return, this time to him, that he might have one last glimpse of transcendence before he died. But neither at Ivy House nor at 14 Sackville Street had there been the slightest intimation of his daughter's presence. She was gone for good, into whatever eternity she had striven so hard to avoid. Jane Franklin was almost twenty years dead now (six Arctic men, McClintock, Collinson, Richards, Ommanney, Barrow and Leigh-Smith had carried the coffin at her funeral), his friends and colleagues all departed, his wife buried in St Augustine's without even a tombstone to mark her grave, and he, well past his allotted three score and ten, retiring to bed each night with little confidence that he would be permitted a glimpse of the following day.

To be incapable of leaving his house was a form of death, an entombment. Yesterday morning from his window he had watched an aged man navigate the street as best he could, one hand clutching a stick, the other, outstretched, pressing against the houses for further support. The sight had pained him; worse still, the decrepitude of another was also a mirror whereby he beheld his own mortality. For what was he now but an animal isolated from the pack, prey to every passing carnivore? Yet he could understand that poor man's zeal and tenacity, for more than anything he too yearned to walk again in the open air, passing along by the river where he might scrutinize the constant variety of shipping that occupied its banks. There was no more forceful reminder that the world continued apace, almost like being afforded an intimation of how life would proceed after your own death, a shade granted special dispensation to return one last time. It induced in him a humility that no religion could replicate.

That sense of living beyond his time had occurred once before, a mere five years ago, with the news that a book had just been published devoted to the details of his daughter Weesy's vision. Entitled *Sir John Franklin: The True Secret of the Discovery of his Fate – a Revelation* and written by the Rev. J. Henry Skewes, vicar of Holy Trinity church in Liverpool, the book was a poor affair, full of overblown imagery and wrapped in a biblical hyperbole. The Rev. Skewes obviously perceived Weesy's brief return as an act of God, authenticated by her revelation of Sir John Franklin's whereabouts. It read, at times, like a work of fiction, and weak fiction at that, and he, William Coppin, barely recognized himself within its pages. As he saw it, Weesy's story needed no further adornment, it was quite astonishing enough without introducing the hand of God at each and every turn. Less was more; tell it simply, stripped of personal interpretation, as he had once told it to Lady Franklin all those years ago.

The visit from the bailiffs would be final proof that he was supernumerary, he would be thrown on to the street with the same carelessness as one might toss away the stub of a cigarette. He knew though to beware of self-pity, why should he be treated with any more consideration than the next man? The world was not a lenient place, hadn't his own experiences made that abundantly clear. Your deeds only lasted as long as they remained within the collective memory; there was a time, difficult though it was to believe, when parents had pointed him out to their children on the streets of Derry, but now, neither his person nor his name stirred the least interest.

Beyond his fear of eviction, he never thought of the future. His mind urged him backwards, ever backwards, rousing him to recall the intensity of his dog days. He sat by his bedroom window, where, should he twist sideways and press his face against the glass he could glimpse the Foyle as it changed from day to day. A new light fell upon it each time he looked, the river wondrous in its mutability. Occasionally the sound of workmen hammering would echo round the street and he would close his eyes and imagine he was back in Ivy House and that it was *his* workforce he could hear, hard at work on the *Great Northern*. He must have looked a peculiar sight to those passing below, this grotesque, aged figure abnormally twisted behind the glass. Perhaps they wondered what it was he saw that they could not?

His day was also lit by the arrival and departure of children to and from the National School opposite his house. He rejoiced in their energy, their enthusiasm, their presumption of all that lay ahead. They brought him comfort too because at last, belatedly, he was paying attention, not to his own children sadly, none of whom were near at hand now, but at least he was paying attention to someone's children, a small private act of atonement for all his years of disregard. Twice a day he was by the window at the requisite time, fondly gazing down upon them like a beneficent god. As he watched them, their irrepressible high spirits breaking through the chill decorum of school hours, he was reunited with emotions he had felt as a child, coming back to him like snatches of an old song he hadn't heard in years, the lyrics of which, to his great surprise, he had never forgotten, rising to the surface from deep within, line by remembered line.

Now when it was all too late, he fervently desired a house full of people, children running everywhere, his wife calling to him above the noise. Where once the children had followed the ghost of Weesy around Ivy House, now it was his turn; in his sleep he walked the familiar rooms, the ghosts of his wife, Dora, and his dead children turning to him and smiling encouragingly, all reaching out to take his hand, all leading him he knew not where.

*

Are you going to tell me or do I have to guess? said Eileen.

Neither. Just try and be patient for ten minutes, will you.

They walked together down William Street, still somewhat awkward in each other's company, through Sackville Street and round the back of the supermarket built on the site of the demolished Ivy House. The *Maiden Tripper* was docked where Coppin's shipyard had once stood.

A boat, said Eileen, we're going on a boat?

We are. Joe eyed her anxiously. I thought you'd like it.

Don't look so alarmed, I'm not put out. Just surprised, that's all. I've never been on the Foyle before.

Exactly. That's why I thought you'd like it. It was Da's idea really, to give credit where it's due.

And what exactly happens? I mean, where do we go?

The boat goes to Greencastle and back again. But we're only going as far as Greencastle because we're having dinner at Kiely's and I've arranged a taxi to bring us back to Derry after.

It gets better and better.

The boat incorporated two tiers of seating and being the first to arrive they had their pick. They chose the upper deck and, fanned by a light breeze coming off the river, waited patiently for their fellow passengers. The city rose and fell before them, bobbing gently.

In twos and threes the passengers came, converging on the quayside like emigrants of old. Except that these emigrants arrived full of smiles and laughter, boarded willingly and cast no last lingering looks back at the city they were departing. A slightly manic air, as of a school outing, held sway.

Beneath them a couple of musicians made some final alterations to the tuning of their guitars. The captain's voice came over the speakers, welcoming them on board and promising, between breaks in the music, to point out places of interest on their journey. As the boat edged out into mid-stream they all shifted in their seats expectantly and began to gaze about them as if seeing everything for the first time. The breeze strengthened and slowly, almost ceremoniously, they proceeded downriver.

The town looks so different from out here, said Eileen, another place entirely.

Why didn't we think to do this with Ciara, said Joe as he gazed at the children leaning on the guardrail, she'd have loved it.

The captain invited them to look to their right, informing them that from the thin spit of land they were currently passing, the monks from the monastic order of St Brechan's had fished for salmon in medieval times, gathering great quantities in the first recorded incident of its kind. To their left were the old docks from which the emigrant boats had departed. On cue the two musicians launched into 'Paddy's Green Shamrock Shore'. As the boat passed Sainsbury's the shoppers loading carrier bags into their cars raised their heads in surprise at the fleeting music as if some coexisting world had momentarily broken through into their own.

For Joe the journey was a teasing simulacrum of his previous desire to leave Derry – how many times had he envisaged the moment of departure, nurtured it in his heart? Now here he was on a pleasure boat going no further than Greencastle and yet his mind was filled with the sensation of leave-taking, of looking past the buildings to the hills beyond, unchanged from generation to generation, the same image visible to him as had stamped itself on the memories of all those who had gone before.

There were occasions when he had comforted himself by likening Ciara's fate to a journey on an emigrant ship and his own to being the relative left behind at the quayside. She was dead to him, he told himself, for he would never see her again, and yet she still lived, existing in a place well beyond his comprehension from where he hoped she had not entirely forgotten her past.

The river broadened and they seemed far from shore. Floating serenely beneath the Foyle Bridge they followed the curve of the river, and the city, with unexpected rapidity, vanished from sight.

Joe stepped below to the bar.

They cruised past the spot where the German U-boat command had surrendered at the end of the war, past the stately Brooke Hall, now home, they were informed, to the novelist Jennifer Johnston, its gardens full of shrubs and trees that two hundred years ago had been gathered from the four corners of the globe, past the small jetty on which stood the remains of the ice-house that had supplied Brooke Hall. They entered the river's narrows, the dense undergrowth throwing shadows across the water, prompting in Joe thoughts of the river journey in *Heart of Darkness*, the alien banks that hid all manner of threat and animus. And doubtless the Elizabethans had perceived the Foyle in much the same way, for these narrows would have been the most dangerous stretch on their journey upriver, too close to the shore for comfort, forcing them to be alert to sporadic attack from natives they looked upon as somewhat less than human.

At Culmore Point, where the river meets the lough, the captain pointed out the famine wall that curved around the bay and back to the city. They took in the nineteenth-century fort that stood on the same site as the O'Doherty town house that Sir Henry Docwra had captured in 1600, giving him control over all those who might want to enter or exit the Foyle.

The musicians struck up the opening chords of 'I Wish I Was Back Home In Derry', a song written by the hunger striker Bobby Sands.

No Protestants on this boat, I hope, said Joe. He sat in silence for a minute. These emigrant songs can get a bit depressing, he remarked.

They're nothing *but* depressing if you ask me. If I have to listen to many more of them I might just throw myself overboard before we reach Greencastle.

They entered the open waters of the lough. The land withdrew, the waves freshened, and yachts with sails unfurled glided past as graceful as swans. Moville came up on their left, its rocky shoreline, a funfair set up on the Bath Green, the bright colours of Sunday daytrippers poised on the shore path like an irregular line of flowers, and past all this they drifted whilst the music of the funfair echoed across the water, the passengers strangely moved as if they were looking in from another world and had been given this brief, passing moment to observe how they had once lived.

As those on board looked shorewards, Joe chose instead to gaze at the profile of his wife's averted face, remembering the first time they had met and how in the course of one evening in the Dungloe Bar he had found himself, almost against his will, staring at her repeatedly, experiencing a tenderness towards this stranger that defied all reason, to such an extent that he had wondered if he could leave her when it came time to say goodbye. But of course she had circumvented this dilemma by asking *him* out, as if knowing instinctively that he wouldn't have the courage. And over the years that followed she had circumvented all manner of difficulties that might have impaired their marriage with a composure that left him gravitating between feelings of inadequacy and wonder.

She had always been the stronger partner, which made her behaviour over the last six months, the way in which she had recoiled from life, all the more unexpected. She had renounced life as if it was a faith she no longer believed in. But no-one can say with any certainty how another human being will react to loss and something in Eileen had sought to forgo the present and reclaim the certainties of her own childhood.

He had blamed her for deserting him, had sat many a night in the dark house and nursed his grievances. To such an extent that anger at his wife's absence had even sometimes displaced his grief.

When he met Katie it had been like meeting Eileen all over again: the same ironic, bantering tone, the way in which affection was conveyed at one remove. He hadn't realized it at first but in talking to Katie he had been talking to his wife again. To say 'I became friends with another woman because I missed you so much' might sound like the lowest of male excuses but nevertheless there was some truth to it. The rhythm of his conversations with Eileen, established over years of marriage, had been replicated with Katie. As if Katie's body had been possessed of his wife's spirit.

But now Eileen was before him again, back from the dead. As he watched her she turned and smiled at him, meaning nothing by it he knew, just a throwaway smile, but his throat constricted and he reached over and took her hand.

Are you all right, she asked?

He nodded. Never better.

The song the musicians were playing had an air that sounded familiar to him, though he could not place it. Perhaps someone in his family had sung it during his childhood. What was it called, he wondered? He listened to some of the words in the hope of finding the answer amongst them:

Our ship at the present lies below Londonderry,
To bear us away o'er the wide swelling sea:
May heaven be her pilot and grant her fair breezes
Till we reach the green fields of Americay.

He leaned over towards the next table. What's this song called, he asked the man sitting there.

'The Emigrant's Farewell', I think they said, the man answered. Something like that anyway.

Before them now were the bright colours of the fishing boats resting side by side in Greencastle harbour. Their boat edged in towards the dock and they disembarked, holding each other's hand for balance.

They bought two ice creams and crossed the street to a bench from where they could look across the Foyle towards the Martello Tower at Magilligan Point, to the long golden strand that, despite the clouds, was still aflame as if blessed with its own sun, to the great escarpment of Benevenagh.

I've taken to reading about astronomy recently, said Joe, glancing at Eileen.

Hmm, she said, noncommittally, taking a long lick of her ice cream.

It seems we have about five billion years left on this earth before our sun dies.

You and me should be all right then.

You know, Eileen, there's nothing like astronomy for giving you perspective. There's a hundred billion galaxies out there and our own galaxy, the Milky Way, has a hundred billion stars.

Eileen bit the end off her cone and began to suck the ice cream out of it.

It makes you realize how insignificant we are, Joe continued. Which is a great comfort, strange as it may seem.

Eileen rested her free arm on Joe's knee. I do so love your idea of small talk, she said, smiling. You certainly know how to chat up a girl.

They sat in silence and watched the car ferry make the

short hop between Greencastle and Magilligan. Joe was reminded of the same pure sensation he sometimes experienced on early mornings when he walked to the corner shop for the newspaper, a gratitude that he had been granted another day, the pristine, unspoiled beauty of it, the hopes that rose in him unprompted. It was as if he'd been forgiven all transgressions, as if he'd never committed any in the first place.

I'm still humming that song from the boat, said Joe. I can't get it out of my head.

They walked up to inspect the remains of Northburg castle, built by Richard de Burgo in the fourteenth century, then stopped for a quick drink at the Castle Inn. They spoke of Eileen's work, of how glad she was to be back, the distraction of being caught up in other people's lives again.

What's the worst thing you ever saw at the surgery, Eileen?

That's easy to answer. It was a couple of weeks after I'd started and a man came in from the shirt factory across the street and said that a rat had bit him. I'll get the doctor to look at it, I told him. The thing is, he said, the rat's still on me. I thought he was having me on, that someone had put him up to it, but he lifted his T-shirt and there was the rat hanging on to his chest like grim death. I nearly fainted. And yet the man was as calm as could be, you'd think he'd no more wrong with him than a cut finger. It turned out that he'd cornered the rat in the factory and it had run up his leg and latched on to his chest. When a rat bites you its jaws lock and you can't shift it, even if you kill it it still won't let go. Eileen shivered. God, the very thought of it gives me the willies.

And what happened to the man?

I've no idea. All I know is that we couldn't get him out

of the surgery quickly enough. Somebody drove him straight to the hospital if I remember rightly.

Well, said Joe, getting to his feet, on that note and assuming you have any appetite left, it's time for dinner.

The summer light was just beginning to fade as they walked down towards Kiely's. It felt like they were strolling through an evening of long ago, taking the same walk along the same shoreline that couples had always taken, relishing the tranquillity, the lap of the tide, the fishing boats rising and falling at anchor, the inquisitive cries of seabirds strutting up and down the foreshore. Experiencing the melancholy that comes from remembering that there were others before you and that there will be others after.

Joe put his hand lightly on Eileen's back, as if encouraging her forward towards all that lay ahead.

In the restaurant Eileen took a good look round her.

Not much to it, is there? she remarked. Considering all the fuss about it, I was expecting it to be a bit fancier. Not that I'm complaining, mind, she added quickly.

They were given seats by the window.

You know, said Eileen, studying the menu, I've always wanted to try lobster. But I haven't a clue how to eat it.

I'm sure if you asked them they'd show you. How difficult can it be?

Have you seen the price of it?

Never mind the price.

When the waitress came to take their order, Eileen explained her predicament.

There's nothing to it, said the waitress, I'll show you how.

They had gin and tonics while they waited, gazing out at the few people that passed by. A young child, briefly separated from its parents, stared in at them then ran away.

I feel guilty when I'm having too good a time, said Eileen. A voice in my head starts chastising me.

Things will get better, Eileen.

No they won't, Joe, they'll stay exactly the same. That's what you have to accept. It's like the view from your bedroom window, you get up every morning, pull the curtains and there it is, a part of your day like any other.

They lapsed into silence again. Sorry, said Eileen, I don't mean to go on, I know you're only trying to help.

The food arrived. God, said Eileen, eyeing her lobster, it doesn't look very dead to me.

You've no need to worry on that account, said the waitress. Now, this is what you want to be doing. She took Eileen through it step by step. You can't go wrong, she said, as she turned to go.

Let's hope not, said Eileen, tentatively picking up the pliers. She levered the lobster off the plate slightly and checked underneath. You shouldn't have encouraged me, she complained to Joe, letting me order lobster. She studied his plate. I don't suppose you'd swap?

The restaurant began to fill up. All colour in the sky moved to the edge, the evening darkened and just beyond the window their spectral twins ate an identical meal, gazing in at them with hands poised above their food as if to make sure they were enjoying it.

You know, said Eileen, vigorously cracking open part of the lobster's shell with her pliers, this is very therapeutic.

She looked up but Joe appeared not to have heard her. When we were on the boat, he said, I was thinking of the first time Ciara went to the pantomime. I had to take her on my own because you were down with flu, do you remember? Well, all through that pantomime she just sat there, very quiet and intense, hardly a laugh out of her. And at the end I said I was sorry she hadn't liked it. But I did like it, she said. So how come you never laughed, I asked her. I never laughed, Daddy, because I didn't want to miss anything.

Eileen offered the ghost of a smile.

She was a strange wee girl, said Joe, gazing off into the distance. I mean, there were times when she didn't seem a child at all, she had such a knowing air about her.

Eileen nodded. For a while there she went through a phase of wanting to meet me in the hallway every day when I came in from the surgery. If she missed me she would insist I go back out and come in again.

We were very tolerant, but then it was hard to refuse her.

Once begun they found they could not stop; through the rest of their meal, through another bottle of wine, through a shared dessert, through coffee and brandy, they told each other stories of their daughter. They searched back for moments when the other had been absent so that each story became an act of union, bringing all three of them together again.

Eventually the waitress brought their bill.

Is it very dear? asked Eileen.

Worth every penny. Joe stood up. Let's wait outside for the taxi.

On the wall opposite the restaurant they sat side by side and Joe put his arm around his wife's shoulder. Engulfed by the darkness they could barely see each other. Behind them the sea stirred and before, lit up as on a screen, the last diners finished their meal. For a few moments it was as if the two of them had stepped out of existence and were gazing enraptured at the white heat that constituted human life.

They heard the car before they saw it and when it pulled up outside Kiely's and the driver stepped out, they jumped down and made their way back into the light to meet him.

Taxi for O'Kane? he enquired, turning towards them.

That's right, said Joe.

Is there just the two of you then?

Yes, said Eileen, taking hold of her husband's hand, there's just the two of us.

*

COPPIN – April 17, at his residence, Sackville Street, Derry, William Coppin. Funeral will leave this (Monday) morning, the 22nd inst. at half-past ten o'clock, for interment in St Augustine's Burying-ground, Derry. Friends will please accept this intimation.

Joe O'Kane stood at the grave, holding in his hand a copy of the death notice and of the *Derry Journal* editorial of 26 April 1895. It went on:

Unhappily Captain Coppin's closing days were harassed by those of his creed and party in terrifying the dying man with the horrors of threatened eviction. The Corporation of Derry has this to add to its long bead-roll of honour. The generation in which Coppin was a giant amongst the men of industrial enterprise had passed away from him in his long and honourable life; those who succeeded to place and power knew him only as a broken man. Why should they bother since his day of usefulness was over? And they didn't. The Corporation has its faults, but fine sentiment of this sort is not amongst them.

Joe could find no record of the burial itself, or of how many attended. As Coppin had died at the age of ninety, it was unlikely that any of his contemporaries had stood at the graveside. A sprinkling of individuals from a later generation, perhaps, to whom the name still meant something. And of course there were the surviving children. Had his two sons, John and William junior, returned to Derry for the funeral? And what of his daughters, Anne and Dora? Doubtless they were present, for, then or later, they seldom appear to have strayed far from home. United in spinsterhood, they would, he had discovered, live the rest of their lives together in a secluded house called 'Ravenscliff' on the road between Moville and Greencastle.

The gravestones gleamed now from a brief shower. Joe moved amongst them, peering down at the names and dates, conscious that Coppin had once performed this same simple act. For him, the graveyard must have been all too familiar, a place to which he returned again and again. And after a short prayer for his wife and children, had he stepped across on to the city walls and stood for a few minutes in contemplation, gazing down at the wild, unpopulated ground that then constituted the Bogside?

Above him would have towered Walker's Pillar; the governor, arm outstretched, pointing down the lough that all might see their salvation. Only the plinth still remained, for the pillar had been an early target of the IRA campaign.

For Joe, as perhaps for Coppin before him, the stress now fell on what was absent rather than what existed. Just as when two seemingly identical photographs are set side by side and you are asked to distinguish what is missing in one of them, so he looked around and noticed all that was gone, the space once occupied, the slight alteration such absences occasioned in the landscape when viewed from afar. And he noted how the eye still registered what wasn't there, as if change had happened too quickly, the object's presence lingering after its demise.

How many times since her death had he stepped outside his front door and, as a car passed, reached instinctively for his daughter's hand.

He imagined a dying man fantasizing of a walk into town, the route he would take, the people he might meet along the way, the shops he would call into. Drawing the pleasure of this imagined walk, like cigarette smoke, deep within. Lying there, staring at the ceiling, and striving to remember each building he would pass, thrilled by the weight of detail that he had effortlessly managed to accumulate over a lifetime.

And were the walk to happen, everything on that day would be slightly altered because of it, the choreography of the town would differ. They would change direction to let him pass. A hand might be raised to greet an old friend on the other side of the street. Conversations would take place and memories be retrieved from the possibility of oblivion.

But of course the dying man never leaves his bed and at first glance the town seems unchanged by his absence. Others fill the space in which he might have walked. Life goes on, as they say. And anyway, how do you measure the loss of what never happened? Perhaps you cannot, perhaps it's simply impossible, even though millions attempt it every day, it being the inevitable concomitant of grief. A world in which the dead jostle past the living to stand full square in front of you, in which the light of day is forever tempered by shadow. A world in which you are never fully present, always a touch distracted, your mind elsewhere, as if you are taking part in two conversations at once and are undecided as to which of the two you should fix your attention on.

Joe stood with head bowed, as if in mourning. William Coppin had become like family to him. There were times upon waking when, for a brief moment before the new day kicked in, Joe was convinced they had spoken together, so powerful was the connection. William Coppin was a man he had once known, he thought to himself. He wondered if he would have got through the past months but for the solace that knowing Coppin had brought him, the recognition of another man's plight on this earth similar to his own. That a hundred and fifty years separated them meant little or nothing – he felt closer to the nineteenth-century shipbuilder than to those he walked amongst every day. It was as if certain emotions – grief, for example – stayed constant in the one place and were handed on from stranger to stranger, from generation to generation; people might change, the names might change, but grief and the enacting of it remained essentially the same. The death of his daughter was no more than a slight variation on the death of Weesy Coppin, just as his own death would echo that of others before him. Through death the city had come alive to him.

Joe picked his way through the graves, pulled the gate behind him, and walked further along the city walls until he stood above Guildhall Square. Leaning against one of the cannon that had, during the siege, pointed towards the Catholic force of James II gathered on the far bank of the Foyle, he watched the activity below, the generations crisscrossing the square, and he thought of a camera capturing this moment and of it becoming an image to be studied years hence, in which those pictured would be considered, from the perspective of the observer, as quaint and innocent and somewhat naive, the almost inevitable conclusion, it seemed, of those looking into the past.

As for Joe, he had acquired, without quite knowing how, an emotional distance that held him apart from the world. He watched the present unfold as if it were already the distant past, requiring no engagement to speak of. He felt as if he belonged to no particular age but could come and go as he pleased. Those below, going about their business, were in no way different from their forebears going about theirs a hundred, two hundred years before; only the fashion told him that this was the early twenty-first century. He had to keep reminding himself that each of these people meant something to someone else, each was irreplaceable.

While he stood there, idling, his thoughts drifting, a familiar figure came around the corner by the Ulster Bank and in a loping walk began to cross the square. There was no mistaking the walk. Joe watched his father stride out, a small rucksack on his back, the only one of the pedestrians who appeared eager and resolved to reach their destination. His father, thought Joe, was a steadfast man. The word had arisen in him from nowhere but it seemed fitting. He found himself unexpectedly moved; he recognized, as if for the first time, the lonely life his father must lead. Perhaps because distance offers a certain poignancy, perhaps because he had just come from the grave of William Coppin, perhaps because his father had no idea he was being watched, whatever the reason, Joe looked upon him with new clarity and respect. No complaint ever issued from his father's lips, no questioning of the role of chance; every misfortune was 'offered up' to God in stoic acceptance, every blessing welcomed but never relied upon. It was an old-fashioned life, one that, in its intrinsic belief in privacy, ran counter to a world in which every autobiographical fragment was tendered without distinction. His father treated his own memories as if they were paintings of great delicacy and fragility, liable to damage each time they were brought into contact with the light, to be viewed by others therefore only sparingly.

Joe thought of calling out but instead he descended the walls and made his way to the bus station. Patsy was seated on a bench, studying his ticket.

Hello, Da.

Patsy raised his head at the words and his face lit up with pleasure. I was just thinking about you, he said.

How come?

I was wondering how your boat trip went. I nearly rang but didn't want to hear if it was bad news.

It went really well. We talked and we haven't done that for a long time. Joe took a seat beside his father. It's like Eileen's come back from some distant place and though she's fundamentally changed I'm beginning to realize the only thing that really matters is that she's back. There were times when it felt like she'd gone as far away from me as Ciara has. Both of them lost to me.

So you're a bit more hopeful?

I am. And that's enough for now.

I'm glad to hear it, son.

Joe toe-poked his father's rucksack. So where are you off to this time then?

I'm staying with an old friend who used to work with me on the building sites. He married a woman from County Mayo and moved there, though she's been dead now a good five years or more He's taking me fishing on the Moy and we're going out on a boat on Lough Conn.

But you've never fished before in your life.

Maybe so but it's never too late to try something new. Sure what could be nicer than being out on a boat in the early evening. It's not as if I care whether we catch a fish.

Well, said Joe, I'm going to miss you. He leaned across quickly and kissed his father on the cheek. Be sure and watch yourself now on that boat.

God, son, said Patsy, a look of astonishment on his face, what's come over you? I'll only be gone a few days.

Joe considered the deep lines cut into his father's face, the broken blood vessels on nose and cheekbones, the patches of grey stubble. Can't I still worry about you? he said.

Of course you can, of course, though there's no need to. Patsy rose to his feet. Here's my bus now.

He stepped on board, handed his ticket to the driver and made his way to the back of the bus. Joe waited for his father to acknowledge him but Patsy had already entered into conversation with a man in the seat opposite.

The engine caught, the bus began to edge out of its rank, and just when Joe was convinced that his father had forgotten his presence, Patsy turned to look out the back window and with a wry, private smile raised his thumb in a gesture of triumph.

*

In 1984 Owen Beattie, a forensic anthropologist from the University of Alberta, applied for permission to disinter the graves on Beechey Island of the three crew members of the *Erebus* and *Terror*, John Torrington, John Hartnell and

William Braine. Beattie wanted to apply modern techniques to an examination of the Franklin tragedy, the same techniques as might be used for any other disaster, to discover how they had died and why.

Gaining permission was a protracted process. Having received archaeology and science permits from the Territorial government, Beattie sought clearance from the Chief Medical Officer of the Northwest Territories whose job it was to assess the health risk involved in disinterring bodies that had been in the ground for over one hundred years. Exhumation and reburial permits were also applied for. Beattie needed permission from the Royal Canadian Mounted Police and from the Settlement Council of the Resolute Bay community. He contacted the UK Ministry of Defence and sent a letter to *The Times*, requesting that any descendants of the three seamen contact him, though none did at the time.

On 10 August Beattie and a small team of researchers landed on Beechey Island and two days later they began work on John Torrington's grave. There was no assurance that anything would still be there, Torrington's body might well have dropped through the ice into the deep Arctic waters, but after two days of hacking their way through the permafrost they glimpsed a piece of blue material and knew that the coffin must lie beneath.

Once they had removed all the ice and silt they discovered a plaque nailed to the coffin-lid, probably made from a tin can, on which a painted inscription read, 'John Torrington died January 1ˢᵗ, 1846.' The coffin was made of mahogany, with brass handles on each side. They sheared through the nails holding the coffin-lid in place and upon removing it were faced with a semi-transparent block of ice within which something rested. They peered through the ice but to no avail.

To thaw the ice, hot water was poured on it. After some time spent heating water on the camp stove and carrying the buckets backwards and forwards to the grave, the front of John Torrington's shirt suddenly came into view, its mother-of-pearl buttons. Next his toes, in a state of almost perfect preservation. The face was covered with the same blue cloth that had draped the coffin and whilst they worked to thaw the rest of the body, one of the researchers, Arne Carlson, concentrated on the delicate task of removing the frozen cloth from the face. Hunched over the body, he pried at the material with a pair of surgical tweezers. When the cloth came away in one go, there, up close to his, was the face of John Torrington.

They all stood back in awe, for it was impossible to believe that one hundred and thirty-eight years had passed since his companions had performed the funeral rites over John Torrington's body. The face was still fully formed, darkened on the nose and forehead where the wool had touched the skin. His eyes were open, the lips pulled back to reveal his teeth; even the veins on his forehead still visible. His expression seemed to convey disbelief at life being over so soon. Only twenty, it seemed to say, and already they are lowering me into the ground.

His body was bound by strips of cotton at the elbows, hands, ankles and big toes. A kerchief around the chin was tied at the crown of his head. He wore a white cotton shirt with thin blue stripes and a pair of grey linen trousers. His feet were bare.

They lifted him out of the coffin to perform the autopsy, the body limp rather than stiff, and as they did so his head lolled against Owen Beattie's shoulder, as a child's might on being carried to bed. John Torrington weighed no more than six stone and when they undressed the body his emaciated condition was evident, with each rib clearly visible.

The autopsy took four hours. Throughout they kept John Torrington's face covered. The internal organs were frozen and warm water had to be poured on them before samples could be taken. Using a surgical handsaw Beattie removed the skull cap. When all was completed they dressed the body, placed it back in the coffin and lowered it into the grave where the remains of John Torrington would return once again to a frozen state. With him in the grave they placed a note, giving the names of the seven researchers, their purpose and an expression of their emotions upon exhumation of the body.

Whilst Beattie had been performing the autopsy, another of the researchers, Walt Kowal, had begun work on opening the grave of John Hartnell. It was soon apparent that Hartnell's grave had been disturbed since burial. The coffin was found at only half the depth of Torrington's, the plaque was missing from the lid, and the right-hand side had been badly damaged by blows from a pickaxe. Hartnell's body was similarly encased in a block of ice but when they poured warm water over it, his face rose as if from the depths. John Hartnell bore the look of a man for whom long years in the grave had been an active torment, trapped like a genie in a bottle. His face had such vigour they might almost have expected him to raise himself up in the coffin and begin ranting about the unconscionable time he had spent underground. A shroud was drawn up to his chin. He wore a cap, beneath which locks of dark hair protruded. One eye appeared to have shrunk and the right side of his body revealed damage from the blows of the pickaxe.

But Beattie and his team had no opportunity for further exhumation, the summer was ending and John Hartnell had to be reburied until they could revisit Beechey Island the following year.

Upon his return to Edmonton, Beattie discovered why one of the graves had been damaged. In November 1852, a privately funded search expedition (which counted Lady Jane Franklin as one of the backers) exhumed the body of John Hartnell. The expedition was led by Commander Edward Inglefield and in a letter he described the exhumation:

> My doctor assisted me, and I have had my hand on the arm and face of poor Hartnell. He was decently clad in a cotton shirt, and though the dark night precluded our seeing, still our touch detected that a wasting illness was the cause of dissolution. It was a curious and solemn scene on the silent snow-covered sides of the famed Beechey Island, where the two of us stood at midnight. The pale moon looking down upon us as we silently worked with pickaxe and shovel at the hard-frozen tomb, each blow sending a spur of red sparks from the grave where rested the messmate of our lost countrymen. No trace but a piece of fearnought half down the coffin lid could we find. I carefully restored everything to its place and only brought away with me the plate that was nailed on the coffin lid and a scrap of the cloth with which the coffin was covered.

It would be another two years before Beattie could return to Beechey Island but in June 1986 they began again the exhumation of John Hartnell. With them this time was Brian

Spenceley, Hartnell's great-great-nephew. They could not be sure the body was still in a state of preservation but, after a day's digging, the uncovered coffin was once again a solid block of ice. After thawing, Brian Spenceley gazed upon the face of his ancestor, an ancestor who had been dead for a hundred and forty years.

They removed the tight-fitting cap, revealing a shock of dark brown hair. Peeling back the shroud, they found two letters and a date embroidered in red on his shirt, TH, 1844, suggesting that it had belonged to his elder brother Thomas who had also been on the expedition. When they removed the shirt, preparatory to conducting the autopsy, they made an extraordinary discovery; a sutured, y-shaped incision running down John Hartnell's chest and abdomen and across to both hips showed that an autopsy had already taken place. It could only have been performed on the *Erebus* hours after Hartnell's death. As far as Beattie and his team were aware, nothing like this – a nineteenth-century autopsy on an intact body – had ever been found before. They surmised that it had been performed on board ship by Dr Harry Goodsir, assistant-surgeon of the *Erebus*.

Now, when they re-opened the original incision, they were able to follow Goodsir's procedure: the removal of the heart with part of the trachea, a cut into each of the ventricles to inspect the valves, dissection of the lungs in search of tuberculosis, a few cuts into the liver. Once finished, he had simply heaped the viscera back into the body; the entire autopsy had taken no more than half an hour.

As before, they took samples and then began the arduous task of reburying John Hartnell.

Finally, there was William Braine, buried deeper than the other two. They worked continuously for thirty-seven hours before the coffin was visible. Once the lid had been removed, an area of bright red seemed to rest above Braine's face. It turned out to be a kerchief and, as the body thawed, they could see the outline of his face beneath. The rest of him was covered in a long, cream-coloured shroud.

William Braine was thirty-two when he died on 3 April 1846. When they lifted the kerchief, a bearded, emaciated face peered back at them through half-closed eyes, as if the sudden brightness of the Arctic light was too much for him. Unlike Torrington and Hartnell, little care had been taken arranging his body in the coffin; he looked cramped and uncomfortable and his left arm lay trapped beneath him. On performing the autopsy they realized that the body had partially decomposed. Lesions along his shoulders and in the groin area were the result of rats tearing at the body when it lay aboard the *Erebus*.

After following the same procedures they'd used on Torrington and Hartnell, Beattie and his team laid William Braine back into the frozen earth. The three graves were just as before, as if never disturbed. For a brief moment the three sailors had been raised up into the present day, into a world that had changed not a jot from the one they had departed a hundred and forty years previous, a landscape every bit as fierce and implacable as they remembered it. As if rudely woken from a dream and then, before they could attune themselves, lulled back to sleep again.

*

Joe and Eileen stood by their daughter's grave. All around them, to the outer limits of the cemetery, the crowd reached; friends and relatives clustered beside individual graves. In their silence and quiescence they resembled the dead themselves, newly arisen on the Day of Judgement, waiting patiently for their final reckoning.

I've never seen anything like it, said Joe, so many people.

It happens every year, said Eileen.

It's like the Day of the Dead in Mexico. When the families all picnic on their loved ones' graves.

Don't be getting any ideas.

On the high ground of the cemetery, half a dozen priests were gathered behind a single microphone. In the gusting wind they struggled to hold down their vestments. The speaker's voice was carried to and fro; fragments of scripture swirled through the air.

Joe and Eileen stood side by side, absorbed in thought. The wording on the gravestone was simple, it gave their daughter's name and the dates of her birth and death, nothing else. A solitary vase of flowers rested on the grass.

Far below she lay in a small white box. Or what remained of her. He remembered the unblemished perfection of her body and the joy and pride with which he had looked upon her. But nature, brutal and indifferent, made no distinction; the same implacable laws applied to his beloved daughter as to any other dead creature.

And yet the day of her funeral had been pure white, the surrounding landscape more appropriate to fable or fairytale. As if they were laying her down for a prolonged sleep, nothing more, in which she would remain as they had last seen her, frozen in time. Like the three dead sailors on Beechey Island who when brought to the surface were still recognizably themselves, capable of being revivified, as if life could be blown back into them again. Hers too had been an arctic burial, the bitter cold that probed deep into the bones, the tortured shapes of the small stunted trees, the tiny coffin lost amid the drifts of snow. Time and again his reading of the Franklin mystery brought her back to him, as if behind every door there was always the same room. In his dreams she wandered through the same landscape as had Franklin, Crozier, Fitzjames and Gore; emerging from a blizzard in the clothes she'd worn on her last day or still identifiable as a tiny speck alone in an immensity of white, too distant for voices to reach her. He had even dreamed of her coffin being dug up, of the lid being prised open and, as he forced himself to look, there before him was the pale face of his daughter, unchanged, a face that showed no evidence of distress or mortality, for whom the grave was no more than a passing inconvenience.

The priests began to radiate out across the cemetery, sprinkling holy water to left and right. As one approached them, Eileen blessed herself, as did those around her. The priest moved on. The crowd began to shuffle and disperse and Joe and Eileen made their way towards the main pathway that would lead them to the cemetery gates. From another direction he saw Declan Brady approaching the same pathway, holding by the arm a woman whom Joe took to be Declan's mother.

As they converged Declan held out his hand to Joe. Joe, he said, I heard tell what happened to your daughter. Saying sorry doesn't amount to much but what more can you say? He turned to Eileen. Are you Joe's wife?

Eileen, she said.

This is my mother. We were just over at the da's grave. Ten years he's dead now. He turned again to Joe. The last time we met, you were on your way to pick the wee one up from school, isn't that right?

It is, said Joe.

My God, how it all changes.

Was she your only child? asked Mrs Brady.

She was.

That's very hard. She shook her head at the thought of it, then reached over and took Eileen's hand. I'll pray for you, dear.

Thank you, said Eileen.

The four of them stepped amongst the crowd and walked together down to the cemetery gates, Mrs Brady taking hold of Eileen's arm and Declan and Joe a few steps behind. The two women began chatting as if they'd known each other for years.

Every time I leave here, said Declan, I promise myself I'll try that bit harder in life. Count my blessings and all. He glanced back up at the banked rows of graves, stretching as far as the eye could see. It seems no time at all, Joe, since we were in school together. But now here I am in my thirties and I feel as if I haven't even properly drawn breath yet. His face took on a bewildered look. It goes so fast, life, doesn't it.

They stood at the cemetery gates to say their goodbyes, a small island of stasis past which the living streamed on both sides.

Time I think, said Mrs Brady, for a bit of dinner. God forgive me but there's nothing like a visit to the cemetery for giving you an appetite.

To Joe's great surprise Eileen laughed. It's the cold, she said, it's always cold up there.

They shook hands and Mrs Brady gave Eileen a kiss on the cheek.

We never did get that drink together, said Declan to Joe, but I hope we will yet. He resumed his grip on his mother's arm, she smiled farewell, and they set off together along the road.

The last time I saw that man, said Joe, I hadn't a care in the world, though I didn't know it then. He turned to look at their receding forms. And what were you talking to his mother about?

Oh, she was telling me about how her life has changed since her husband died, how she doesn't have enough hours in the day now for everything she wants to do. Isn't it well for some. Eileen leaned in against him and slipped her hand into his coat pocket. Can you feel how cold I am? she said.

He took her hand. Like ice, he said.

She pressed her body against his. It's up to you to keep me warm, she said, her breath upon his face, I hope you realize that, Joe O'Kane. You'd better keep me warm.

EPILOGUE

HE SAT AT the desk in their bedroom, his research on William Coppin spread about him. He had everything he needed, everything there was to find. He knew more about William Coppin than any man alive and beyond the facts there existed the speculations, the drift of a man's thoughts in the long ago.

Every now and then he would glance out the window, his eye caught by movement in the street below. He expected Eileen back at any minute. Across the river the moon rested briefly on the brow of a hill like a giant prehistoric white boulder before clouds swept across to obliterate it.

Their car slid into view and stopped in front of the house. Eileen climbed out and smiled up at him before reaching in for her bag. But rather than immediately coming indoors she stood at the car for a moment, gazing into the darkness of the playground across the street. The alertness of her manner told him that something had caught her attention. He watched her for a moment with some puzzlement, wondering what she could see, then returned to his work.

When she finally entered the house she called out his name and started up the stairs. Joe, she called again, upon reaching the bedroom door.

He turned to face her.

There's a child sitting on its own on one of the swings in the playground, she said.

Eileen, it's after eleven, it's probably some drunk on the way back from the pub.

It's a child I tell you.

He turned back to the window and peered out. I can't see anything

How do you expect to see anything from up here? I want you to go over there and check.

You're not serious.

Oh but I am. How you can think of just sitting here when there's a child out there on its own in the dark.

Holy God, Eileen. He sat on the edge of the bed and put on his shoes. It's like being married to Mother Teresa so it is.

Once outside, he stopped at the gate for a moment, aware that Eileen was watching from the bedroom window. A few doors down a man sat on a low garden wall eating a bag of chips.

Hi, mucker, he called to Joe, his voice slurred, d'you want a chip?

No thanks, said Joe.

Please yourself.

Joe approached him. You weren't by any chance sitting on one of them swings over there a while back, were you? he asked.

The man peered across at the playground. Swings, he said, do I look like a man who sits on swings? What do you take me for? Just because I've had a few jars doesn't mean I'm going to be messing around in the first wean's playground I come across.

Fair enough, I was only asking.

Is this some kind of neighbourhood watch or what?

Sorry?

Making sure no one goes in your playground at night. I would have thought you'd better things to do with your time.

It's nothing like that.

Come to think of it, this isn't even your wall I'm sitting on. Why don't you knock on the door though and get the man who lives here to throw me off. That should keep you happy.

Jesus, said Joe, you're a right little ray of sunshine.

Aw fuck off, said the man, going back to his chips.

Joe crossed the street, trying to shake off his irritation. Arsehole, he said to himself with heat. He made his way down the dark lane that ran alongside the playground towards the entrance gate. The moon was still hidden and he stepped carefully on the uneven surface. As he drew parallel to the swings he saw her. He stopped for a moment in the darkness and watched. It was a young girl, maybe five or six, and she sat very straight and precise in the seat, barely moving her body as she swung gently to and fro. He could hear the chain creak with each oscillation. Were she to remain undisturbed, it looked like she would continue to swing until the end of time.

He walked on a few yards to the side gate and crossed the playground slowly so as not to frighten her.

Hello, he said, you must love being on the swings to be still here this late.

She looked up and smiled as if she'd been expecting him. I do, she said, I could sit here for ever. She continued swinging, unperturbed by his presence.

I used to like the slides best when I was your age.

You can fall off the slide and hurt your bum, she informed him.

There is that. He lowered himself on to the adjacent swing. Do you live nearby?

Not far. Melmore Gardens.

In Creggan? He looked at her in astonishment. That's a fair walk. I don't suppose your mammy knows you're here?

I sneaked out the back door when I was supposed to be in bed. Everyone was watching TV.

Do you not think they'll be missing you now? he asked.

They might, she conceded.

I could walk back home with you if you like.

She slid off the swing. I'm not supposed to go anywhere with strange men.

Well, what if you walk home and I just walk alongside you. How does that sound?

That might be OK.

And I'll give your mammy a ring to let her know you're all right.

The girl considered this. I have to speak to her too. You could be only pretending to ring her.

You know, I hadn't thought of that. Aren't you the sharp one. What's your name?

Molly. Molly McKevitt.

Hello, Molly. I'm Joe. He took his mobile phone from his pocket. First of all though I'm going to ring my wife or I'll have her worrying too. He smiled at Molly as he spoke and when Eileen answered, his voice took on an exaggeratedly breezy tone. Eileen, I'm over in the park with Molly. Yes, she's here all on her own and I've offered to walk back home with her. Don't worry, I'll not be long.

He stared down at Molly. I'm ready if you are.

Was that your wife?

Yes.

Is she nice?

Joe laughed. I certainly think so.

They walked back up the lane on to the main street. The drunk was slumped on the opposite wall but he perked up when he saw Joe. Now what are you up to? he shouted across. He leaned forward to take a good look at the pair of them. Are you making a citizen's arrest of that wee girl for being in your playground? He cackled at his joke. My advice to you, fella, is to lighten up. You need a hobby or something.

I don't like that man, said Molly.

That makes two of us.

He's rude.

They walked quickly on, the drunk's shouts dying behind them.

Now, said Joe, I think we'd better give your mother a ring in case she's worried about you. Do you know your phone number?

Of course I do, she said indignantly, aren't I six.

He rang the number and it was answered almost immediately. Hello, he said, is that Mrs McKevitt?

It is, yes.

Mrs McKevitt, you don't know me, my name's Joe. I'm ringing because I'm with your daughter Molly and we're on the way up to your house right now.

She's all right, is she? Is she all right?

She's fine. I think she just strayed a bit further than she intended.

There was a muffled thump and then a moment later her

voice again. Are you still there? Sorry, I dropped the phone, I'm such a bag of nerves. I was afeared I'd never see her again.

You don't have to worry and if you just hold on Molly wants a quick word with you herself. Joe handed over his mobile.

Hello, Mammy. Molly's face scrunched into a look of intense concentration. I know you did, she said. Yes, loads of times. I know, Mammy. No, I won't forget. With a weary sigh she handed the phone back to Joe. Mammy wants to speak to you again.

Where was it you found her? asked Mrs McKevitt.

She was in the playground in Bull Park.

Bull Park? What in the name of God was she doing there?

I haven't a clue but you can ask her yourself soon enough. We should be up at your house in about ten minutes.

He hung up and smiled at Molly. You might get a wee bit of a telling off but your mother's just glad you're all right.

I didn't stray, she said.

What's that?

I didn't stray. You said I strayed but I didn't, I knew exactly where I was going.

Her fierceness surprised him. He studied her for a moment, not quite knowing what to say, remembering how Ciara would also become worked up over some apparently innocuous misunderstanding. Children seemed to be moved by their own peculiar rationale as to what was and wasn't important.

Fair enough, he said.

They turned on to Bligh's Lane and began the climb up into Creggan. What took you to Bull Park? asked Joe.

Molly shrugged, as if her actions were as much a mystery to her as they were to everyone else. I don't really know, she said. It just came into my head, me sitting on that swing in the dark. She glanced up at him. I knew the noise it was going to make, the swing, even before I got there. I could hear it. One noise going forward, another noise going back. How did I know that, d'you think, she asked wonderingly?

Most swings make a noise, said Joe, they get rusty from being in the open all the time.

Um, said Molly, looking unconvinced.

He had not walked alongside a child since Ciara's death and the rhythm of their movements, Molly's slight physical presence, the brief spurts of conversation, brought back memories of walking to and from her school with his daughter. The sense of quiet pride that fatherhood had aroused in him and that had now left his life. How on those walks Ciara would ask him questions about everything under the sun, how she would look up and incline her head as she awaited his reply, the blithe confidence in her face that he'd been terrified of extinguishing. He felt a small hand slip into his and for a moment he was back with his daughter, his life restored, all the attendant emotions sweeping across his brain as across a flood-plain. He looked down at her, smiling, and it was Molly who smiled back at him and he realized that it was Molly who had taken his hand.

At Melmore Gardens she led him to her front door. He let go her hand and rang the doorbell. A young woman in her mid-twenties opened the door and behind her a child could be seen crawling with frantic intent down the hallway in their direction. No-one spoke for a moment and then the woman said, Come here you, and pulled Molly into her arms, hunching her body over her. I can't thank you enough, she said to Joe, my husband has been all round town looking for her. He's on his way back now. Will you come in?

No thanks, I'd better get home. Fascinated, he watched as the baby, panting with excitement, got closer to the door.

You really scared us, love, Mrs McKevitt said, looking down at Molly. Her daughter said nothing and Mrs McKevitt shook her head in bewilderment. Why you had to go the whole way to Bull Park I don't know. She turned to Joe. I don't think they understand the risks at her age, though God knows I tell her often enough.

Joe reached down and picked up the crawling baby just as it was about to reach the front step. He held it in front of him at arm's length and a tiny red face, distorted with rage, made more noise than he could have imagined possible.

The wee rascal, said Mrs McKevitt, reaching out to reclaim the baby, I didn't even see him. Now, she said to Molly, say thank you to this kind man for taking care of you.

No, said Joe firmly, she doesn't have to thank me. In fact, if anything, *she* took care of me. He held out his hand to Molly. It was a pleasure to meet you, Molly. But mind now, no more late-night trips to Bull Park.

She shook his hand solemnly. I promise, she said.

He walked back down Bligh's Lane, the sky spread before him. A low moon lit the thin clouds that covered it, like an X-ray of the rib cage held up for inspection. He could make out Orion's Belt and he tried to discern the Hunter from the other surrounding stars. Everything had to be given shape, as if randomness was more than we could bear. He marvelled again at how some of the stars he could see were long dead, marvelled at the persistence of their light. Not that it mattered, for human beings were incapable of telling the difference. The living and dead stars mingled together without prejudice in the night-sky, their light still reaching us, still guiding us.

ACKNOWLEDGMENTS

The following books have been of considerable help in the research for this novel.

Sir John Franklin's Last Arctic Expedition by Richard J. Cyriax (Methuen, 1939); *Search for Franklin* by L. H. Neatby (Walker, 1970); *Unsolved Mysteries of the Arctic* by Vilhjalmur Stefansson (George G. Harrap, 1939); *Sir John Franklin – the Secret of the Discovery of his Fate* by Rev. J. Henry Skewes (Bemrose & Sons, 1889); *The Voyage of the 'Fox' in the Arctic Seas* by Francis L. McClintock (John Murray, 1908); *Portrait of Jane: A Life of Lady Franklin* by Frances Woodward (Hodder and Stoughton, 1951); *Frozen in Time: the Fate of the Franklin Expedition* by Owen Beattie and John Geiger (Bloomsbury, 1987); *Unravelling the Franklin Mystery* by David C. Woodman (McGill-Queen's University Press, 1991); *The North-West Passage* by George Malcolm Thomson (Secker & Warburg, 1975); *Captain William Coppin* by Annesley Malley and Mary McLaughlin (Foyle Civic Trust, 1992); *I May be Some Time: Ice and the English Imagination* by Francis Spufford (Faber and Faber, 1996); *Arctic Dreams* by Barry Lopez (Picador, 1987).

I'm grateful to Graeme Harper and Annesley Malley for their suggestions after reading earlier drafts of the novel.

My thanks to everyone at the Marsh Agency and at Bloomsbury, in particular my agent, Geraldine Cooke, and my editor, Rosemary Davidson, for all their advice and support. And special thanks to Rachael.

A NOTE ON THE AUTHOR

Liam Browne was born in Derry. He works as a
literature festival programmer and
currently lives in Brighton.

A NOTE ON THE TYPE

The text of this book is set in Linotype Sabon, named after the type founder, Jacques Sabon. It was designed by Jan Tschichold and jointly developed by Linotype, Monotype, and Stempel, in response to a need for a typeface to be available in identical form for mechanical hot metal composition and hand composition using foundry type. Tschichold based his design for Sabon roman on a font engraved by Garamond, and Sabon italic on a font by Granjon. It was first used in 1966 and has proved an enduring modern classic.